T0277966

HEIST ROYALE

ALSO BY KAYVION LEWIS

Thieves' Gambit

The Half-Class

HEIST ROYALE

KAYVION LEWIS

NANCY PAULSEN BOOKS

NANCY PAULSEN BOOKS
An imprint of Penguin Random House LLC
1745 Broadway, New York, New York 10019

First published in the United States of America by Nancy Paulsen Books,
an imprint of Penguin Random House LLC, 2024

Visit us online at PenguinRandomHouse.com.

Library of Congress Cataloging-in-Publication Data is available.

Printed in the United States of America

ISBN 9780593625392 (hardcover)
ISBN 9780593859469 (international edition)
1st Printing
LSCC

Edited by Stacey Barney
Design by Suki Boynton
Text set in Mundo Serif

For Keithen. I’m your biggest fan.

ONE

IF I PRETENDED hard enough, I could almost believe the fireworks bursting over the stadium were for me. According to my phone, it was still 11:47 p.m. But that was Rio time. Back on Andros, it was January 13 already. Close enough. It was my freaking birthday and all I wanted was to see one debonair, vest-wearing traitor destroyed.

"He's really doing it up with the choreography, don't you think?" Devroe's voice, frustratingly nonchalant, buzzed from the com in my ear. From my spot in the wings, I couldn't help but glance toward the stage, where Saint Santi, one of Brazil's biggest pop stars, somersaulted over one of his backup dancers during the instrumental of "Eruption." The crowd lost their minds. The floor shook as over forty thousand fans seemed to screech at once.

I didn't respond, but Devroe kept talking anyway. "'Eruption' is such a powerful song. It'd resonate more if he let it breathe, don't you think?"

"Thirty seconds before I'm headed your way. Don't get distracted."

"I'm only ever distracted by you—"

I muted the com until I was sure he was done talking. Six months later and he was still *flirting*. Acting like he didn't have a world-shattering wish stashed away to play against me at any time. I thought he'd get tired of this game after a month or two of working together, but the icier I got, the more steadfast he became. It was enough to drive a girl crazy.

It was enough to pummel my heart into pieces.

I had to get rid of this boy before he ruined me in one way or another.

"Eruption" ended with an explosion of confetti and streamers over the pit. The stage flashed to black, and within seconds Saint Santi was replaced with his body double while the real deal was offstage, engulfed by an entourage of costumers, makeup artists, and assistants.

With my standard-issue stagehand jacket and Santi's favorite energy drink in hand, I slipped into the posse. Before I knew it, we were deep backstage. In the dressing room, Santi shoved the energy drink back into my hands before two other posse members started stripping him out of the sequined jumpsuit he performed in. A man with perfectly arched eyebrows wearing a belt of makeup brushes like an ammunition strap gripped Santi by the chin as he caked on fresh foundation. A mushroom cloud of hairspray fogged out the dressing room, and I saw my chance.

Joining the myriad of hands plucking and primping Santi, I finagled my fingers into the waistband of his pants and fished out the palm-sized leather notebook within. I pressed the book up my jacket sleeve and deposited the replica in its place. Santi fanned the cloud away while two assistants draped a sweeping coat over his shoulders. He patted his waistband, just like my recon saw him do between every costume change. Satisfied that his notebook was still in place, he allowed the stagehands to shove fingerless mesh gloves on his hands before the whole gang rushed out into the hallway toward the next set.

"I hate that we're going to miss 'Salacious Seduction.' That song is so very *us*."

Slowly, I slid my gaze across the now-empty backstage corridor until it landed on the threshold across from Santi's dressing room.

I'd decided a few months back that Devroe's unrelenting aesthetic appeal was another reason to be pissed with him. He was giving James Bond's more laid-back little brother tonight, in all black from his form-hugging jeans to the fitted black blazer and the V-neck Santi T-shirt underneath. He knew what he was doing; the magazine spread pose in the doorway with one foot up and his hands in his pockets was enough to tell me so. It was impossible to look as sexy as he did and not know what he was doing.

"'Irredeemable' is much more *us*." I shoved past him into the space, a storage room for Saint Santi merch and stage equipment, cluttered with plastic boxes overflowing with shirts and posters, tangled black wires on the floor, and what looked like a miniature volcano for the second act in the corner.

"The pocket's near his left hip." I tossed the notebook to

Devroe. He pressed the door shut and immediately started skimming through the pages and snapping pictures. Saint Santi's precious songbook. In true artist fashion, he scribbled lyrics as they came to him and always kept the notebook on him. It would've been pretentious if the last six or so of those scribbled songs hadn't gone platinum in the last year. Someone in the organization wanted the newest songs.

I did my best to ignore Devroe, cologne model appeal and all, while I changed into the new hoodie he had brought in a backpack for me and twisted my braids into a bun. On the off chance Santi or anyone did notice his precious notebook was missing, it wouldn't hurt to be a little less recognizable on my way out. I eyed a box of red-and-black Santi socks beside the hoodies—they'd look amazing with my checkerboard kicks, but the box was XXS socks only. I sighed.

"As stunning as a scarlet sunrise and as intriguing as a moonless midnight," Devroe whispered.

I tugged my new orange Santi hood down. My face flushed. "What?"

Devroe nodded toward the notebook, flipping a page. "Just the lyrics. They're quite beautiful. No wonder he's raking in so many awards." Devroe looked up. There was a crushingly tempting sparkle under his silky lashes. "They resonate—"

I forced myself to roll my eyes. "Nothing to set the mood like stolen words. Move."

He was strategically blocking the door. As expected, he didn't budge at first. "It's midnight." He maintained piercing eye contact, like that was going to be the thing to finally break me.

"Move."

"January thirteenth." He straightened a braid behind my ear, tickling my skin and making my breath catch.

"Move."

"Happy—"

I grabbed him by the arm, twisted it, and sent him spinning behind me as I opened the door and got the hell out of there before my heart could do something treasonous.

Happy birthday was something only people I loved had ever said to me. I couldn't let myself get that giddy flutter hearing it come from him. Not when he could cash in on his wish at any second. Not when I still had another six months of teasing and flirting and seductive posing to deal with.

The only person who could wish me a happy birthday was me, and that was because I was making it happy myself.

No one paid me any mind as I slipped into the wings of the stage. The getaway car would be waiting around the back of the stadium—a brisk walk through trailers and tour buses, through a checkpoint, and out into the street. My half was done; it was up to Devroe to return the original songbook after Santi's finale. It was preferable if Santi didn't notice the target had ever been missing at all.

But that didn't mean he couldn't notice something else was missing.

"Hey!" I butted in to the stage manager's drill sergeant routine, yelling over the roar of the crowd. Our research told me she was one of the bilingual Spanish-speaking crew members. Necessary since my Portuguese was less than fluent. "Do you know where Santi's firework mic is?"

"Of—" She squinted at the stage. The manager screamed.

"It's gone! Where's the mic? Goddamn it, where's my firework mic?!"

The wings shattered into acute chaos. It might as well have been the apocalypse. Two songs left until Saint Santi's finale and the TikTok-famous microphone he was supposed to belt his final note into while literal fireworks exploded from his palms was missing from its spot tucked in his heeled boots.

It'd been missing since I swiped it in the dressing room earlier and left it in the hidden pocket of Devroe's backpack. But if they hadn't noticed that yet, a hint wouldn't hurt.

"There was a guy in a black blazer eyeing it earlier," I added into the chaos. The manager nodded. She flagged over two backstage bouncers who looked like they were begging for action, and the swarm straight-up sprinted backstage.

I left smiling. What a pity for Devroe to have to waste his wish bailing himself out of a Brazilian prison. The best gifts really are the ones you get yourself.

Despite my insistence that we could take off, the driver of our black Tesla getaway car didn't budge—to be expected. The plan said Devroe was supposed to be back before 12:45, so unless Count herself was telling him to hit the gas, he wasn't going anywhere until then. Or so I thought. It was surprising when the touch screen flashed a message in Portuguese and he pulled out at 12:38.

"Where are we—" I cut myself off. We weren't on the route back to the hotel, but I should know by now that asking wasn't going to get me anywhere either.

I ran my fingers over the links of my meteor bracelet, already wary of where I might end up. But before I could really start to fret, we pulled around to the opposite side of the stadium. It was another restricted area, but to my surprise, with a few words in Portuguese, we were waved through and rolling up to another staff exit. The back doors pushed open. The stage manager, now laughing up a storm, stood with some of her lackeys holding the doors open.

Then Devroe and Santi himself were leaving, grinning like they'd been friends for years.

What the actual hell?

Seething, I watched Santi pat Devroe on the shoulder. Devroe, now missing his stylish blazer and wearing an orange hoodie like mine, shrugged before gesturing to the car, prompting Santi to wave in my direction. I ducked even though the windows were tinted to the point of being painted black.

Despite myself, I couldn't take my eyes off Devroe as he slid into the back seat with me.

He was supposed to be in cuffs right now. How the hell did he get a private escort out? I wouldn't ask, so instead I settled for gritting my teeth and glowering.

And Devroe only smirked. "He was so grateful when I returned the mic to him. Was waiting right on the edge of the stage. Truly I caught him in the nick of time. Thank god I found that thief in the black blazer. He got away, but I managed to wrestle the mic from him."

How did—

I plucked the com out of my ear. Unmuted.

He won this round.

"I'm sure you'll get me next time." He presented something from his pocket. "Consolation prize."

"I don't want—"

It was a pair of the firework socks, just like the ones in the storage room, only actually my size, and with Santi's fresh signature across the ankles.

The only gift I might get for my birthday . . .

I snatched the pair and chucked them out the window, already mourning the loss of such uniquely gorgeous footwear.

Devroe blew out a breath. "I figured you would do something like that." When I looked back, he was holding an identical pair. "I'll hold on to these until you come around."

TWO

Details on the next job incoming.
One week out. ☺

A string of attachments followed Count's text. Something about Montreal and some Monets. I skimmed the files before tucking my phone away to deal with them later. Devroe was not of the same mind.

He held the door for me as we entered the hotel, a cutesy boutique in a swanky corner of Rio. The type of place where string lights crisscross the streets and the upcycled furniture in the lobby is totally posh.

"Let's discuss the next job," Devroe offered.

"Tomorrow."

"I'm busy tomorrow."

I scoffed. "Doing what?"

"Thinking of new ways to impress you."

How was it that maintaining my iciness was getting harder as time went on, not the other way around?

Ignoring him, I made for the elevator, but a petite woman in red pumps and a matching pencil skirt threw herself between me and the doors, explaining something in Portuguese.

"The main elevator is out of service," Devroe translated.

I sighed, turning toward the stairs. The woman blocked me yet again, speaking just as insistently.

"They just started polishing the stairs. She says we can take the penthouse elevator and circle back down the emergency stairs." He winked at the woman as she offered a key card. She flushed. I rolled my eyes.

"Whatever." I let Devroe lead the charge into the private elevator, not that I had any other choice. The petite woman waved at us, a mischievous look on her face.

"Do you know her?" I asked.

"Not at all."

With a chime, the doors opened. I stopped a single step out.

In a dim foyer, a candlelit table was waiting. As intimate as they come, with a white tablecloth and an unassuming single-layer cake in the center.

That woman. She knew what Devroe was planning. He probably told her he was my boyfriend or something.

"You're such a liar," I said.

"Like you didn't know that."

I turned on my heel to dip back into the elevator, but he grabbed my wrist. "Don't spend your birthday alone. We're going to have to talk about the next job anyway—you might as well eat cake while we do it."

The twist of my lips probably translated my *hell no* before a sound left my mouth, but he was quick to interject. "It's pineapple upside-down cake."

I froze. Though I hadn't given the cake a close enough look before, the scent of condensed milk and pineapple was unmistakable now. Mom and Auntie had made me that cake every year since before I could remember. My mouth watered at the thought, and my heart shuddered with a pang of longing. I didn't think I'd be having it this year.

It wasn't for him—god knew how he found out what flavor to get—but just for the cake, I reluctantly drifted toward the little table. Devroe's eyes were alight with excitement as he sat across from me.

"This isn't a date." I blew out the two candles between us. He swatted my hand away from the cake cutter, insisting on doing it himself, undoubtedly so I had to watch him tantalizingly roll up his sleeves.

"Not working," I said.

"Not even a *little* flutter in your stomach?"

"I haven't dug in-depth into the files Count sent yet, but if it's a private gallery, I'm thinking something along the lines of a traditional break-in—"

"We have a week. No need to worry about the next job now."

"You just said—" Groaning, I rubbed my temples as he placed a perfectly cut slice in front of me. "I hope this is poisoned so I can be done with you."

He licked a smudge of condensed milk off his finger, and that *was* enough to send a flutter through me. "If it is, we're going down together."

I bit my lip and fingered my silverware while he cut himself a similar slice. "Do you think toying with my emotions is fun?" I asked quietly. "Isn't having your wish enough?"

Devroe paused, locking eyes with me. Then, uncharacteristically, he averted them. "I would've used it already if I was going to . . . you know."

"There's no point in all this. You don't have anything else to gain from me," I said.

"Except your forgiveness." He moved like he would reach for my hand, then thought better of it and resorted to straightening out one of his folded sleeves instead. "I feel . . . rather bad about everything."

A bead of anger, let's call it that, swelled in my chest. "So it's about you. Wanting to make me smile a little so you can feel less crappy about yourself."

"No, that's not what I meant. I mean . . . I feel awful because I care about you. Can't you let me try to make things right?"

"Give me your wish."

He blinked.

"You want to make things right. I'll forgive you, here and now, if you give me your wish." I cocked a brow.

As expected, he didn't move.

". . . I can't."

"Well, you must not feel that bad." I stood, leaving my precious pineapple upside-down cake untouched. "Email me your thoughts on the next job."

He didn't try to stop me from leaving this time, and I didn't look back.

I LEANED AGAINST my suite door, finally alone, and blew out a slow breath. Devroe felt bad. What was that worth?

Why was I even thinking about it now? This would've been easier if he'd just gotten arrested earlier—

Something moved near the window. City lights snuck in through sheer curtains, enough to backlight an armchair and whoever was standing behind it.

I moved slowly, trying not to give away that I'd seen them, and carefully unraveled my bracelet. Whoever this was, if they were hiding in my room, they should've known what they had coming.

I gave myself one more breath, then shot forward. The shape was a blur, but I could make out where a neck should be. Just as I snapped my bracelet forward, the person's arm flew up, catching my attack. It was like they'd known exactly where I was aiming for.

Probably because they did.

A lamp clicked on, lighting up the room. For the first time in six months, I was face-to-face with my mother.

"Happy birthday, baby girl!"

I yanked my bracelet chain, trying to tug her off-balance. She knew me too well. With just the right twist, the chains slinked off her wrist. Mom held her arms open like I would hug her. She'd switched up her weave. Six months ago she'd been in a down-your-back, wavy phase. Tonight, she was wearing quarter-width curls. Still voluminous and eye-catching. Still more glamorous than I could ever be in high-waisted black jeans and a chest-hugging black top. Still with her full lips and clever eyes and delicate nose. Still Mom.

Her same cocoa butter scent wrapped around me. The trained comfort response to that smell was almost hard to fight.

"I'm not talking to you."

I started wrapping my bracelet around my wrist. How did she get here? How did she know where I was at all?

My gaze shot to the door. Where would I even go if I stormed out . . . ?

"If you leave, you're going to run into the Kenzie boy again. He's pacing through the lobby right now." Mom held her phone landscape, flashing me CCTV footage. Devroe was indeed lingering downstairs, looking surprisingly downtrodden. The same petite woman from before was trying to comfort him. Not that I cared.

"Must have been a disaster of a date, baby girl."

My face suddenly felt like a firepit. "It wasn't a— How long were you watching me?"

Mom ignored the question, instead twirling her finger toward the bed.

On the duvet sat a black-and-gray-striped box topped with a silver bow. I flipped open the top, if only so I could tell her how much I hated the gift. She'd been horrible at birthday presents since I graduated from being happy with baby dolls and toy cars. But inside, I was shocked to find a pair of purple high-tops with gold shooting stars sewn into the sides. Tiny gold diamonds circled the rims of the soles, and even in the dark I could tell they were real. These kicks were . . . absolutely stunning.

I shoved the box away. "Ugly."

Mom pursed her lips. *Really*, they seemed to say.

"How much of a dent did these put in your new half-a-billion-dollar fortune?"

Mom flinched, clearly dreading where this conversation was going. Lucky for her, we didn't have to talk at all. "Get out," I said.

"I just want to explain." Mom pouted as if I was the one being cruel. "I think I deserve that."

"Deserve? Did I deserve to be abandoned in the middle of the ocean? Or to be almost gunned down in France? Or to almost fall twenty stories in Egypt?"

"I never put you in any situations I didn't know you could get out of," Mom said. "Look at you—you're fine! I don't understand why we can't just talk now that it's over."

"It's not *over*," I said. "Devroe still has his wish. He could blip us out of existence in a second, and if he did, it'd be your fault."

That shut her up. She sunk into the armchair, fiddling with her gel nails.

"Why did you do it?" I asked. "Did you really betray his mom and let his dad just die?"

Mom examined me for a long moment, like she was taking in every change since the last time she saw me. "I didn't know that he was Diane's boy. I didn't know all of that was going to happen at the end of the Gambit."

"That doesn't answer my question."

Mom paused. "It's very quiet back home without you and Jaya. I've always hated quiet."

I stumbled in my anger for a second. I understood how grating quiet could be, all those years alone back home. The silence of loneliness has a certain heaviness. Had Mom ever really felt it before? Before me, she had Auntie, but after Mom let her get kidnapped, she'd taken off. "I still want you to go." I moved toward the door, but the handle went slack under my palm. The screws holding the knob in place were loose. Mom must have removed the spring inside. She'd never given me the option to leave in the first place. Always making sure she'd get what she wanted no matter what.

"Argh!" I stormed toward the window instead.

"Oh, Rossie, come on." Mom grabbed my shoulder as I heaved the third-story window up. "I'm sorry, really."

Mom had never said sorry before. Six months ago it would've taken my breath away. For all I knew, I might be the only person on Earth who'd ever gotten a sorry from Rhiannon Quest. But there was something unsettling about that. What was it worth?

I shoved her under the throat. Hard. Mom stumbled into a coffee table. "Leave. Me. Alone."

Not caring that there was a sidewalk speckled with witnesses below, I slipped onto a drainpipe and slid to the ground. Jamming my hands in my jacket pockets, I started walking into the night.

THREE

EVEN AT NIGHT, Rio de Janeiro is hot as hell in January. Or maybe it was just because I was fuming.

I don't know how long I walked. Pointlessly, in fast, storming steps, from one snug street into another. I left the posh little area around our hotel and found myself venturing through the vibrantly painted downtown shopping districts, where banners connected the rooftops and vendors sold fresh fruits and travel photographers came to get the most exotic-looking pictures. At least, that would have been the vibe during the daytime. Hours past midnight, the city was slumbering. Trucks were packed up, vendor carts were pushed to the side, and only moonlight lit the streets. I wasn't totally alone; a few people were also out for past-midnight journeys, but for the most part, it was just me and my thoughts.

And my phone.

Kyung-soon

Hey . . .

did you know?

IT'S YOUR BIRTHDAY??!!

I made a sharp turn onto another street, this one with cobblestone sidewalks. A two-door car playing a muffled Saint Santi song, ironically, passed slowly. Its wheels crackled over the cobblestone.

Kyung-soon sent a GIF zooming in on some K-pop star under a storm of confetti. There was a caption in Korean, but I wasn't quite at reading level yet. I'd promised Kyung-soon I'd learn Korean after the Gambit, and had been, but speaking and reading were two totally different skills.

Smiling, I walked around a middle-aged woman in a smothering wool scarf, waltzing in the opposite direction, who smelled like the weirdest citrus and savory perfume. **I'm aware, lol**, I added into the group chat.

Mylo

You can now be tried as an adult in almost every country! 👏

I turned another corner, and a steady beat of steps turned with me. Curious. I pretended to stretch and glanced over my shoulder. A figure made a quick turn into a doorway. It would've looked totally normal if I hadn't known what it looked like when someone was tailing you.

"What part of 'leave me alone' do you not understand?" I spoke loud enough that I knew she could hear me. Not that difficult, since she was only a block behind at most. Mom didn't come out of her hiding spot. I rolled my eyes and paced even faster in the other direction. Just ignore her. It was a matter of days before Count whisked us away to the next job, and I doubted Count was going to allow anyone to follow us that easily.

It took her six months to find me the first time. Hopefully it'd take her longer the next time around.

Behind me, the steps disappeared. Fat chance of her giving up, though. She probably just trekked back to the hotel to wait me out. Guess I'd be crashing in the lobby if the alternative was dealing with her again.

A man passed me on the sidewalk. That scent again, citrus and meat. It was so distinct. Too weird.

And the same scent I'd whiffed off that woman.

My heart sped as I tucked my phone back into my pocket. I did my fake-stretching trick again, getting a quick glance behind me. The man, casual in plaid shorts and a brown T-shirt, turned onto a branching street.

He was with that woman who passed me earlier—the one in the scarf. They had to have been in the same place to get that weird scent, but they were dressed in totally different types of clothing. They were trying to look like they hadn't come from the same place.

It wasn't Mom. I was being tailed by someone else. At least two people.

Which way had the woman gone? Had she taken a right

behind me? And if it wasn't Mom tailing me from behind, then I still had the pursuer to my back. They'd probably just learned to be quieter after I stupidly called out to them.

One behind. One to the right. And if my instincts were correct, there was probably one other person coming in from the left. They were setting up to intersect me.

Four blocks before the avenue ended.

I kept my steps steady. My chain was begging to be unraveled. But I couldn't yet. It'd set off whoever was tailing me from behind. Then the chances of me getting the jump on whoever the hell this was would be gone. Three on one, the element of surprise was going to greatly increase my chances of winning this.

The street narrowed. One block, then two passed. The narrow intersection was getting closer. That was where they would do it. I wouldn't have anywhere to run.

Three blocks. One more.

I pretended to pop my knuckles, using the chance to unclick the ball of my meteor bracelet.

Three steps left.

Two.

One.

That same bizarre scent stuffed the air, this time twice as strong.

Let's do this.

I stepped onto the corner and immediately ducked and spun out of the way. As expected, the woman with the scarf was there waiting to pull me into what looked like a bear hug. She stumbled, having thrown most of her weight where she thought I was going to be. I grabbed her scarf and yanked hard, pulling her totally off-balance. She crashed to the ground.

Her scarf: The fabric was padded. Thick. Meant to protect her neck.

Protection—against someone who might be prone to strangling people with her chain? They were prepared for me specifically.

Fast steps crunched over the cobblestone sidewalk. Man with the plaid shorts. I swiped my arm back. The link of my meteor ball unraveled. The weighted ball at the end cracked right into his nose, drawing a splatter of blood. With him distracted, I sent an aggressive kick into his knee. He screamed. A bone cracked, and he dropped to a broken kneel. I sent another kick into his chin, keeling him over.

With two down, for now, I braced to run, but arms tackled me from behind. Hooking a long forearm around my neck, this new attacker pressed a com in his ear with the other hand. "Bring the car!"

Headlights skidded into sight blocks down. A car meant more people. Not good for me.

I tried to buck him off of me to no avail, so instead, I grabbed one of his fingers and twisted it back. It snapped in my grip. He screamed. I grabbed another finger, ready to break it too. This time he pulled his arm away, and that let off enough weight for me to successfully scramble out from under him. Even with his broken finger, he tried to drag me into a stumble, but I sent a palm into his nose, buying me enough time to clamber to my feet.

The car squealed to a stop.

Run.

I meant to set off in the fastest sprint of my life, but a desperate grip wrapped around my ankle. I tripped. The scarf woman dropped a knee into my back. Before I could twist around, a needle pricked my jugular.

I could feel the woman relax on top of me. Whatever she'd injected me with meant the fight was over.

Car doors opened. The woman got up. My limbs were heavy. Drowsiness set in fast.

Well, if I was lucky, this was just another fake kidnapping.

FOUR

A SIZZLING SOUND WOKE me up. And too many smells to break down. Butter? Salisbury steak? More citrus? And was that . . . sugarcane?

I winced and sat up, rubbing my eyes. There was a table under me? No, I was *sitting* at a table. My butt was half asleep, so who knew how long I'd been here.

A few other tables, all painted in bright colors, filled the rest of the room. Wind blew a sheer white curtain through open French doors on one side of the room. On the other side was a tiny, empty bar, and behind that, an open door—the origin of all that sizzling.

A pan clattered, and glasses clinked. People were speaking too.

I sat up, thankfully not as dizzy as I would have guessed,

and crept toward the open French doors. If there was a balcony, this would be an easy escape.

No such luck. The balcony was encased by glass windows, so spotless I didn't notice them at first. Past them, a tumbling slope descended. The view was spectacular, overlooking a twinkling city below.

A loud clang made me jump. Someone snapped in Portuguese, "Clean that up, Marc."

Using my lightest steps, I peeked into the kitchen, the only place another exit could be. It was chaos. Plates and saucepans and mixing bowls were stacked in comically high piles by a sink, where that man I'd face-kicked was scrubbing furiously. The scarf woman, who I could now see was a big-boned redhead whose face was smeared with freckles, was transporting dirty cookware to the industrial sink. The guy in plaid shorts, whose nose I'd broken with my chain, was now wearing a splint and stood at attention between an open pantry and an industrial freezer. There was a gun at his hip.

They all had guns at their hips. I didn't know what the hell was going on here, but if I could get one—

"Go sit down, Ross. I'll be out shortly."

I stiffened. Scarf Woman jogged toward the freezer to fetch something, revealing a fourth person in front of the stove. He was around my age, or twentyish, in surprisingly tasteful tan trousers. His silk dress shirt was starting to come untucked, and the sleeves were rolled up. He had golden-brown skin and voluminous black hair that stuck to his forehead, likely due to the steam from the four different pans he had going.

He spared me a glance. "Shoo, now." With a spatula in his hand, he gestured me back into the other room.

Biting the inside of my cheek, I retreated. There were too many of them in that room. Not to mention, they were armed. Also . . .

I twisted my wrist. My meteor bracelet had been stolen.

Call me a hypocrite, but having your belongings taken really sucks.

I patted my back pocket, expecting to find my phone gone, but it was still there in its waterproof *Starry Night* case. The signal was scrambled, though, so it was pretty much useless.

About ten minutes later, Nose Splint and Scarf Woman exited the kitchen to set up two tables with tablecloths and silverware. The guy in the silk shirt came out to drop two plates at the table nearest me, while the last goon, a wiry, tall guy with a five-o'clock shadow and an intimidating scar slashing his neck, waited by the kitchen, hand on his gun holster.

Yes, sir, I get it. No escaping or whatever.

The man in the silk shirt fell exhaustedly into one of the multicolored chairs at the table, wiping his brow as one who'd just been cooking up a storm would.

Scarf Woman returned to the kitchen and came out balancing three more plates between her lithe arms. She left one with the guy guarding the kitchen and the other two at a table for her and Nose Splint.

Maybe, having been involved with too many kidnappings in real life, I was now dreaming about them.

"Sit." Silk Shirt gestured to the chair beside him. I flipped him off. He sighed and dragged a rose-gold chain out of his pocket. My meteor bracelet.

"I'll give it back if you sit down." He dangled it like I was a cat he was playing with.

I stomped up to the table and reached for it, but he jerked it back at the last second. "*After* we talk." He nodded to the seat again.

Guess I was going to have to play along until I could figure a way out of this.

I sat.

"Wonderful!" He grinned in the self-satisfied way people who are used to getting what they want do, then glanced around. "What is everyone waiting for? Eat."

All three of the goons picked up silverware and did as they were told—even the guy standing by the kitchen found a fork on the bar. I glanced down at my plate.

I had no idea what the hell I was looking at.

Meat? Something definitely smelled savory, but it was so smothered in red and brown seasonings that I couldn't make out what animal it was, let alone a cut. And some kind of . . . salad? Mush? It could have been rice porridge, but there were specks of orange in it. I leaned down and took a whiff. Yes, definitely citrus in there. And was that fried sugarcane and plantains on the side . . . with gravy? Mole?

I side-eyed the man in the silk shirt. He steepled his fingers under his chin . . . watching me.

Hesitantly, I picked up a fork and, like a poison-conscious girl, switched his plate with mine before flaking up a corner of the maybe-meat.

It melted like butter in my mouth. Probably because there was way too much butter; it almost overwhelmed the kick of the spices. Venison, I thought that's what it was.

"Too much butter," I said. "But otherwise, surprisingly all right, I guess."

The man in the silk shirt lit up. Since he seemed to be expecting it, I tried what looked to be a burnt plantain next.

The mushy disaster in my mouth was definitely not a plantain. I spit that mess into a napkin as fast as I could.

"So you *did* bring me here to kill me . . ." I mumbled.

He scoffed. "Nonsense. Marc. Maria. How is everything?"

Marc, the man with the scar and the five-o'clock shadow by the kitchen, shook his head as he swallowed. Maria's eyes were watering as she scooped up another spoonful. "Excellent, sir. As usual," she forced out.

I never thought I'd feel bad for the people who kidnapped me, but here we were.

"Who are you?" If anything, talking was an excuse not to eat. "I don't get invited to dinner with strangers that often."

"Strangers?" He huffed and took a bite of the venison, leaving a messy sprinkle of spices all over the tablecloth but somehow managing not to get anything on himself. "You've been in my hotel room, seen my dirty sheets, hacked my computer, and we're still strangers? You break my heart."

"I've never—" I thought back to the kitchen, and the tornado he'd whipped it into. In a matter of minutes, his side of the table was covered in crumpled paper towels and crumbs. This dude was naturally messy. I had been in a messy hotel room before. In which I hacked someone's computer.

During the Gambit. Phase two. I was supposed to delete a list of organization members off his laptop.

Oh, crap.

"It's all coming back to you now?" he said with a less genuine smile. "You can call me Baron. You've been screwing me over for quite a few months now."

Was that what this was? Petty revenge?

"Look," I said carefully. "I'm just a hired hand. If you're looking for someone to be pissed at, there are a lot bigger, slimier fish than me."

He chuckled. "I've never heard someone refer to Count as a fish before, but I'll have to use that the next time I'm unfortunate enough to speak to her. Let's do a speed run of all your questions," he said. "No, I don't work for Count. Yes, she hired you to steal from me. No, I don't like her any more than you probably do. Yes, I'm with the organization. Does that clear things up?"

"All except for why I'm here and why Count had us stealing from you."

He raked his hands through his hair, which looked like it was cut to be worn as a stylish mess. "You and that Devroe boy screwed me out of a quarter million dollars tonight. I own Saint Santi's record label." He tapped his knife against his plate. "I also owned the mansion you stole a Monet from last month, as well as the stocks you tanked by leaking information you hacked out of an office building in New York two months ago. You've been ruining my life since you entered the Gambit. Well, ruining my life as much as a fly can ruin an elephant's life, but you know, still so annoying."

All those jobs Count sent us on . . . they were hit jobs on this Baron guy?

"What'd you do to piss her off?"

He shrugged. "Pretty understandable, actually. I'm trying to replace her. And I want your help."

FIVE

YOU WANT TO replace Count. As . . ."

"You know what I mean," Baron said.

I did know. To be honest, I'd never been entirely sure if Count was just a mouthpiece for the organization or if she was a lot higher up than she let on. She certainly didn't act like a lackey. But this confirmed it. She wasn't just a key player, but I guess the . . . ?

"You're telling me Count is, like, you guys' leader?"

"Something like that."

For now.

"If she's the top woman, why is she still doing things like sending emails and texts herself and personally rendezvousing with nobodies like me and Devroe?"

"Because she's a chronic micromanager, obsessed with

keeping a personal eye on everything. Of course she fails, because it's impossible for one person to manage all the tiniest details of an empire this large. Hence how she allowed you to trip her up at the end of the Gambit. I never would have let something that embarrassing happen, which I knew would eventually." He got up and started pacing, dropping his hands on his hips. "She's as paranoid as she is obsessive. I was using the master list to start fishing out who I knew would be loyal to her in the event of a proposed change of power, and I suppose she guessed correctly what I was up to and had you wipe my drive. It delayed me for a couple of months."

"What do you want, an apology?" Victim of my crimes or not, this guy was top-tier organization. Anyone in the organization was permanently on my hate list these days.

"I'd respect you less if you said sorry. And it's not necessary. Count and her little antics have only been slowing down the inevitable. I'm getting more and more members on my side every day. Losing a few hundred million here or there isn't going to stop that, no matter what she thinks."

Yes, because when has losing a few hundred million ever stopped anyone?

Baron quit pacing and shot a glare at Marc, who'd only finished half his plate. Marc quickly picked up his silverware and started eating again.

"I'm close to tipping the balance, I think," Baron said. "I just need another key member to side with me for a change of power. We're around fifty-fifty right now. But I've done all I can with persuasive words and bargaining. Everyone left on her side is too loyal. They're not going to switch unless something happens to show they're not as safe under her rule as they think. I need someone to hit her where it hurts. I need someone they think Count has in her pocket to attack."

"Me?" I shook my head. "I don't even know you. Why the hell would I want you in power?"

"You prefer Count?"

"I'm saying I know her."

"Oh?"

"More than I know you, *Baron*." At least I knew Count's real name, and that she had a son and an ex-wife. Maybe that wasn't much, but don't they say something about sticking with the devil you know? My devil was a passive-aggressive control freak, but at least she didn't make her lackeys scarf down her culinary disasters.

I bit my finger. "Why do you want me anyway? There are a lot of other thieves familiar with Count who have a freer schedule than me." One was presumably still staked out in my hotel room. "Actually, I can AirDrop you my mom's number right now." Wouldn't I love for her to have a distraction.

Baron shifted. "I did think about your mom for this job first. Oh, how I would have loved to have her. I've heard she's absolutely the best." A sour sort of look twisted his face, and he shook his head at me. I squirmed, sinking at the thought that he was disappointed I wasn't her for a second. "However, even I am a bit apprehensive about working with someone so notoriously conniving. I'll admire her from afar, and hopefully you'll be good enough."

Good enough shouldn't have stung as much as it did, but I pushed on.

"Why not the actual Gambit winner in Count's arsenal?" I asked, biting back my bitterness.

"The Kenzie boy's not cut out for this. You have a vested interest in helping me. For the same reason he never would."

I sat up a bit straighter. Okay, he had me curious now.

"You're not the only one Count's been throwing at me over the last six months," Baron said. He cocked a brow. "Have you wondered what Ms. Abara has been up to since the end of the Gambit?"

Diane. Devroe's mom. The woman who wanted him to wish all of my family into their graves.

No, I certainly hadn't forgotten about her. But I guess I'd been a little too busy trying to keep an eye on her son to worry about what she was doing. No wonder Mom was Baron's first choice for this. Screwing over Diane was at the top of her résumé.

"She's . . . working for Count?"

Baron circled the table. "She's managed to do three times as much damage to my personal assets as you and Mr. Kenzie have all by herself. If I know Count, she'll squeeze as much work out of her as she can before giving her what she wants. But Count *will* give her what she wants, and I'm pretty sure that's still, you know, the end of everything you know and love."

I burst up from the table, pressing a hand over my heart. Count had seen us every other week for the past six months while she was courting Diane?

I paced over to the balcony. Why did I think Diane would just . . . stop? I'd been so worried about Devroe's wish, I hadn't thought that she could find another way to get what she wanted.

I pressed my forehead against the glass. A phantom chill

brushed my skull, pushing through my braids. That barrel, pressing against my head and the heads of my entire family too.

Baron approached. I could see him in the reflection of the glass, thumbs hooked into his pockets. "She has quite the grudge, I've heard. I can't imagine what that feels like hanging over your head, every single day." He clicked his tongue in mocking sympathy. It was a good thing he'd taken my bracelet, because I wouldn't have been able to resist strangling him.

He leaned against the glass beside me. "As you can see, it might be in both of our best interests if Count wasn't the one in charge anymore."

I shook my head. "Until you cut a deal to help this woman murk my whole family too?"

All of these organization members were the same. Heartless. Cold. Ruthlessly pragmatic. I was convinced that was the only type of person that could lead a group like this.

"No, in fact, I can promise you the opposite. Help me overthrow Count, and I'll give you guaranteed protection. All the Quests will be safe as kittens under me. For life."

I turned to face him. Was he for real? I scanned his face for a hint of deception. All I found was determination in his eyes.

He meant this, at least for now.

"How do I know you're not lying?"

He huffed a laugh. "If there's one thing we do in this organization, it seems to be keeping our promises. We wouldn't have quite the reputation we do for our Gambit wishes if that wasn't the case. This is real, Ross Quest. I want your help, and you need mine."

Did I? He could be lying, no matter what he said. What kind

of fool would I be for just deciding to trust this stranger that kidnapped me?

What would the consequences be if we failed and Count was furious with me? But that sure as hell wouldn't be worse than if he was telling the truth about Diane and I did nothing. Just imagining everyone being hunted down. Me . . . dead before my next birthday. I'd only ever get to eighteen . . .

Baron shook his head, breaking in before I could start spiraling. "I really thought it would be an immediate yes. I'm sure Rhiannon would've said yes immediately. She's so very good at getting what she wants."

He was baiting me, but he was right. Mom would've agreed immediately. Psychotic or not, she was excellent at winning. Wasn't that a trait I wouldn't mind adopting?

"Give me the details."

SIX

ARRIVING IN NEW Orleans during the biggest party of the year was more chaotic than I was prepared for.

It took me a whole thirty minutes just to fight my way through Louis Armstrong Airport, decked out in purple and green, to the rideshare pickup area, only to find the nearest Uber wouldn't be available for an hour. A guy in a THROW ME SOMETHING MISTER sequined T-shirt and a woman with a jester hat got into a shoving match at the back of the dizzyingly long taxi queue. The worker at one of the rental car kiosks laughed under her feathered mask when I asked if there was anything available.

Could you blame me for hot-wiring a Prius from the long-term parking lot?

Mylo and Kyung-soon had beat me by a day somehow, and their texts since I'd landed weren't super helpful.

Mylo

are you out of the airport? We're waiting at the Airbnb. (PIN DROPPED)

Hey we're going to get beignets meet us at this cafe (PIN DROPPED)

Left the cafe. Saved you some beignets

Kyung-soon ate ur beignets

Kyung-soon

Mylo ate your beignets

Mylo

Meet us at this wax museum (PIN DROPPED)

They're closed. Now we're going here (PIN DROPPED)

Nvm we broke into the wax museum meet us here (PIN DROPPED)

We got chased out of the wax museum we'll meet you here (PIN DROPPED)

After a two-hour-long game of tag, I finally managed to catch up. The last pin dropped led me to a strip mall in Metairie, one of New Orleans's swankier boroughs, where I found myself walking into a low-lit, laughter-and-chime-filled place called Throwback.

A huge, two-story arcade. I didn't see any giant touch screens or dance games; instead there were rows of standing quarter machines. Ah, I got it now. *Throwback*. A vintage arcade.

I moved around the floor, dodging between kids running with glow sticks, waiters wearing Mardi Gras beads and jester hats, and honestly way too many older folks slurping colorful slushies, all insisting that they were the best at this game back in the day. I found Mylo hunched over a *Pac-Man* console.

At least, I thought it was Mylo.

"'Scuse me, sir, have you seen my friend?"

He jumped, then immediately got eaten by a ghost. Luckily, he didn't seem to care.

"Yo!" Mylo knocked the breath out of me with a bear hug. "Ross Quest in the flesh again! You're shorter than I remembered."

I snuggled into him for a beat longer than necessary. I *just* got friends to snuggle into. There'd been way too few of these moments in my life. I could probably count them on one hand. If Diane got what she wanted, I was going to die pitifully unhugged.

"Are you okay?" Mylo tried to pull back. Apparently when you start squeezing the life out of someone while contemplating your mortality, they notice.

I blinked back any tears as I let him go. "Yeah. You're, uh, more clean-cut than I remember. What the hell happened to your hair?"

I'd thought he was growing it out. At least that was what I remembered from the last time we FaceTimed a week ago. But now he'd chopped most of the shoulder-length glory into a short-cropped, young-gentleman style. He'd even dyed it a dashing russet brown. No trademark loose-hanging suspenders. Less eyeliner too. If it hadn't been for the distressed jeans and T-shirt, I'd have thought he'd been body-snatched.

Mylo ignored my weird huggy moment for now and let his shoulders slump. "Yeah, yeah, I know." He rustled his hair, only for it to settle neatly back into place. "I got this long con coming up at UCLA next semester. I told you, don't you remember?"

He had? Was I paying attention? "Yeah. Slipped my mind."

"I had to interview a few days ago. Must look like a presentable young man." He stuck a finger in his mouth and gagged.

"Right . . ."

"Do I look that bad?"

"No, I just wasn't expecting a prelaw student."

With how pale he got, you'd have thought I told him he looked like a goblin.

"But, you know, on your day off. With a hangover," I added.

"I'll take it." He gestured to the machine behind him. "Wanna play? I need more quarters, though." He scanned for any staff, then gestured for me to guard the machine. With lightning-fast talent, he twirled a certain familiar pen out of his pocket and lasered open just the right spot in the back of the machine. A basket of quarters sat inside. He gave me a handful and collected a handful for himself. A few seconds later, he had the piece clicked back in place and I was starting my very first game of *Pac-Man*.

I was not good at it.

Gobbling up dots? Could do. Avoiding the pesky little ghosts? Not so much.

"There aren't any, like, secret rows I can sneak into?" I complained.

"Is the great escape artist Ross Quest having trouble getting through a single screen of *Pac-Man*? This is not how I predicted things going."

I groaned, dropping my forehead on the console after getting hit with the Game Over screen for the fifteenth time.

"Get away from the screen before you waste hours there. Trust me, I know." Kyung-soon, carrying a sickly-sweet-smelling paper bag in one hand, twinkle-waved at me with the other. At least she looked the same. Well, except—

"Am I the only one who didn't get a haircut?"

Her copper-color hair stopped just above the headphones around her neck now. Still familiarly frizzy, though.

She shrugged. "I did it first. Mylo's the copycat."

Mylo sniffed the air. "You got more beignets!"

Kyung-soon jerked them away before Mylo could grab the bag. "For Ross. Eat them before he steals them too."

We made our way to a peeling faux-leather booth in the back. After making Mylo watch with hungry eyes as I ate one puffy, powdered-sugar-caked beignet, I was merciful and shared the bag. Kyung-soon had dumped the contents of her backpack on the table and was fiddling with a transparent sticker with wiring running through it. She caught me eyeing it and sighed. "Biometric sensor. I didn't know it was assembly-required."

"That's her way of saying she accidentally spent twelve grand on a pile of junk."

"It is not!" Kyung-soon insisted. She was comparing the device to a picture on her phone. "I trust the engineer who sold it to me. She's a friend of my mentor's. Once this is done, I'll be able to get past any biometric lock, so long as I have a sample from the target." As an example, she pressed my thumb over the center of the sticker. My skin tingled, and a light on Kyung-soon's phone flashed before sputtering out.

"If only it was actually functional," Mylo said, lips coated with powdered sugar. He nodded toward me. "Anyways. What's your catastrophe?"

I frowned. How did he jump to catastrophe?

Mylo and Kyung-soon exchanged a look. "Why else would you be here in person? It's not like you just wanted to see us," Kyung-soon said.

I opened my mouth, but Mylo beat me.

"You must have twisted Count's arm for a break, since we all know she wasn't gonna be, like, yeah, go take your two weeks PTO, no prob. And if you did that, then it must be for something important," Mylo explained.

Well, that was better than telling me I'm the friend who always has problems. We'd have to make sure that wasn't what they actually thought later.

I spilled about everything. Baron, being sort-of kidnapped, Count being a way bigger fish than I'd assumed, and the vote of no confidence Baron was trying to initiate. Oh, and, you know, Devroe's mom still being hell-bent on wiping my fam off the face of the earth.

Mylo rubbed his chin. "I always suspected Count was at the top of the organization."

"No, you didn't," Kyung-soon said.

"Well, it makes sense now. Those power suits she wears don't exactly scream underling." Mylo took a breath. "What makes you think this Baron dude is going to be better than her, though?"

"I don't care who's 'better.' I care who's on my side." My phone buzzed.

Devroe

Count said you took some days.
Missing you already

Haven't been to New Orleans in a while.
Maybe I'll follow you.

I muted the conversation. How the hell did he know where I went?

Kyung-soon licked her teeth. My phone had been on the table; they'd clearly read the texts too. "Diane is Devroe's mother. What is Baron going to do to someone who's been working for an enemy if he takes over?"

"I dunno. Does it matter? I'm a little more worried about stopping her, not her retirement plan."

"Okay, but . . . we shouldn't participate in anything that's going to hurt her."

"Hurt *her*? The woman that tried to get Devroe to have the organization blow me and my family's brains out six months ago?"

"Devroe's our friend," Kyung-soon said quietly. "If we told him about—"

"He's not our friend!" I yelled, louder than I meant to. A lady with a toddler gave me a stank look.

"Devroe is a playboy traitor who might maybe have enough empathy to back out on family genocide, but that doesn't change the fact that he was manipulating us throughout the entire Gambit and now he's just holding this wish over my head, and for all we know he's already well aware what his mom's been up to. We're not telling him about this. End of conversation."

Kyung-soon folded her arms. "Sure. Your decision is final. All of our relationships should get greenlit by Ross Quest first. Everything revolves around you, anyway."

I balked. "What does that mean?"

Kyung-soon stayed silent. We just glared at each other.

"Aaannyways." Mylo looked to Kyung-soon. "Maybe we don't tell Devroe, for practicality, don't want this getting leaked back to Count, but . . ." He turned his attention to me. "Maybe you hit up Baron and make sure he's not going to have all his political enemies beheaded at the end of this? Or at least not the mom of the guy who, for whatever reason, decided *not* to have you and your family murdered? Seems kinda fair if you're getting lifetime protection in return? Eh?" He gave us both a goofy smile.

"Fine," we said in unison. Only Kyung-soon answered in Korean.

"I don't know what that means," I said without thinking. I had been learning Korean like I promised, but letting her know I'd been loyal enough to learn a whole-ass language for her when she couldn't even get behind shunning my ex-crush-turned-almost-murderer was too pathetic.

Kyung-soon got up and slid her headphones on. "Text me the details." She left.

"That wasn't cool, Ross," Mylo said, and I felt like a real jerk for a second. Wasn't I just lamenting all the time with friends I was going to miss out on if Diane got what she wanted?

I bit my lip, suddenly regretting how impulsive I'd been. "I'll say sorry later." I could probably catch her now, but . . . ugh, awkward.

"Okay, but— Never mind." Mylo clapped as if nothing had happened. "No worries. She'll be back. Now, didn't you mention this job involves costumes?"

SEVEN

I THOUGHT I WAS sick of balls and galas. Devroe and I had infiltrated quite a few over the past six months, all involving the same tasteful quartets, sleek evening gowns, and well-mannered but highly punchable rich people.

The krewe of Cherus's Mardi Gras ball was nothing like any of those.

The parade rolling through the French Quarter outside was loud, but somehow the party inside overwhelmed all that noise.

The second floor of the refurbished Toulouse Theatre, now renovated into a posh ballroom, was a wonderland of purple, gold, and green, from the tinsel dripping from the high ceilings to the confetti on the floor. The few tables around the edges of the room were dressed in iridescent tablecloths. The bar had been spray-painted gold. Overhead, a thin net held up a sea of gold and purple balloons. Who knew when those would be released.

Waiters in jester costumes kept dropping fresh cinnamon-scented king cakes on any free table they could find, and every few minutes a new person announced that they got the baby. The jazz band was playing at top rhythm: trumpeters and a drummer and a man with an accordion, performing so vigorously sweat dripped off their faces. The dance floor—which was pretty much the whole ballroom—was overflowing with people spinning and two-stepping, and every now and then converging into line dances everyone seemed to know so well I wondered if they taught this sort of thing in school here.

Oh, and the costumes.

Gowns and waistcoats made of shimmering golds and purple feathers. Capes stretched like wings every time their wearer lifted an arm. Elizabethan-like collars a foot and a half tall. Dozen-layered skirts that shimmered like water. Jester hats with tinkling bells. Not to mention the masks.

From half masks accented with feathers to quieter porcelain doll faces frozen in expressions of delight or horror. We took full advantage. My mask, pink and sequined like the rest of my costume, but thankfully lightweight for practicality, covered me from forehead to chin. Mylo had somehow convinced me to spray-dye my braids a flattering rose-gold. So here I was, in a glittering dress with a ruffled high-low skirt and puffed sleeves, with matching Mardi Gras beads strung like bracelets over my forearms. They helped my meteor bracelet blend in, though now I realized how stupid I'd been to be worried about that. I should've been worried about the way the night-vision filters in my mask aggravated my pupils. Mylo didn't mention how annoying they would be when he was helping me fasten them in place. I'd also opted to wear the shoes Mom bought me, but only because they matched and after I sent them through a run in the washer just to be sure they were properly debugged.

Mardi Gras was alive and gorgeous in a Technicolor kind of way. I wanted to come back for fun one day. I mentally added it to the list of reasons I had to stay alive.

My phone buzzed.

Still waiting.

Kyung-soon passive-aggressive text tally: three. Me and Mylo were doing the hands-on work—I eyed him in his leprechaun-green-sequined three-piece suit line dancing near the stage with a few guys who looked like they'd walked straight out of their frat house—while Kyung-soon would handle the getaway. Having someone with a motorbike hidden in the alley outside waiting to transport the target was a necessary part of the job I'd planned, but let's not kid ourselves by pretending she picked that part for any reason other than getting to spend as little time with me as possible. I'd been planning to apologize before, but I refused to do it while she was acting like this.

A text from Devroe distracted me.

Time for dinner?

He dropped a pin to what I assumed was a restaurant in the quarter. As if I'd be able to make it there through the chaos of the parade outside. And it was only supposed to get more chaotic when the krewe of Cherus's royalty ditched this party for their own larger, grander parade. Though they'd be missing one of their showstoppers once Mylo and I were done.

Swiping a goblet of champagne from a jester, I looked over the edge across the ballroom. There, our target, dazzling in a sea of silver and white rhinestones that somehow shaped into an evening gown with a sweeping cape and tall collar, was showing off her glory. Well, that and the blinding tiara crowning her cream-blond curls and the matching diamond necklace dripping into the low cut of her gown. Gotta say, she absolutely shimmered.

Louisiana Senate Majority Leader Louisa Robicheaux. The most powerful person in her state's congress. But tonight, she was the queen of Cherus, and wearing authentic jewelry borrowed from the Napoleon collection. The set's value sat comfortably in the eight-figure range.

And all I had to do was take it.

I remembered the articles Baron had sent as he'd explained the job to me during my layover yesterday. Dozens of local news outlets were covering how Senator Robicheaux was going to rule the Crescent City this Mardi Gras, with genuine jewelry once worn by Napoleon's wife bringing an air of true royalty to scene.

The organization's primary purpose is to make our members' lives perfect, Baron had explained. It was almost hard to hear him over the blender whirring in the background. *They deserve to be worry-free, get whatever they want, have their enemies destroyed, and every now and then be entertained by less valuable people like you.*

Offense taken, but I was an insignificant little thief, so what did it matter?

The whirring stopped, then restarted before Baron continued. *Count's job is to keep everything running smoothly. If something disastrous were to happen to one of its founding members, something like a multimillion-dollar tiara getting snatched off her head right before she was supposed to publicly show it off, and by someone Count was supposed to have a leash on, well, that'll probably make her look more than a little unfit for the job.* The blender stopped. *Marc, drink this . . .*

Across the room, the senator laughed, emphasizing the lines around her lips. Her necklace glinted in the light. I pursed my own lips under my mask. Rob her. Make it public. Easy work, but crossing the Rubicon too. I was going all in with Baron once I touched that crown. But whatever faith I had in Count dissipated when I learned she was working with Diane.

After what felt like an eternity of king cake and cheers and bumping into drunk krewe members, the senator decided to enter the dance floor. I instantly started circling the floor myself, brushing past Mylo and his emerald-green top hat along the way. His eyes were coated in want as he gazed at the senator's tiara set.

Mylo flexed his fingers under his chin. "Do you think Baron would notice if we kept—"

"We're delivering what he asked," I reiterated. "Every single piece."

Mylo let out a little whimper.

"I'll make it up to you. For now, stick to the plan." I clapped his shoulder. He nodded.

Mylo disappeared into the crowd. The band had started up again, now playing a waltz that honestly sounded like it could have been straight out of a Cajun fairy tale, accented with accordions just as much as the violin. Courtiers were swirling around the dance floor, showing off their chosen partners. The lighting dipped low, until it was akin to candlelight.

I waited the song out, still circling as nonchalantly as I could until people started to file in for a line dance. I'd gotten here early just to make sure I could get the steps down enough to participate.

The numbers evened out, so I was partnered facing a princess from the court. She gave me an up-nod, and I returned it, then looked over her shoulder. Mylo was right where I'd expected him to be, near the tech booth. Pretending to casually lean against the side of the booth, he whipped off his top hat. He plucked invisible lint from the inside, popping open the false compartment inside. We'd been practicing this all afternoon. Only about five yards away from me. Perfect distance.

The conductor counted the band in, and the music started up. The dance began. Suddenly the whole floor was a swirl of motion and steps and claps. The steps were simple. Each verse, partners switched positions. Everyone was moving so often, spinning and swirling next to each other. It was only a matter of time before I was right next to the queen.

I spun. Our skirts brushed. I shot half a glance at Mylo. *Now.*

The lights blinked out, leaving only the lights on the Mardi Gras trees. Delighted *oohs* sounded through the room.

The night-vision lenses in my mask activated, glossing the world over in shades of green and gray.

Swiftly, I reached for the senator's ears. The earrings were clip-ons, according to Baron's file. Just as fast, I tossed them to Mylo. He caught them in his top hat.

He flicked the lights back on. Delighted laughter mixed with the music. The dance went on. I spun arm in arm with my princess partner. The senator frowned.

The effects technicians were buzzing with confusion. Mylo hit the lights again. This time, I went for her necklace. In half a second, I had the clasp unclipped. I tossed in a high arc, and Mylo caught it like his hat was a bucket.

He let the lights back up. The technical people scrambled around the booth, fiddling with switches and cords, trying to figure out what was going wrong. The crowd clapped giddily. The music played on.

My partner and I switched spots. The senator stopped, bumping into another couple in the chaotic dance. She patted her neck, and her eyes went wide. "No, wait!" Her voice got lost in the gargle of laughter and music and stepping feet.

Too late. Mylo knocked the lights out one last time, and I went for the last piece, that dazzling crown. With an expert toss, I arced it over the heads of the crowd. Mylo held his top hat out, braced to receive. This was it: He'd catch it, dip out to one of the smoking rooms, then drop the target out the chosen window, where Kyung-soon would be waiting to catch it, buckle it into her moped, and deliver to the drop-off point. Even if the senator had the entire party locked down and questioned, it wouldn't matter. She wasn't getting her set back, especially not before the parade, when she'd teased to show it off to all of New

Orleans. What an embarrassing night it was going to be for her. It was all locking itself into place as I watched the tiara soar overhead—until a hand punched the air, grabbing the tiara midair, killing its momentum and ours.

What?

The lights came back up. Mylo looked around frantically; he gave me a sort of what-the-hell look.

Yeah, same.

"You, kid, get off the wires!" one of the tech maestros snapped at him. His jig was up. Putting his top hat back on, Mylo smiled awkwardly and backed off, though one of the techs reeled him in for a stern Southern talking-to.

I had more important things to worry about, like *who the hell took my crown?*

Senator Robicheaux had the same concerns. She shuffled across the floor, pushing people out of the way, scanning the confetti-covered dance floor. "Where is it? Where is it? Where is it?"

I studied the crowd outside of the dance floor, then bent down, scanning people and costumes at around thigh level. If someone was holding the crown, they wouldn't be carrying it above.

There. A sparkle in the light. A woman's arm, a Black one, against the black satin of an evening gown. She slipped out of the ballroom.

Yeah, I don't think so.

I pushed, squeezed, and shoved my way out of the ballroom, lifting my skirts so I could pick up the pace as I went. I got through the crowd and into the sparser hallway just in time to see a flutter of a black evening gown turning the corner. She had to be headed to the storage room. There weren't any windows or exits in there; it was a dead end.

Her mistake. I followed until I burst into the room, in all its mirrored-walls, stuffed-clothes-racks, and cluttered-marble-countered glory.

Empty?

The door clicked shut. I jumped, spinning around in a noisy rustle of fabric. I staggered back a few steps.

I'd only seen her picture once, but I recognized her instantly.

Diane Abara. Devroe's mum.

The woman who wanted me dead.

EIGHT

WHAT DO YOU say when you find yourself face-to-face with your family's mortal enemy for the first time?

Hello.

I think I hate you.

Can I have that crown back?

None of those seemed right, not that it mattered. My tongue was rooted to the roof of my mouth, and my feet were in quicksand. I'd been the one chasing, but Diane's harrowing stare made me feel as if I was the one who just got caught.

My tongue decided to come off hiatus. "I—"

"Take off that silly mask," she said. I did, not because she told me to, but because I felt childish wearing a pink night-vision mask in front of her, in her elegant black evening gown and lacy half mask.

My eyes took a second to adjust to normal vision. Loose articles of costumes hung on racks, and broken float pieces, plaster heads and hands, and spray-painted planks of wood and plastic were strewn around the room, some of it piled from the carpet to the low ceiling.

In real colors, not the greens and blacks of my night-vision lenses, Diane was even more surreal. Not just because of who she was, but because, loath as I was to admit this, she was *stunning*. Tall with flawless deep brown skin and waves of silk-pressed hair behind her shoulders. There was a distinct lack of laugh lines on her face. Something told me she was one of those people who, when she did smile, it was all the more radiant. Mourning eyes were hooded under long lashes. She was heartbreakingly gorgeous, the flavor of beautiful that people write sonnets about. So drastically different from Mom's pretty, which was all boisterous and loud and glamorous.

I wondered, during their Gambit, was Mom ever jealous of her quietly gorgeous competitor?

Diane tilted her head to the side. "You don't look like her much. Not even when she was younger. So lanky. Are you sure you're Rhi's daughter?"

Was she teasing me? Why did it almost sound like she was serious?

Whatever. Two could play that game.

I licked my teeth. "I can sort of see you in Devroe, but he has more lively eyes. Did he get that from his father?"

She tensed at the mention of Mr. Kenzie Senior and tightened her grip around the tiara.

The tiara. If she was working for Count, no way was she here to steal it. "I'm guessing you're here for, what, guard dog duty?"

Diane started circling the room, holding the crown with a deceptively light touch. With her other hand, she carried a black clutch.

"How is Devroe doing?"

The question took me aback. Devroe really hadn't been talking to her?

My peripheral gaze trailed the tiara. Maybe I could make a move for it if she stayed distracted. Keeping her talking wasn't the worst idea.

"He's having the time of his life disrupting mine. You raised a shameless flirt."

"With you? Still?" She ran her thumb over the bottom row of diamonds stacking up the crown. "I hoped if I stepped away from him for a while, it would help him get his priorities figured out, but maybe I'm just not the priority anymore."

"You're beat up because he decided he wasn't cool with murdering a whole family for you. My sympathy is overwhelming."

She cut a cold glare at me. "I'm not the one who struck first, and not the one who threatened to come back and do worse."

I paused. "What do you mean?"

"I figured Devroe was going to fall for someone someday, but never could I ever have imagined this." Diane grimaced, and I knew the distasteful *this* was me.

Distasteful to her, but was she serious about Devroe? Was she joking when she said he'd fallen for me? If anyone would know the line between teasing and genuine interest, it would be her.

I wanted to probe more, but Diane was already moving on. A threadbare smile broke through her scowl. "You may not look like her, but you sound identical. I was always so happy to hear her voice. Rhi can be so engaging when she wants to be." Still holding the tiara, she sighed, stopping in front of a massive grated fireplace, a remnant from when this used to be a smoking room in the theater's older days.

Cautiously, I followed her. Her grip on the tiara seemed looser than before. She was so melancholically magnetic, but I told myself I was only getting closer for the target. One well-done swipe was all it would take, surely.

I stopped about a pace away from her. Never once in a heist had my target or team or anyone just stopped to . . . gaze sadly into a fireplace.

"Can you answer something for me?" she asked softly.

"I probably shouldn't." A patient silence stretched between us. "What do you wanna ask?"

The tiara was only a few inches from my fingers.

There was a desperate glow in her dark irises.

"Were you happy, you and Rhiannon?"

That wasn't the question I was expecting, not that I knew what I was expecting.

But the way she waited, as if she was desperate to know . . .

My gaze slipped toward my kicks, the champagne diamonds glinting under the hem of my skirt, and an unexpected fondness swelled in me. I'd been living with a chronic liar and manipulator for eighteen years. Most of my life before the Gambit was spent being smothered under her wings, trapped on that island.

That was the knee-jerk answer. But if I was being honest with myself . . .

I didn't *hate* our isolated island. There were more good times than bad. Days building sandcastles and topping them off with rubies and emeralds. Nights falling asleep in Mom's lap when I was tiny enough to fit snugly between her legs while I doodled our house's blueprint on an Etch A Sketch. Watching trash Netflix shows with her and Auntie. Some of those memories weren't even that far back.

"Yes," I said quietly. "I was happy, and she was happy."

Saying that out loud felt like taking a kick to the chest.

It . . . made me want to talk to Mom. For just a second, all practicality was gone, and even though this was obviously not the time, it made me want to call her.

My gaze was still focused on Mom's gift, trying to ignore the sudden urge to be wrapped in cocoa butter–scented arms.

I looked back up to Diane, expecting to see her still staring hopelessly out her window, still expecting that same melancholic expression. But that Diane was gone. I was looking at the hurricane again. A furious, vengeful storm. So angry, she was practically shaking.

It startled me so much I took an instinctive step back—or I tried to. Something clanged and kept my arm jerked in place. My meteor bracelet. It pulled taut and tight from my wrist to the fireplace grate. The end of the chain was a tangled and knotted mess. She'd tangled the links around the wrought iron so the second I moved, I pulled it into a knot myself.

Oh no.

Gritting my teeth, and with more pettiness than logic, I tried to shove her back. She grabbed my hand and twisted. I winced. My breath caught as she grabbed me by the braids and tugged so hard, she might have ripped some out. My back arched painfully. I sucked in air through my teeth, snarling at her.

"Happy, hm? Good for her."

I bit my lip, tasting metal, and still she just kept twisting.

Diane cocked her head to the side, watching me with a cruel distaste. "I heard you've been trying to frame Devroe. That's cute. Obviously, you haven't been doing it right." She twisted harder, making me yelp. "Let me show you how you really frame someone."

With that, she let me go and started striding out of the room, as if nothing had happened. But before she left, she tossed her black clutch at my feet. With the clasp open, the contents spilled out over the carpet. Bracelets and watches and cell phones and car keys.

She'd been planning this since I got here.

Her phone buzzed as she opened the door. "I have the crown. Please let Madame Senator know I'll meet her at the floats." Diane opened the door and raced into the hall. "In there . . ." And now she was siccing the dogs on me.

This was just not my night.

NINE

THE WAY I saw it, I had two options. One: tell these incoming whoevers the truth, that I did not steal all these things conveniently left at my feet and I had been framed. Or two: run.

One was never really an option.

I contorted my wrist. My meteor bracelet was tightly wrapped around it, but the sound of approaching footsteps spurred me on. My hand twisted out of the tangle of chains at the last second. I hurled myself through the door right as it opened, crashing past a jester and a guy in a golden bodysuit before breaking into a sprint.

"Ay! Stop that girl!" one of them roared. I kept pumping my legs, my train fluttering behind me. I needed to get out of here, but I needed that crown too. Like hell was Diane just going to take the W.

I skidded around a corner. Feet pounded the carpet behind me. "Hey, Chris, stop that girl!"

Who the hell is Chris?

Before I got to the ballroom, a bear of a man dropped into a tackle pose, legs wide, knees bent, right in my path.

So that's Chris.

Still running, I hoisted up my skirts and slid like a batter between his legs. A few feet past him, I rolled into a crouch. A trio of partygoers sipping daiquiris from actual chalices cheered at my impromptu move.

"Run, girly, run!" One of my fans whistled, but I was already dashing back into the ballroom. I could lose the pursuers in the crowd, maybe, but after that? Diane said she was meeting the senator down at the floats. Their parade was probably about to start.

I needed to get that crown back before they hit the streets.

Ducking and weaving and twisting, I worked my way through the chaos of low lights and glitter and sweating bodies and rustling costumes. But the room was less dense than before. The royal court had left, along with at least half of the krewe.

So much for getting gobbled up by the crowd.

I attempted to hide between a tinsel-wrapped pillar and a woman in a hoopskirt and matching crop top. Maybe they wouldn't see me.

"Hey!" a man called out. "That girl! In the pink! AY!"

Half the ballroom froze, and all eyes followed the man's pointed finger to land on me.

Suddenly, the door was blocked by two more partygoers. Damn Southerners and their hero complexes.

A loud pop sounded overhead. The crowd gasped, then cheered. A sea of gold and purple and green balloons rained over us, flooding the room.

There was yelling by that technical booth, where a large string dangled loose. Mylo, a dynamic flash of green, winked at me before hightailing it into the balloon camouflage and away from the booth jesters, who looked like they were going to strangle him.

In the chaos, my instinct was to race for the exit, but I stopped myself midstep.

Fighting a storm of balloons, I raced to the balcony doors instead.

The parade crowd had multiplied. Directly below, lights on the floats burned bright, while krewe members fluttered about.

Holding on to the railing, I leaned forward to get a good view farther down the street. Past a princess float with papier-mâché turrets and another that looked like the top of an erupting gold volcano, I saw it. A silver-and-blue float styled like a giant cloud. The queen's float. It'd only be a minute until she was turning onto the parade street.

Too many krewe members on the ground. I wouldn't catch up on the sidewalk.

Holding up my train with one hand, I got a running start and bounded onto the adjacent balcony. This one was empty. I kept running. So many Spanish-style balconies in the quarter were right next to each other, and jumping the railings was like jumping hurdles.

I didn't stop until I landed on the corner balcony just before the turn onto the parade street. Everything was moving and alive. I watched the princess float slow as it turned left into the parade, veering close to the corner.

It was close enough to jump, as long as I timed it right.

The queen's float was approaching. She primped her tiara and took deep breaths. This was my chance.

I took a step back, shook off any nerves, and bounded off the balcony.

I thudded onto the back of the float, breaking into a shoulder roll.

One of the queen's courtiers, dressed in a silver-and-blue cupcake gown, gasped. She almost tripped over the edge of the float in shock, the piles of beads around her neck probably throwing her off-balance. Two other courtiers rushed to help her.

The senator's dais was at the top of the float. I slipped into the small staircase at the float's center, where beads dangled from hooks on the walls and plushies and plastic cups and scepters rattled in boxes. Ducking, I slid between the containers of favors and pushed aside the blue curtain at the top.

Her back was to me, but she was standing on a platform all by herself. The queen was fluffing out her overwhelmingly large skirt and primping, her last chance before entering the parade street. The tiara was planted firmly on her head.

Grab the crown, jump the float. Kyung-soon should still be waiting behind the ballroom. I'd just need to get back there.

My fingers were outstretched. The float started to turn. Right before the parade street, it was perfect.

But a hand wrapped around my wrist.

Diane had changed clothes and was now in the same silver colors as the krewe. In one swift movement, she twisted my arm behind my shoulders and pulled me away.

I tried to work myself out of her grip while throwing a punch at her. Diane parried my fist away, then executed a well-placed kick behind my knee. I doubled over, and she yanked me back into the curtained space. I guessed she was going to try and keep me under wraps until the end of this.

"Don't be difficult," she said. Something cracked. What was that smell?

She was bringing a knockout stick up to my face.

"No!" I bucked and squirmed, but damn, her grip was iron. I was this close and about to drop the ball.

Everything compressed into this one furious moment. Who was to say she wouldn't just take me out while she could? I'd be unconscious and defenseless.

With a scream half muffled by the crowd, I kicked my foot out, tangling my toe in the fabric of the queen's train, and tugged. It wasn't much force, but it was enough to pull her weighty costume off-balance. With a yelp, she tripped backward, landing in a jumble of cloth and sequins right at Diane's and my feet.

I punched my head back, butting into Diane's nose. Her grip slackened. I slithered out and plucked the crown from the queen's head, then made a mad dash for the lip of the queen's dais. I'd jump onto the level below, then the street, and get the hell out of here.

Diane's hand grazed me, but I slipped it and leapt.

"Stop her! Stop the float! Call someone!" The senator's voice was an octave higher than the roar of the crowd. The float's courtiers were jostled as it abruptly stopped. All the better for me. I raced to the back of the float, 100 percent ready to bolt over the back and into the alley where Kyung-soon would be waiting.

Ahead of me, Diane shoved through two courtiers, one of those knockout sticks in hand, cracked and ready. How the hell did she get down from the senator's dais so fast?

I tried to skid to a stop, but at this point collision was inevitable.

Screw everything . . .

An arm looped around Diane's throat before a gloved hand snatched the knockout stick and held it under her nose. It happened so quick, even Diane couldn't keep up. Her eyes rolled back, and she collapsed into a pile of limbs and costume. Unable to slow down, I stumbled into the whole thing, only getting a good look after.

My savior, wearing iridescent white slacks, a tapered vest, and a trimmed jacket, looked back at me. Their face was a milky white mask.

"The hell's wrong with you, let's go!"

She spoke in French. I knew that voice.

She jumped off the edge of the float, and I followed, glancing down at her shoes. White boots, with silver and purple fleurs-de-lis shimmering on her soles.

"Noelia!" We simultaneously hurdled a crowd-control barrier, sprinting side by side. "What the hell are you doing here?"

"Working. But I probably just got fired."

She threw away a job for me.

When we were out of this, I'd buy her the prettiest shoes I could get my hands on.

"What's your getaway? I'm guessing you have something near?" We raced past the row of floats.

"Behind the theater." I rerouted us between the buildings, through a slender alley, and toward freedom. It'd be a tight squeeze on Kyung-soon's moped, but we'd make it work.

"Here!" I raced into the back lot . . . and immediately skidded to a stop. Noelia slammed into my back.

"What . . . ? Oh."

Kyung-soon's bike was knocked over, and in its place was a black SUV, the back door already open, and two guards, a man and a woman, with pistols out on either side.

"Hey." Kyung-soon, looking thoroughly annoyed, showed off her zip-tied hands from her seat inside the SUV.

I backed into a fighting stance.

A gun clicked behind us, and I turned just enough to see a woman in all black bearing down on us. Noelia grabbed my wrist. "Not a great idea," she whispered.

"Ms. Quest." The woman guard used her gun to gesture inside the SUV. "You too, Ms. Boschert."

"Oh?" Noelia's knees bent just the slightest. For someone who was telling me not to fight two seconds ago, her opinion sure did shift fast when she realized *she* was about to get ushered away somewhere too.

"You couldn't even get another SUV?"

My head and Noelia's shot around. Striding toward us—well, more like being forcibly escorted by her own armed bouncer—was Diane. There was a groggy sway to her steps.

One of the goons snatched the tiara from me and hightailed it back toward the parade. All those hijinks for nothing.

Diane slid into the SUV across from Kyung-soon, complimenting her haircut in Korean.

Without much of a choice, Noelia and I piled in too, and I prayed we would all get wherever we were going without killing each other.

TEN

IT WAS AT least an hour until the SUV came to a jostling stop. All of the doors opened at once, revealing even more armed goons. Delightful.

Diane, Kyung-soon, Noelia, and I were herded like very dangerous cattle toward a building of whitewashed stone.

I craned my neck, examining the whole thing. And it went up.

Like, fifty floors up. A lone skyscraper set in the middle of a grassy lawn.

This was the Louisiana capitol building. That was why we were in the car so long—an hour's drive from New Orleans to Baton Rogue. Louisiana's congress didn't convene until March; they had to be out of session now.

"Gauche," Noelia tapped in Morse code on the back of my hand, lip curling at the unnecessary height of the building. I'd learned while on one of my documentary binges back in my lonely days that Louisiana's capitol building was only the tallest United States capitol because Governor Huey Long wanted to make it look like a giant penis.

A few years later, he got shot inside his own giant penis.

If the tension hadn't been so high, I might have snickered as we passed the stairs where it happened. Sadly, we weren't headed up, so I didn't get to see the famous bullet hole. Instead, we crossed the lobby's marble floor toward the tall doors leading into the chambers.

Noelia nodded at Diane and Kyung-soon a step ahead of us. She tapped my hand again; we'd been talking in silence the entire ride, mostly about her not realizing she'd been outsourced on a job with Devroe's mum and apologizing in the same way a friend might if they realized they'd accidentally slept with your ex. It'd have been funny if all of this weren't so decidedly unfunny.

"What are they talking about now?" Noelia asked. Diane and Kyung-soon had been chatting in Korean about everything from AI to gelato shops in London's Soho district during the ride. I hadn't been paying too much attention . . . until now.

"Devroe does miss you, you know," Kyung-soon was saying. "He brings you up every day . . ."

I slowed, before a guard pushed me back into motion. "What? What?" Noelia tapped frantically.

Every day? How would Kyung-soon know . . . unless she'd been in contact with Devroe this whole time? No wonder Devroe knew my birthday. The pineapple upside-down cake. That

I was in New Orleans. Kyung-soon had been spying for him this whole time.

Gritting my teeth, I answered Noelia with a rough thrumming. "Liars."

The senate chambers were gorgeous, in an official sort of way, with navy-blue carpet, veined pink marble pillars between high windows—curtains drawn tonight—and gold molding running across the ceiling. At least a hundred oak desks, each proudly displaying a mini American flag and Louisiana State flag, with a corresponding blue leather chair with gold studs, sat empty facing the speaker's desk at the very front.

Armed goons were stationed at every window, bracketing us in from all sides.

We were far from the first to arrive to this little party. Count was there, for the first time ever with her hands tablet-free, and so was Baron, leaning back casually against the podium while pointedly ignoring whatever Count was saying to him. There was a scent like cream and sugar and baking spray, and I just knew it was coming from him.

He frowned as our entourage entered. "What the hell are they doing here?"

"Witnesses for whatever hysterics you've been concocting—"

"You really are getting desperate, calling in the help." Baron pulled out his phone, pretending Count didn't exist again.

A spark of green flashed from one of the front-row desks. Mylo raised a hand, still in its emerald glove.

"Yo!"

Someone was sitting next to him. He stood. "Mum?" Devroe's eyes flashed through a whole coterie of emotions from confusion to concern to anticipation back to confusion as they flickered from his mum to me.

"My god, it's like the worst high school reunion ever," Noelia whispered. She shrugged Mylo's hand away as he came in for a dap-up.

"Ross, are you . . . all right?" Devroe's fingers flexed, but he refrained from reaching out. Diane walked right past him, not meeting his eye. Kyung-soon cleared her throat and gave him a look that said he should tend to her.

"I . . ." He turned to his mum, then me. "I'll be back." And followed her to a desk across the aisle. As if I cared.

"Noelia! What's up?" Mylo beamed. "Crazy night, amirite?"

"You look like a discount leprechaun," she told him.

"Are you going to tell us why we're here?" I projected to the room.

Baron ignored me, though I wasn't as irked at being ignored as Count seemed to be. She stormed down the pair of steps from the speaker's raised platform. "Deception and betrayal." Count cut a glare my way, like this was my fault.

"Don't look at me like that. You're the one who screwed with my family first, and I hope you're about to get chewed out for it," I sneered.

"Excuse me?" She looked genuinely flabbergasted.

"Chewed out," Mylo said slowly. "You know, it means dragged, beaten up verbally, punished—"

Count raised a silencing finger right in front of Mylo's face, her jaw clenched in that say-something-else-and-you'll-regret-it look that only someone who has a teenage son can master.

She stepped close enough that I wished I still had my chain.

Not that I thought I couldn't take Count without it, but you never knew.

"What do you mean, 'I screwed with your family'?"

Why did she sound almost like she didn't know what I was talking about?

"You've been employing Diane in exchange for granting her wish to destroy the Quests," I said.

Count rubbed her temples and muttered some French words even I didn't know, but from the way Noelia blanched, I guessed it was something particularly profane. "I haven't hired Diane Abara for anything. Ever."

I straightened. "Baron said you were going to offer her a wish in exchange—"

"I would never offer someone a wish so frivolously."

"Bull!" I sputtered. "What about the hit jobs you had us do on Baron?"

"Yes, yes, every now and then," Count admitted. "But I don't know what that has to do with Diane."

"Then who hired us to protect the senator at the parade? Papa said it was an organization request," Noelia interjected.

Baron had one arm up on the speaker's desk. He winked at me, smirking.

Of course. Diane was never employed by Count; that was just a lie to goad me into this botched job tonight. Baron had said he initially thought of Mom for this, but probably figured she would have been harder to dupe. Still, as long as one Quest was on the scene to butt heads with Diane, it was guaranteed to turn into the disaster he wanted.

Mom never would have made this mistake.

The chamber doors groaned open. Senator Robicheaux stormed in faster than a sixtysomething woman in a full Mardi Gras costume should have been able to, hauling her skirts in handfuls.

"Start the call!" she barked, and to who I wasn't exactly sure until all of the goons by the windows and doors pulled tablets out from their jackets and started queuing up what I guessed was that call.

Count put a smile on real quick. "Good evening, Madame Senator. Perhaps we could speak in private for a few—"

"No." The senator kept walking until she was at the speaker's desk—her desk, I supposed.

Baron, on the other hand, gave the senator a playful but respectful bow. "Your Majesty."

The senator huffed, but it was better than what Count got.

Tablets were shoved into all of our hands. A video call, hundreds of icons littering the screen. More than hundreds, it had to be thousands.

In the top corner of the screen: 1,480 participants.

"Oh boy," Mylo said, straightening his top hat. Noelia sucked in a breath, holding the tablet up at a more presentable angle.

I swallowed hard. Was this . . . the entire organization?

"Emergency session," the senator said, her Southern drawl sharp. "Tonight has been one of the most embarrassing nights of my life. It's unacceptable that I or any of us should have to put up with anything less than sublimity—that's the entire reason this esteemed group exists."

"I couldn't agree more, Madame Senator," Baron cut in. "But

that's what you get when you have someone incompetent running things for you."

Count, red as the fires of hell, retorted, "Tonight's incident was intentionally orchestrated. The only way to get rid of the problem is to get rid of the dissenter—"

"A competent leader wouldn't allow a 'dissenter' to cause so much trouble." Baron shrugged.

The senator slapped her hand on the speaker's desk. "*Both* of you are to blame," she said decidedly. "We know you've been launching petty attacks against each other for the past year, and now it's starting to be an inconvenience. One of you has got to go."

Her attention had returned to the video chat. Of course, the *important* audience in this.

"Exactly what I was thinking." Count gestured back to us, pushing through a tremble in her hand. "Baron is the seed of discontent in this organization. That's why I asked for the remainder of our associates to be brought here as well. A thorough questioning will prove that all the trouble that's been caused has been instigated by this disloyal traitor—"

"Loyalty, treason, blah blah blah." Baron rolled his eyes. "What do any of us care about that? The point is, who can get the job done cleanest? Dragging in a bunch of underlings to plead her case for her isn't just a perfect example of how sloppy Count's become. She's pathetic and desperate." Baron turned back to us, hand on his heart. "No offense, underlings."

"Honestly, a lot taken," Mylo said.

Messages flooded the chat, all of them coming in under the name **Anonymous**.

Baron has a point.

Ha! I never liked him before but . . .

I heard Count wasted a week visiting her brat last month.

Count's tablet shook in her grip. The senator nodded along to the incoming messages.

Diane held her tablet gently in her lap. The hint of a smile was forming on her lips as well, despite Kyung-soon's worried frown and Devroe's pacing in front of her.

She was about to get what she wanted too.

Baron reeled me into this mess by telling me that Count had promised her a wish come true in exchange for helping crush the competition. Count would never make that promise—what leader would give someone a blank check like that? But a would-be leader . . .

Baron had offered her the wish. Once he was crowned, he was going to take us out for her.

A new message dropped into the anonymous chat. It was bolded.

Shall we put it to a vote?

"No!" The messages stopped, and everyone in the chambers looked to me. A couple of goons waiting against the walls slid hands inside their blazers.

They were probably wondering what the hell I was doing.

I was wondering what the hell I was doing.

"A vote," I repeated. "Now, really?" I stepped up to the senator, my tablet clenched tightly at my side.

"Look—" I cleared my throat at the senator's sneer. "Ma'am." She gave me the most annoying that's-better look I'd ever seen.

"Opinions are obviously biased right now. Count dropped the ball tonight, but that doesn't mean Baron's the overall best choice to run your . . . group."

"Thank you for that unsolicited opinion, Ms. Quest. Madame Senator, maybe we should get the help out of the proceedings. If Count wants to babysit, I'm sure she'll have plenty of time for that now." Baron circled my way just to put a hand on the small of my back, like he could guide me away that easily.

I twisted his wrist into a bone-breaking lock.

The sound of half a dozen guns being cocked at the same time filled the chambers. The goons were suddenly circling in fast. Devroe tried to rush my way but was blocked by one of the goons.

"You don't look so competent now," I said.

"Oh, like you couldn't get Count in a poor-man's armlock," Baron said through gritted teeth.

"Count's smart enough not to get this close."

I let him go, splaying my hands to the guards so they knew I wasn't fighting anymore. Baron tried to hide his embarrassment, but the red on the tips of his ears gave him away.

If I hadn't been on Baron's chopping block already, I sure as hell was now.

The senator tilted her head to the side, and the guards begged off.

She thrummed her fingers against the side of her desk.

Okay, no getting ushered away for me. So that meant she was at least curious about me, or maybe my little attack on Baron had entertained her. "Awfully loyal to Count, are we? You must really like her."

"No," I clarified. "But I . . . respect how suited she is for the job she does."

The senator scoffed. "And yet you still betrayed her. Why?"

I swallowed. How did I keep it from sounding like I was only Team Count for the sake of my own family?

I went on, feeling thousands of invisible eyes on me. "Have you spent a month with Count before? I wanted to slam my head against a steel safe." That got me a smirk and some laughter in the chat. "But look what happened the one time I didn't listen to her."

A new message buzzed into the chat. This one bolded too.

Gambit?

And just like that, the messages flooded in.

Yes, let's test it.

Who can do the most for us in a week? Two weeks?

I like it.

Yes, a Gambit to decide the winner.

Less like a Gambit, more like a gauntlet.

"Oh, come on," Baron said, scrolling through his tablet. He let out a wry laugh. "You can't be serious."

"I like it as well." The senator nodded, looking through the comments.

"Managing the Gambit is one of the most important events of the year," Count said, having, mostly, found her composure again. She straightened the edges of her hair behind her ears. "Are you saying you wouldn't be able to manage that responsibility?"

"Of course not," Baron spat.

"How are you going to plan one if you can't even win one?" Noelia added from behind me.

Mylo pointed at her. "What she said."

"I'm not a thief. I don't do that grunt work any more than you do," Baron said to Count, his composure starting to frazzle.

"Obviously no one is expecting you to get your hands dirty, Baron. But it appears some of our favorite talent has already created factions," the senator said, waving him off. "How does a little team versus team sound?" The senator was speaking to the tablet again. Her gaze flicked to me, then my friends behind. "I think it's clear that Count already has her own gaggle of in-house supporters. Perhaps Baron does too? If they come as a package, let's see whose package is superior."

The messages were now a near-overwhelming yes.

Diane stood.

"Mum?" Devroe asked.

"I would like to support Baron's team," she said. "If I'm allowed to play."

The comments approved.

"We're with Ross!" Mylo said, grabbing Noelia's hand and raising it along with his.

Noelia wiggled her hand away and cleared her throat, placing a hand over her heart. "I would be honored to enter another Gambit, in Count's favor."

She gave me a little nod.

Devroe fidgeted on the other side of the aisle, twisting his cuff link. "If I'm allowed to play . . . I . . ."

Our gazes caught, and I almost crumpled seeing how quietly distraught he was. Back at the ball, Diane implied she hadn't talked to him since the end of the Gambit.

She also implied that she thought her son really was on my side. Would he prove it now?

"I'd like to join Baron's team."

I couldn't say that was a surprise, but it did ache.

Kyung-soon rose and gave Devroe's hand a friendly squeeze. She spared me and the rest of our friends, or maybe just my friends, a sliver of a glance before returning her attention to the senator.

"Baron, please." Her voice was quiet, but it still hurt.

I knew we were having beef right now, but . . . really?

Then again, she'd been in contact with Devroe this entire time. I needed to stop being so gullible. Maybe Kyung-soon was never really with me, not when compared to Devroe, at least.

No freaking way I would cry here. So I blinked away my tears and turned my full focus to the senator.

In the most dramatic fashion possible, she clapped her hands and smiled. "Then we've got a game. Whoever's team wins this gauntlet will have the honor of leading us, or continuing to lead us. And the other one . . . Well, you know how retirement works in this organization."

Count took a shaky breath, paper pale. I could see in her face the look of someone tallying their life achievements along with all the things they hadn't done yet.

"We'll arrange specifics within the next few hours," the senator said.

Whoever won got to lead. Whoever won got to live.

ELEVEN

IT'D COST OVER two thousand dollars for me, Mylo, and Kyung-soon to get a studio Airbnb during Mardi Gras season.

Count had a penthouse suite booked in under two minutes. Perks of the job, while she had it.

After the most awkward car ride ever, Count told me, Mylo, and Noelia that she'd have someone get our things and bring them here—because of course she knew where all of our things were—then retreated to the upper floor of the penthouse.

So now I was sitting at the dining table with my head in my hands, moping . . . for lack of a better word.

Oh, and still in full Mardi Gras costume. Let the good times roll, amirite?

In the living room, Mylo was ordering so much room service I suspected he was reading the menu back to the staff.

On my own, I found myself tracing the edge of my phone.

Not that it was important at all . . . but I found myself opening the text thread with Devroe. He'd looked so . . . conflicted. Would he even text me back if I texted him right now?

Hey . . . I sent. Just as an experiment.

The bubbles started dancing immediately. But then they disappeared. The hell?

I should've left it at that, but . . .

Are you guys okay?

This time, he did commit to a response.

Devroe

Fine.

No thanks to any of you.

I glared at the screen. Where the hell did this come from?

Me

My bad, I see we've switched back to temper tantrum mode. Sorry for asking.

I waited a whole minute, until I was sure I wouldn't hear back from him at all.

Devroe

Talk to your crazy mom.

I have to protect my own family.

I dropped my phone. I guessed if there was a day to be butthurt about my mom's past transgressions, it was today. Feeling particularly pathetic, I opened the notes in my phone.

REGRETS AND OTHER STUFF TO FIGURE OUT IF I LIVE:
Wth is going on with Devroe and me?

Noelia settled into the high-backed seat next to mine, bringing a barely sipped bottle of spring water with her. I flipped my phone facedown.

"Sorry about Kyung-soon." She worried her lip. "I know you thought you were friends, so . . ."

I sat up and dragged my fingers down my face. "Whatever. I should probably be over the whole 'oh my god, that person wasn't really my friend' thing now. It's not like it's the first time."

She winced, and I realized my mistake.

"Not that I was talking about you! I mean, I kinda was, but you didn't know back then, so, not your fault."

"Right."

We sat in cricket-chirping silence for a few seconds, punctuated only by Mylo's "Does that come with onion rings?" in the other room.

"You didn't have to do this for me," I finally said. "Not that I don't appreciate the support, but I know you've probably got other assignments with your family—"

Noelia put a hand up. "First, believe it or not, but you *do* have some friends who aren't in the market to stab you in the back and just want to help for the sake of helping. I'll use baby terms since you're new to the friendship thing, but that's what friends do, Quest."

I flushed and hid a smile.

"Second"—Noelia held up two fingers—"this might actually be good for my family situation."

She took a sip of water and some time to gather her thoughts. Like a good friend, I waited. "Since the end of the Gambit, things haven't exactly been fantastic for me. Losing was bad enough, but apparently not even trying to win the final phase was . . . particularly disgraceful."

"The final phase was kidnapping! Not to mention you saved your own brother from being snatched."

Technically *I* did, but semantics.

She pressed her hands to her eyes. "Papa says if I'd gone through with the phase and won, then I could've wished for Nicki back and everything would have been fine." Her forehead scrunched, like she was suddenly fighting a headache. "Nicki ended up being unceremoniously dismissed from Hauser. All of his records were 'mysteriously lost.' His devices got 'accidentally' wiped. They even scrubbed all his social media accounts. Which of course Nicki thinks is *my* fault." She rubbed her eyes, so hard I was a bit worried she'd damage them. "I thought he at least would be over it by now, but six months later, and he's still calling me Witch Bitch."

"You know your family is being a bunch of Monday-morning-quarterback dicks, right?" Never in my life could I understand the logic of "it's your fault for not just letting your brother get kidnapped."

Noelia shook her head lightly. Even if I was right—and I was—she wasn't in a place to hear it.

We were quiet for a few seconds. Was this the type of moment where you would pat someone on the shoulder? Maybe, but I waited too long and missed my opportunity.

Instead, I said, "You did the right thing."

"Yeah, I know," she said. "But that doesn't change the fact that all of that . . . crap that happened knocked me down from heir apparent status to lackey sent on bodyguard work."

Hence how she ended up in New Orleans, I guessed.

She turned away, as if the wet bar on the other side of the room demanded her attention. "Everyone in the family knows I'm on the outs with Papa. I bet even Nana Cati knows."

"Is she usually out of the loop?"

"She's dead."

"Oh."

"Second Cousin Trevor is probably higher on Papa's list than I am right now. Trevor couldn't steal a Kleenex from a rubbish bin. Recovering my reputation by winning this new game isn't the worst idea. Who cares if I fail? Once you hit rock bottom, there's nothing else to lose."

I huffed an awkward laugh. "You're Noelia Boschert—you and rock bottom are like the repelling ends of magnets. You couldn't hit it if you wanted to. And your papa is probably just pushing you around for a little bit until he takes you back."

"You don't know that." Noelia's voice cracked. Her shoulders trembled. Was that a sniffle?

I went stiff-still in my seat.

Cautiously, I snuck around her chair to peek at her. Noelia's eyes were red, swelling with tears. Her cheeks were a blotchy color. She bit back sobs.

"Are you crying?" I caught myself too late. That was totally not the thing you're supposed to say to someone who actually was crying, and definitely not in the stupid-ass tone I just used. What *were* you supposed to do when your friend was crying?

"No, of course not. Don't be ridiculous." Noelia swatted tears from her cheeks, but more fell.

Oh man, how did I deal with this? "Uh, there, there." I tried the shoulder pat, which did absolutely nothing. I nearly tripped over a chair bringing her a pile of napkins from the wet bar. She took one and blew her nose, but didn't stop sobbing.

"It's, um . . ." I could try and give her some advice about her family again, but that hadn't worked before.

"It's okay, you're totally allowed to cry." I was still patting her shoulder with as much natural skill as an animatronic.

Noelia blotted away the freshest tears, blinking her red eyes. "You're awful at this."

"Uh . . . yeah. But I'm here?"

That earned me an almost smile between the sobs.

Out in the living room, the sound of one of the double doors swooshing over the plush carpet announced someone was here. The rattle of a cart followed.

"Wow, you guys are fast," I heard Mylo say. "But I guess it *is* the penthouse. Set up wherever."

I heard Mylo shuffling over the carpet before sliding into the dining room, still in his green dress pants, button-down, and vest. "Hey, I ordered all the food—"

He stumbled to a stop, scanning the disaster I'd somehow turned Noelia into. I was going to shoo him away, but instead he sighed, locking eyes with Noelia, who had enough pride to attempt a poker face.

"Family stuff?" he asked.

How did he—

"How'd you know?" Noelia asked, sniffling.

"People only cry that hard about family stuff or breakups, and when breakups are the culprit, it usually involves more anger or looking at old texts or pictures of 'better days.'" He hopped in the chair on Noelia's other side.

Was everyone this tuned in, or was it just me who didn't know what the hell I was doing when it came to comforting friends?

"Well, aren't you an expert . . ." Noelia rolled her eyes.

"Ignoring you or being too pushy?" Mylo asked.

"I don't know. Both. Maybe more the first one," Noelia said.

"Sucks, doesn't it?" Mylo sighed. "Sometimes you feel like you're yelling into a void trying to get your family to listen to you and they just . . . don't?"

I expected Noelia to snort or say something dismissive, but she blotted the newest tears away and gave a little nod instead. "You wish they would notice everything you're doing, but instead—"

"You're totally invisible. Preaching to the choir, my friend," Mylo said.

And just like that, they fell into their own conversation,

venting about the woes of being a minimal priority to one's parents. Or parent, in Noelia's case—I'd never heard her or anyone in the industry mention where *Mrs.* Boschert was.

I slowly eased myself out of the room. Maybe that was why I hadn't been able to help. If anything, my problem was the opposite. Whatever the case, it felt like a conversation I wasn't meant to be a part of.

Addition to my new list:

Regret not getting to understand my friends better.

I rubbed my neck as I stepped into the open living room. The waiter was taking her sweet time setting up all the food. It looked like she'd barely started. What had she been doing for the past five minutes?

I scanned the plush carpet. Faint impressions, shod, not barefoot like Mylo's, led from the dining room doors back toward the cart behind the sectional sofa.

Was she snooping on us?

I walked toward her. The closer she got, the more obvious it was that she was wearing a fake crochet wig, and the more familiar the curve of her lips under her festive Mardi Gras half mask.

That undeniable cocoa butter smell hit me a foot away.

I ripped her wig off, and waves of weave fell out. She at least had the dignity to take the mask off on her own.

"You have no chill and no restraint."

As I spoke, Mom sat on the back of the sectional, crossing her ankles. She loosened the top button around her neck. Whoever she stole this uniform from wasn't precisely her size.

She did the finger quotes thing. "No mother 'has chill' when they don't know where their child is."

"But they 'have chill' when they chuck them into the ocean and traumatize them for life."

"You've gotta get over that, baby girl." Mom rubbed her temples like I was the one stressing her out.

"No, *you* need to get out!" I pointed toward the door, coming off way more petulant than I intended, but it had been a long-as-hell night and I was starting to emotionally malfunction.

Mom pouted. "I'm only here to help."

"With what?"

She hadn't been at the capitol building—how would she know what I needed help with?

"How long have you been following me?"

She shrugged. "Oh, you know."

"Since I got here?"

"Sure."

So since Brazil.

"Jesus Christ," I groaned.

Mylo peeked out of the dining room. Noelia stepped out beside him.

"You're still here?" Mylo frowned at Mom. "Did Ross not tip you? You know they let you Venmo tips now."

Noelia shushed him. "Are you . . . Rhiannon Quest?"

Mom gave her a twinkle-finger wave.

Mylo lit up. "Hey, you're Ross's mom! What's up?" He bopped over like he was going to ask for her autograph. I cleared my throat and cut him a glare. Mylo stopped. "Oh yeah, I mean, shame on you for everything you did to Ross." He gave me a reassuring half nod.

"And you're here because . . . ?" Noelia cocked a brow.

"She's leaving," I said.

"No, I'm not," Mom said.

"Yes, you are."

"No, she's not." Count emerged from the hallway leading into the bedrooms, trademark tablet in hand, her hair a touch disheveled. "Rhiannon contacted me asking to supplement my team. I've accepted her."

"But she's—"

"Lament your personal issues later. I want her on my team. End of story."

I wanted to protest, but it'd make me look petulant again.

"How about a little gratitude for the girl who just saved your job?" Noelia said, tone sharp as knives. Her claws were back out, and I was glad she was on my side.

"Gratitude is for people who are helping you out of the goodness of their own hearts." Count looked to me. "Don't act as if you're here for anything except our intersecting best interests."

"I'm actually just here for Ross, and the food." Mylo lifted one of the silver trays on the cart. His face distorted when he found it completely empty.

"The organization has decided on the rules of this . . . Gauntlet." Count touched her tablet. My phone buzzed. So did Mylo's and Noelia's and Mom's. "It's to be a showcase of jobs, unfortunately chosen without my input, that will be considered high-ticket wins for the organization as a whole."

"So we're not just knocking items off your personal hit list anymore?" I asked.

Count bit the corner of her lip, not responding.

I looked at my phone. A picture cued up from the link Count

had sent. Ice—sheets of blue-white ice and glaciers. A tundra stretching farther than the eye could see. The only sign of life was a speck of a building nestled alongside a large body of water. I zoomed in on it, just to make sure I wasn't imagining the sliver of concrete in the snow. But it was there, a flat building with snowmobiles to the side and a matching outbuilding a short distance away. A thin antenna, fuzzy in the low-definition picture, punched into the sky.

"Three phases, best of two takes the win," Count said. "This is number one."

"That's a lot of snow on flatland." Noelia tilted her phone to the side for a new angle. "What is this . . . Russia?"

"There's no body of water that big in Russia, baby Boschert," Mom said.

So the only place this could be was . . .

"Antarctica!" Mylo said with so much enthusiasm I thought a *ding ding ding* would follow his answer.

"The edge of Antarctica, technically," Count said. "This is a lab specializing in converting nuclear reactions into a completely perpetual and renewable energy source."

"Cool." Mylo nodded, rubbing his chin. "How do they do that?"

"If the science is over my head, I promise it will be over yours," Count said. Mom pressed her fingertips to her mouth, hiding the laugh I knew she wanted to let out.

"All you need to know," Count continued, "is that their work involves research and technology that could revolutionize energy conservation in the coming decades, and therefore change the landscape of profit and power in the very lucrative energy sector."

I knew where this was going already. "And this is the part where you tell us that, sadly, the organization doesn't have any investments in this lab that managed to ace this breakthrough, right?"

"That would be the case, yes," Count said. "Select members of our organization hold significant portions of their fortunes in the energy sector. We've attempted to buy out this lab with no success. And then they made this breakthrough. Not good for us. Unless they were to lose ownership of the new prototype technology they've just perfected."

Stealing from scientists in Antarctica. Could honestly say I'd never done that before.

"When does the phase start?" I asked.

"Don't you know the drill by now? Be downstairs in ten." Count strode out of the suite.

Mylo grumbled, heading for the door too. "Guess I'll have to steal some crepes from that bakery by the lobby." As he left, Noelia headed back toward a guest room, mumbling disparagingly about American crepes, leaving me and Mom alone. I was going to follow Mylo, but comforting cocoa butter arms wrapped around me from behind. "I'm sorry about your friend turning against you," Mom said. "And the Kenzie boy too."

I should've wiggled out of her grasp, but another part of me stayed still. "You don't care about my friends."

Mom sighed. "No, but I care about my baby girl, so I'm sorry they let you down."

"Not the first time someone has."

Mom only squeezed me tighter, and I was feeling so exhausted that I just let her. Until Devroe's text popped into my mind. "Devroe said to talk to you. He said something about protecting his family, but it didn't seem like he was talking about the organization. You don't know anything about that, do you?"

Mom tensed. She petted my hair. "Why would I know?"

I turned and narrowed my eyes, but Mom's poker face was impenetrable. "I haven't seen Diane in twenty years," she swore. "I don't know what he's talking about. *That's* the truth."

Maybe it was the nostalgia of being in my mom's arms again, but she seemed genuine.

I made a mental note to add to the list again.

Figure out how I feel about Mom.

TWELVE

A YEAR AGO, IF anyone had told me I'd be atop a mountain in full ski gear, wiping flecks of snow off my goggles and fighting a relentless ice-cold wind in the middle of the Antarctic night, I would have said, *Yeah, maybe*. Weirder jobs had happened.

If you'd told me I'd be doing all of that with Noelia Boschert, and happy to have her too, that's when I would have called bull. Funny how drastically things can change within a year.

An artificial vortex of wind blew up snow behind us. Noelia scrambled to catch her unruly double-plaited braids, which were, quite hilariously, slapping her face like it owed them money. I was suddenly grateful I'd pulled my braids into an efficient ponytail.

"Are you sure they can't hear this at the lab?" Noelia yelled over the thrashing of the helicopter blades. I turned to watch the copter, dark except for the speckles of light from inside the cockpit, rise back into the air. It was a relative tornado dropping down in the middle of the silent continent. Copters aren't exactly the stealthiest ride out there, so they're typically repulsive to thieves. But when you need to get to the bottom of the world, the options are limited.

"Chill." I stage-gestured to the valley of the mini mountain. Down the slope, past another expanse of flat snow and nestled between scraggly rocks on each side and a glacier-filled sea behind it, were a slice of concrete and faint twinkling lights. "We're miles away. They're not gonna hear anything, and with the lights off, they can't see this far either."

At least, I was 90 percent sure that was the case . . .

"I'm looking at the feed the American boy is sending in from the shore." Mom's voice buzzed in my ear. Hundreds of miles away, on a freighter, she was running coms. Despite being on the team, she was not down for the cold. So she said, but I suspected she didn't want to risk running into Diane. "The helicopter was practically invisible."

"I'm listening and watching. Over and out." A tiny click sounded in my ear as she turned off her mic.

"She knows no one says *over and out* anymore, right?" Noelia twisted her braids into her goggle straps.

"Mom plays by her own rules." I checked my watch: 2:55 a.m., but the sun had set only an hour before we dropped in. Most of Antarctica is trapped in daylight this time of year, which would have been a nightmare. However, the Antarctic Peninsula gets a couple hours of night, a small window of time for infiltration.

Noelia and I would ski down the mountain, navigate the

lab—then we'd leave through one of the side exits and maneuver around the nest of rocks toward the shore, where Mylo was waiting in our cold-weather-proof Zodiac. From there it would be a brisk ride to our helicopter pickup spot. There was no way we were hauling ourselves back up the mountain to this drop-off spot.

That was if everything all went according to plan. There was also, you know, the other team to worry about. But you couldn't plan for everything, except that was the reason both Noelia and I were here. Two thieves may be less covert than one, but they also kick more butt than one, even if neither of us were particularly out for blood or anything—

I turned to Noelia, about to ask if she was ready, only to find her tucking a gun into her marshmallow-white waistband.

"What the hell? We don't do guns!"

"Said who?"

You'd think she'd be done with guns forever after what happened with Yeriel. I breathed in a painfully cold breath. "Lia . . ."

"Will you relax? It's not *real*." With clumsy hands—I attributed that to the thickness of her gloves—she popped open the mag, revealing dual rows of tiny capsule-sized canisters filled with clear liquid, each with its own baby syringe.

"Sedative. Fast acting." Noelia popped the mag back into place. "I won it in left right for Christmas."

I cocked a brow. "Left right?"

"That game where everyone brings a gift, and you pass them around in a circle until the music stops."

"Someone brought a sedative gun—"

"Christmas is always interesting in the Boschert household." She resituated the gun at her hip.

"Don't hesitate to shoot."

Noelia and I startled. I hadn't even heard Mom click her mic back on.

She continued. "Trigger-happy people get a bad rap, but at the end of the day, they're the ones who are alive."

"Okay, thank you, over and out," Noelia said. There was a short pause before Mom clicked off again. Noelia sighed. "With advice like that, I'm surprised she doesn't carry a gun."

"Mom's deadly enough without one." Weirdly, a little spark of envy hit me. In terms of efficiency, it was a shame Mom wasn't here. No one won like her.

Shaking the thought off, I adjusted my goggles. Noelia clacked her ski rods together for luck. Staring down the miles of slope and snow ahead of us, I blew out a cloud of air, and we took off.

By the time I was folding my skis and rods up and tucking them into my backpack, I was unreasonably pissed at whatever asshole architect dropped this lab at the edge of the water, forcing us to trudge across tundra for over an hour. If only all this had gone down a couple months earlier, we could've cut time by sneaking across the frozen-over ocean, but the slightly warming temperatures increased the chances of becoming a human game of Skee-Ball on the ice. So that was, sadly, a no-go.

Creeping onto the roof of the lab, which, thanks to a slope of snow, was as simple as walking up, Noelia and I set a drop line to propel into a window. Noelia swung down and shaved away at the glass, carefully handing me the pane before shimmying inside. I gripped the rope, about to follow, when Mom's voice buzzed back in my ear.

"Just to you, baby girl. There's a time to do things your way, and there's a time to do things my way. If you want to win, do as I say. Be brutal this time around."

Brutal. No hesitation. Were those the parts of Mom that ruined all her relationships, or were they the parts of her that always got her what she wanted?

Winning was something I wanted too.

Noelia tugged the rope from below, probably wondering what the hell I was doing.

"I understand. Over and out."

THIRTEEN

WHILE STUDYING THE lab's blueprints, I'd been imagining the set design from *The Thing*. The reality was a little less sci-fi.

I led the way across the scuffed white tile of the hallways. Multicolored Arctic coats and boots hung on hooks here and there. Disorganized shelves were stacked with books with intimidating scientific titles like *Nuclear Fission and Atomic Subdivision*, Vol. 12, but also a few well-worn Dan Brown novels and Twilight paperbacks with the covers nearly disintegrated. The lab was giving off a lot more ragtag crew of young scientists instead of corporate sterile lab vibes. No wonder they turned down all the organization's proxy attempts to buy them out. I bet they were the found-family types that wanted to unveil their stunning prototype together.

My heart ached for taking this from them.

I bet Mom wouldn't have wasted a millisecond on a thought like that.

We took a quiet route through the research sector of the lab. We needed to get to the main research and storage unit toward the shore. Half the building was residential. As long as we stayed on the lab side, there was no reason we should run into anyone in the middle of the night. Noelia was one step behind me, hand on the hilt of the gun in her waistband, scanning for any surprise attacks.

After creeping through a few more corridors leading into messy offices and mini labs, we slipped through a pair of saloon-style swinging doors and into a darkened mess hall. Arctic moonlight squeaked in through slit-like windows inches below the ceiling line, illuminating the metal tables and mismatched steel and plastic chairs.

I pointed toward another saloon-style door on the other side of a serving counter near the back. This shortcut was going to save us about five minutes.

I weaved through the well-loved chairs and tables, until a sliver of sound broke into the otherwise-silent mess hall.

On instinct, I ducked behind the side of a counter, reaching to pull Noelia down too, but she was already dropping into a crouch. A whisper of footsteps echoed beyond the door on the other side of the counter. Light steps. Trained steps.

They were here.

Worrying my lip, I looked at Noelia and mouthed: "Team Kenzie."

"Maybe," she mouthed back.

Those quiet steps were getting closer. They must have

come in through another entrance. There were dozens on the residential side they could have taken advantage of. What were the chances they cared just a little less about getting caught by the staff than we did?

They could've been less worried because they were better prepared to mow down anyone in their way. That was the way Mom would think of it.

I wanted to win like Mom, didn't I?

She wouldn't hesitate.

Noelia still hadn't moved. Instead she was waiting to react. That kind of crap was probably what got her an L during the Gambit too.

"Gun," I mouthed.

She frowned and shook her head. "Too drastic. Wait."

"Gun. Now."

"No."

She really wasn't going to do anything.

I flexed my fingers, pretended to gesture at something, then pivoted directions and swiped the sedative gun from her grasp. Noelia's eyes widened. She reached to snatch it back, but I shoulder-rolled out of the way. Landing on the balls of my feet, I prowled toward the door and the nearly there footsteps. How many of them would be coming through? One? Two? All three? It only sounded like one, but who knew.

My grasp was surprisingly still on the gun, and my finger right on the trigger. I thought I didn't like guns, but maybe I didn't know what I could do. I'd been choosing not to be this brave for so many years. Choosing to be so easy to get one over on.

A pale light slipped under the crack of the door. I raised the gun. *Come on.*

Noelia crashed into me. Her arm snaked around my neck. We collapsed to the floor. My grip on the gun slipped, and she easily twisted it from my fingers, all while managing to tug me to the side. I flailed at her arm around my neck, but she managed to drag us between an industrial fridge and a trash compactor anyway.

Furious, I opened my mouth to protest, but she covered it, using her finger to tap Morse on my cheek. "Look."

Reluctantly, I ripped the goggles off her head and angled the reflective lenses to spy on the half-open door.

A short man with a thin beard, wrapped up in flannel, peeked in skeptically.

Not Team Kenzie.

Noelia cocked her head at me in a way that said more than any Morse code taps could. I'd overreacted, at least in her view. But I couldn't feel that sorry about it. I was just trying to be ahead of the enemy. Trying not to be so soft. Those were the traits that always got Mom what she wanted.

I watched our guest for a few moments longer, noting the revolver holster. Count's intel was spot-on. They were scientists packing heat. I suppose getting into a gunfight with one of them . . . wasn't in our best interest.

Mr. Flannel opened the door of the fridge opposite us. He peered around the room one last time before fishing out a bowl of leftovers labeled *SARAH* in big bold letters on the side. Guess that explained his cautiousness on the way here. The guy who eats everyone else's food is hated by all. In about five minutes, he'd eaten Sarah's soup and Akshi's fruit salad, then retreated the way he came.

Noelia slipped out of the hiding place first, giving me a once-over as she kept a tight hold on her weapon.

"Good?" she asked.

I forced a nod.

DESPITE MY PARANOIA, things continued to go as planned for the remainder of the job. Almost too well, which was only increasing the sense of dread. We made it into the inner chamber of the lab undetected. The target looked exactly as it had in the picture included in the file Count forwarded us. A fairly large piece of machinery. Well, portable but still a decent size—a contraption that reminded me of one of those cube gaming consoles my mom said were all the rage in the early 2000s. About half the size of my torso, stainless steel, and with a small fan in the back.

Noelia got to work making sure all of the cords were disconnected and the security RFID tags disabled, while I used Mylo's laser pen to carefully shave off the security tag welded to the side of the cube.

Tag-free, the cube wouldn't catch any of the scanners at all the windows and doors. We'd be able to walk right out—as long as no one saw us.

I bit the inside of my lip as Noelia held open my reinforced backpack and I deposited the cube inside.

"I don't like this. Where are they?" I whispered.

"Don't complain. Focus on not tipping over," she mouthed back.

She had a point. This was like carrying a backpack full of bricks. Even with the reinforced shoulder straps, I felt like there was a whole house hanging off me. I buckled an additional round-the-waist strap over my snow coat and around my torso for extra support, but still, damn. My legs were already sore, and now no doubt my upper body would be too. I tested out a few steps with bent knees just to make sure I didn't waddle.

Maybe Noelia was right. I should be glad we hadn't run into any drama yet and pray it stayed that way. I wasn't exactly in fighting condition at the moment.

We retraced our steps through the mess hall back past the smaller research labs and a submersion tank room, until we branched off in a different direction, following my exit route. We maneuvered around to the north side of the facility, the side facing the outbuilding near the frozen ice. Around the rocks toward Mylo's Zodiac we'd go.

Every step I expected Devroe or Diane or Kyung-soon to appear, ready to take us on somehow.

What if . . . we had just gotten here ahead of Team Diane? Even I had to catch a lucky break every now and then, right?

As we passed the north service door, halfway to the exit we were planning to use, the universe reminded me, *No, Ross Quest doesn't really get those.*

Fluorescent lights came to life, blinking a furious bloody red. The same lights flicked on behind us, turning the hallway into a scalding-red hellscape. A shrieking alarm blared.

Welp.

FOURTEEN

THERE'S ALWAYS A shard of a second when something like this happens—pure disaster on a job—when an alarm goes off, a gunshot rings out, you feel someone's got their hands on you, when you don't move. For me, it isn't panic that freezes me up, but high-speed reflection. *What did I do wrong?*

Noelia turned toward me in a flash of motion, her braids whipping her face.

"The tags?" she asked. More lights were coming. The residential area wasn't exactly what you would call close, but it wouldn't be long before someone followed the very obvious path of blinking lights.

"We turned them off . . ." I said. No way I would've made a mistake like that.

Noelia, biting her lip, flicked her eyes at my lead backpack. "Are you sure those were the right type of tags?"

"Yes!"

"Okay, but were you sure you were looking at the right research to disarm them?"

"I didn't mess this up—" My eyes caught on the side of the door. Pushing Noelia aside, I bent down until I was eye level with the thin, transparent device pasted just under the security sensor.

I almost laughed. Kyung-soon did get her DNA-triggered sensor to work. And I'd already given her my DNA.

"Whatever, doesn't matter." Noelia peeked outside. "The residential side of the building is awake. I can see the lights on. They're expecting whoever the hell it is to go toward the west exit." A.k.a., the exit we had been on our way to. So much for that.

Noelia reached for the strap around my waist. I slapped her fingers away. "What the hell are you doing?"

"We can't use the west exit now, it'll be swarmed with people!" Noelia whisper-yelled. "The only option left is back through the window. This won't fit through the window, so we have to abandon it."

She tried to unbuckle my backpack again. This time I ripped her hands off me.

"So we're just gonna leave the target here?"

"Yes!"

She was out of her mind.

What was their game plan? Even if Noelia and I ditched the target, the facility was going to be on alert now. According to the lab's security protocols, they were supposed to transfer all prototypes and valuable materials out of the main lab and into the secure outbuilding in the event of an "emergency."

I pushed open the door that had just tripped the alarm. Brisk cold and a stretch of glassy ice welcomed us. Out in the darkness, I leveled my gaze on the detached outbuilding. Smaller than the main facility, only a narrow strait of frozen ice between us and it.

It should have been empty . . . but past the stillness of the night, I thought I could feel a tingle, the weight of someone's eyes on me.

There was already movement inside the other building. If I couldn't see it, I felt it, colder than the Antarctic night itself.

They were there. No . . . she was there.

I didn't know how, but they were going to swipe the target from the more secure facility. All the more impressive.

Was she in there, watching me too? Smiling, maybe? All of them, perhaps?

"Ross . . ." Noelia pleaded. We couldn't have more than a minute or two until the facility was fully awake. "We need to hustle now. The window is our best shot. Drop the stupid backpack, and let's win the next phases."

I kept my back to her and instead looked out over the ice. Smooth and glassy and black as ink.

There was a reason we were supposed to pass this exit. It led straight onto the ice.

No one would be crazy enough to leave out of this door. That would be suicidal.

The ice *looked* solid enough.

I tightened the waist strap Noelia had tried to remove, cracked my neck, and slid my goggles back on.

"No, no, no, you can't!" Noelia swooped in front of me, putting both arms out. "The ice is a couple inches thick at the most. There's a reason you didn't pick this route."

"Yeah, well, I didn't know the situation then."

"Yes, you did!" The distant sound of voices. Time slipping away.

With Team Kenzie waiting for me to drop the target and turn tail so they could swoop in for the first easy win. One win closer to wishing away my family.

Mom would do it.

And that sealed the deal for me. Mom had beaten Diane once before, and I was sure it wasn't by playing it safe.

"Get to Mylo. Bring the Zodiac around to the edge of the ice." I shoved past her. "I'm going out."

FIFTEEN

ICE CRACKLED UNDER my boot.

I sucked in a sharp breath. My brain screamed to jump back onto the safe ground behind me, but I fought it, taking another baby step.

The ice made another unsettling crackle. But no spidering, not that I could tell.

It was solid. I was fine.

Inching forward, I quickly glanced over my shoulder at the facility. Already, I'd made it farther than I thought—at least five yards now. Maybe my adrenaline had carried me this far. Noelia was gone; only a closed door was left behind.

My breath blew out in an icy cloud. I slid forward. The ice crackle-popped under me, making my heart stutter. I gripped my shoulder straps and kept going. Carefully. Slow wasn't so bad. Since the idea of anyone breaking in through the water side was a new level of insane, there weren't any cameras facing this way to worry about. I could take my time.

One step, then another. Smooth, easy. Don't lose balance. The pack strapped behind me felt even heavier with the all-encompassing cold pressing in and numbing my limbs. I almost felt myself teetering when I was at the halfway mark, but I caught myself.

Chill, Ross.

No pun intended.

Almost across—I could do this.

A streak of a sound broke into the night. I stilled, arms out to keep my balance. Even over the blaring of the lab's alarms, my ears were honed to recognize a sound like that. Hinges moving.

The back door where I'd left Noelia was still closed, a threadbare layer of snow now beginning to cover my messy footprints.

If not that door, then . . .

I turned my gaze toward the adjacent facility. Rounding the back came a figure. Tall and wrapped snugly in all black. We were too far apart to see each other clearly, but I knew she was looking at me, just like I knew I'd felt her eyes on me earlier.

Diane. Again. And just like last time, she was headed straight for me.

Oh, no you don't.

I had a head start—all I needed to do was keep moving. Gripping my shoulder strap with one hand and keeping the other out for balance, I inched forward again. Diane hesitated for less than a second before sliding onto the ice. Catching on to my short and careful movements, she mimicked me, sliding over the ice in an annoyingly graceful way.

I gritted my teeth and looked toward the edge of the frozen water. The collection of rocks was, what, one hundred feet up and to the left of me now? It'd be an easy climb to the cove behind them. I just had to get there. Having exited the safe way, Noelia should already be waiting with Mylo.

Get to the cove. Don't break the ice. Don't let Diane catch up. Those were the only three rules of my life right now.

I slipped forward. The ice groaned. No time for fear.

Diane was getting closer.

My breath did catch when I risked a look back at her. Distance was double-timing me, but Diane was featherlight, while I had what might as well have been a bag of dumbbells strapped to me.

I bit my lip, though it was so chilly I hardly felt it. I needed to speed up, but it wasn't like I could take bigger steps. I tried to just move faster. Slide, maybe. My boots blazed through the crunchy, paper-thin layer of snow above the ice. I ignored the hollow hum of sound waves bouncing against the ice beneath me. If it cracked, I'd just have to outrun that too. Stopping wasn't an option.

What would happen if Diane caught up to me? Hell or high water, ice or snow, I wasn't handing this target over. But it didn't look like she was just going to rock-paper-scissors me for it either.

Letting her catch up to me meant an altercation. Altercation meant movement.

Too much movement meant shattering ice.

She was playing chicken with me. Little did she know how reckless I was these days.

I kept gliding, pushing myself forward over the ice like I was on slow, miniature skis. But I wasn't fast enough. Diane was getting closer and closer. It was like in a horror movie when each time the lights click back on, the slasher is even closer than before.

The rocks were maybe twenty yards ahead. Diane was more like four behind me.

At this rate, she'd catch me.

Glancing back again, I saw her pull something out of her coat pocket. Small and silver, it glinted in the moonlight. She pressed the side, and a blade punched out the top. A switchblade.

She wanted to use it to cut the straps. That had to be what she was going for. It was what I would do.

As she drew closer, I felt that phantom barrel from the end of the Gambit at the back of my head. The point of the blade was precariously sharp, gripped in her thin gloves with intent . . .

Or maybe she wasn't going for the straps. After all, she was doing all this because she wanted my mom and me dead. Who would stop her from doing it now?

Oh crap.

Panicking, I turned around. Her lower face was hidden behind a mask, but those furious eyes, now close enough to make out, would have been enough to raise my hackles even without the knife.

In that same split second of panicked reflection, I focused

on the sheet of ice under my soles. Why does ice crack? There's too much force on it. Force is weight divided by area. If I could redistribute my weight, it would decrease my chances of breaking through the ice or catching an already-splintered part.

I unclicked the straps of the backpack, slinking it off, then unclipped the ski rods weighing down the pack. Like a starfish, I sprawled over the ice. Only ten or so meters away now, the turn of events even made Diane's steps stutter for a second, and it was just the kind of momentary slipup I needed. I javelined the ski rods in Diane's direction. She threw her hands up in defense, but I wasn't aiming for her. One, and then the next landed point first into the ice. The splintering sound might as well have been as loud as an avalanche. Diane dropped into a crouch. I kept my weight sprawled and held my breath. But the splintering drew to a stop at my feet.

Carefully, I tilted my head up. A long and precarious crack divided me and Diane. It had worked.

Irritated but not defeated, Diane was already going the long way around the lengthy splinter. Really, I'd just bought myself time. I scrambled on my back a few yards away, then carefully stood, restrapped the target on my back, and resumed the pace I'd been at before. Sprawling was safer, but I needed speed again.

The edge of the rocks beckoned me ahead. I flew forward.

Ice still surrounded me; in a warmer month, I would have been on the edge of a lagoon, but now there were just the rocks wrapping around me. Ahead, a smaller patch of them jutted into the air, begging to be climbed. I panted, unsmudging my frosty goggles.

To the rocks. Over the rocks. To the Zodiac. I had the target.

I was going to make it.

Then a thunderous crackle roared behind me. My head snapped around just in time to see the ice buckling and shattering like fractured cubic zirconia.

I ran. The frozen air dug into my throat. My heart pounded into the cold. More ice was splintering under my weight, but screw it. I needed to get away.

A few more yards until solid ground. And I was sprinting.

The rocks were almost close enough to jump onto. Just an arm's width away. I blew out one last time, and grabbed on to the first bumpy crevice.

It happened like a dream. The ground underneath me was there . . . and then it wasn't. The crashing and buckling sound of the ice reached a crescendo. And the next thing I knew, I wasn't standing on anything at all.

SIXTEEN

THERE WAS COLD, and then there was this.

Ice. Pinpricks all over my skin. It was like the water, personification of cold itself, had reached up, wrapped its fingers around me, and squeezed. Everything was ice. Was I ice?

And black. The only light was a small hole above me now. And I was sinking farther from it by the second.

My lungs constricted—I'd already been out of breath, but now I really couldn't breathe.

I kicked frantically. Each movement felt like dragging my legs through sand. No, slush.

My skin was numbing.

And the surface was still getting farther away.

I looked down, darkness stretched beneath me, and I wanted

to scream. Dark was okay. Deep was okay. Dark and deep and cold was terrifying.

My legs were still moving. If some monster from the deep did grab them, how long until I couldn't feel it at all?

My lungs burned. Ironic.

Why was I still drifting down?

My arms and hands were a frantic flash of movement above me. Just swim, Ross, damn it.

The package on my back fought every upward movement, its weight tugging the straps so carefully tethered around me. They might as well have been ropes tied to the bottom of the ocean, reeling me down.

I moved my hands down to the straps around my waist. Where was the clip? It was just a button, like a car seat strap. I just had to press it. Where was it?

Where was my waist? Where were my hands? Where were my fingers? My sense of everything was slipping away, erased by the vortex of cold.

I pressed a hand, I think, over my nose and mouth to keep from taking an instinctual breath in. My chest was the only thing on fire. One breath in, and I could quench that.

One breath in, and I was never getting out of this water.

I might already be dead.

That thought sparked a burst of adrenaline. I kicked and strained and stretched for the surface with the last of everything in me. The gaping ice wasn't that far. I only had to kick. What was one yard, two yards, ten yards? Forget the burn, forget the cold, forget the numb. I wanted to see my mom again, and Auntie. My friends. Even . . .

I could see my arm reaching for the surface. I was almost there.

With one last burst of adrenaline, my hand punched the surface. Yes. I had one hand out, I could do this.

My hand slapped down on the ground. Only it wasn't the solid rock I'd been hoping for. I grabbed a piece of ice, breaking it away from a larger chunk. My weight pulled it down into the water with me. Without getting a lick of air, I slipped back away from the surface.

My legs quit on me. My hands were done moving too. That was my last shot, and I wasted it.

Nothing would move. And I stopped trying.

I think my eyes were freezing too. Water was seeping past my snow goggles. I closed them. I guessed this was how Ross Quest died. I couldn't help it—I took a breath, and water flooded my lungs. It honestly didn't even hurt . . . that much.

Until . . . it did.

A rush of cold returned. Brisk and unforgiving, like a blast of freezing air had just hit me all over. I forced my eyes open. The all-consuming darkness was gone—

I tried to breathe, but nothing would go in. Panic. There was ice water in my lungs . . .

Oh god—

I coughed, hard. Water spat out of my mouth. Someone was hitting my back, aiding the process.

They stopped hitting my back, and through my blurred vision, I could see that someone was rubbing my arms. The echo of warmth fought through the cold, and I could feel the heat starting to return as they pushed their bare hands up my sleeves to heat my arms.

The only thing making it through my numb ears at first was a steady beat of static. But as those heated up too, the static morphed into a warbled jumble of words. And within seconds, the volume slowly increased until I could hear a clear voice and feel a cloud of heat on my ear.

"You're okay, you're okay, you're okay." He repeated it again and again, like he was talking to himself more than me.

"Devroe?" I tried to ask, but I could only mouth the words.

I blinked a couple of times, and my vision cleared enough to make out the shattered ice.

Devroe . . . saved me.

I wanted to smile. I wanted to cry. I wanted to thank him. I couldn't speak, so I just focused on the little bit of warmth I could feel coming off of him. That huff of air on my ear. The way he tucked my head into his neck, the friction of his hands on my arms. It didn't even bother me to admit that it all felt really, really nice right now.

"You're going to be fine, love." If I had been capable of it, I might have shuddered. Love—did he mean to say that? He hadn't called me that in his months of teasing. If he was trying to melt me with words too, it was certainly working. He said it like a desperate promise, and even though I still couldn't feel my toes, I believed him.

The numbness was slowly giving way to feeling again. He shifted behind me, and I felt my waterlogged coat being stripped off. Then he kicked off my drenched snow boots with his own. My limbs shivered. My teeth rattled. Devroe, still cradling me in front of him, slipped his fleece-lined boots onto my feet, and even with the extra space from the larger size, it was enough warmth that I almost swore I could maybe feel my big toes again.

He slipped a coat over my shoulders—his coat?—still toasty with his body warmth, and guided my shivering arms into the sleeves. It wasn't a perfect fit. My undershirt was damp, but already I felt a little farther from death than I had been a minute ago. He wrapped a gray thermal scarf snugly around my neck, one that I was happy to find smelled just like his familiar cinnamon-and-spice scent.

"Absolutely fine," he promised. And I let myself almost nod. Whatever he said, I believed it. I appreciated it. I liked it.

Why had I been so angry with him all this time? *How* could I have been?

His arm snaked around my waist, cocooning me in the coat still toasted with his body warmth. I was still shivering, my teeth still chattering, the sensation on my skin still far away from what it should have been, but this was better and he was here and I could work out how I felt about all that later but right now it was okay.

"You need to get to somewhere warm soon," Devroe said. I felt him shift behind me. Was he going to carry me? Where?

Oh gosh, I thought I might die if he bridal-style picked me up and carried me through the snow.

A familiar sound cut through our quiet. The metallic click of a gun.

"Get away from her."

Battling my shivering and my shaky breath, I followed the voice. Atop an ice-encrusted rock, backlit by the Monet-blue sky, Noelia was glaring at us.

No—at Devroe.

And she had her sedative gun with her, finger on the trigger with a certainty that made me wonder why she hadn't shot yet if she was that determined to.

"Lia . . ." My voice came out small and weak and hoarse. I felt Devroe tug me tighter into him at the sound of it. I coughed once and tried to raise my hand to wave her off. It was like raising a quivering twig. "Stand . . . down."

Yeah, okay, he was the enemy. Team Kenzie. But couldn't she see Devroe was helping? For five minutes, couldn't we cool it with the drama? Maybe . . . he was even going to switch teams.

"You're not going to shoot me," Devroe said, more taunting, meaner than I would have expected. "You don't have the stomach."

"Not with a real gun, no," she admitted. "But I assure you I don't have a single problem pumping every vial into you. I'm only going to tell you one more time." She hopped down to a slightly lower rock, never so much as blinking. "Get away from her, and the target you're trying to swipe."

Target?

I turned around. My neck ached from the motion. Yes, one of Devroe's arms was around me, but the other hand was busy detaching me from my heavy-duty backpack. The straps had been silently severed. A slender switchblade, not unlike the one Diane had been carrying, rested over the snow. I should have realized the backpack was off of me when he had no trouble replacing my coat with his own. Of course I hadn't felt it. And if I did, the overwhelming relief of warmth was enough to easily forget about something like that.

Devroe hadn't been saving me. He saved the target. And he wasn't warming me up—he was distracting me.

I needed to get away from him.

My arms and legs barely worked, but I tried my best to scramble out of his embrace.

"Ross, wait—"

"Let . . . go . . ."

I heard Noelia making the final jump onto our level of rocks. She wasn't messing around. She shot. The yellow-white vial landed in the snow just beside Devroe's knife, but it was close enough. He let go of me, and I instantly tumbled over myself. I hadn't realized how much he'd been supporting me.

That made me want to cry even more.

"Step back," Noelia ordered. I focused on trying to get to my feet while he shuffled up, the rustle of snow telling me he was taking cautious, if not reluctant, steps away.

Noelia grabbed the target backpack by the only unsevered strap, then haphazardly swung the same arm around my waist. It was clumsy, but I could lean on her to walk.

Devroe was a few feet away, his hands up. His bottom lip trembled as he looked at me. It almost looked like he wasn't faking it.

"Ross, I—"

"Shut up," Noelia said for me. "Say something else, and I'll shoot you for real."

Devroe bit back a grimace, before sighing. I had to look away. Everything was too painful. My lungs, my legs, my heart.

Devroe didn't try to speak again, but he didn't leave either. I could sense him watching us as Noelia helped me up the rocks, until we were out of sight, headed toward Mylo and the Zodiac.

SEVENTEEN

TWELVE MISSED CALLS. Thirteen missed calls. Fourteen missed calls.

Devroe

Please answer.

I'm sorry. Please let me explain.

Fifteen missed calls.

I watched the notifications rack up under the mountain of heating pads the medical officer layered over me. According to this Argentinian military freighter's doctor, I had been on the cusp of full-blown hypothermia by the time we got here. Probably explained why I barely remembered the Zodiac ride or anything, really, before coming back to myself in this windowless triage room. As soon as I had phone connection again, it was vibrating nonstop.

Sixteen missed calls. Seventeen missed calls.

Finally he stopped, and I thought he'd given up.

Devroe

What choice did I have? You're trying to protect your family, and I'm trying to protect mine.

I sat up a little in my heap of heating pads. What did he mean, protect his family? No one was trying to slaughter his.

Was I missing information? Maybe, but I'd jump back into the ice before I actually returned one of these calls.

With a yell, I hurled my phone against the wall. Noelia, having arrived at just the wrong time, twisted out of the way. She picked up my phone, brushing it off. "This is the same phone you had during the Gambit. You must have the sturdiest phone case on earth."

I huffed in place of a laugh, sinking back into my heated cocoon. Thankfully, Noelia said nothing about the missed calls and texts. Instead she opened up Netflix, scoffing at my Currently Watching list. "Are K-drama romances all you watch?"

"You got a problem with that?"

"They're so slow-paced. And melodramatic. Unrealistically fantastical."

"That's what makes them—" I sighed. "Never mind." Guess I wouldn't be having any K-drama watch parties with Noelia in the future. Now that Kyung-soon was gone, maybe I'd never get to do that again.

Noelia sat at the foot of my bed, now in joggers and a turtleneck instead of snow clothes. She looked perfectly airy and composed, which was probably quite the juxtaposition to me right now.

She gave me a pitiful smile. "Kenzie sucks."

"Yeah."

Why hadn't I reached out to Noelia sooner? Even if we wouldn't have watched K-dramas together, I wasted so much time because I thought being the first to reach out would be uncomfortable.

Another note for the list:

Get to know Noelia better.

A notification on my phone stole both of our attention.

Count

tablet ☺

What tablet?

"Someone needs to ban this woman from emojis," Noelia said.

Before I could voice my thought about the missing tablet, Mylo burst into the triage room, waving said tablet. "Looky what I found! Okay, I didn't find it, some lackey in the mess hall gave it to me." He offered me a Styrofoam cup. "Drink coffee. It'll warm you up."

The "coffee" was more like a cup of sugar milk teased with coffee, but I appreciated the gesture, so I took a few sips before handing it off to Noelia. Just in time, a video request lit up the tablet. Mylo swooped to the other side of my bed, and I felt perfectly cuddled between my friends.

The screen clicked on. Count, sipping tea in some sort of baroque foyer, filled the screen. "Acceptable work. Phase one has officially been declared my win." She raised a hand, and a uniformed maid retrieved her teacup and saucer. "We're only one win away from us all getting what we want now."

"You're very welcome," Mylo said. "Maybe some of us deserve a high-performance bonus for this one?"

"Being on my good side is a generous bonus."

"Why isn't my mom on?" I asked.

"The senior Ms. Quest is on her way to meet you. I've already briefed her on the next phase. What do you know about casinos?"

"YES," Mylo said.

"I'll translate that to 'a lot,'" Noelia said.

"Casinos in Monte Carlo specifically." Count's video minimized, and a new image overtook the screen. A vibrantly colored building that looked like it was rising out of a sparkling sea. It wasn't the type of place I would've thought was a casino, actually. Instead, it was reminiscent of a resort or castle. Though the trim of lively lights did lean toward something more electric than a stuffy old castle.

"Oh!" Mylo closed his eyes briefly in contemplation. "That's Hart's Caye. Most profitable hotel in Monaco. They're totally high-end. There's a dress code just to get to the lower-tier slot machines. And the levels of exclusivity go up from there."

"So I'm guessing you've been there?" Noelia asked.

"Once. My French wasn't that great at the time, so I didn't have as much fun as I could have."

Count's eyes sharpened into a glare. "You didn't do anything to be remembered, did you?"

"Course not!" Mylo threw his hands up. "Never in my life have I been tagged at a casino for anything, and you can put some money on that, Your Countliness."

Count inclined her head a touch. Good enough for her . . . for now.

"What's your beef with the casino?" I asked.

"The owner of the property, one Quinton Hart. He's become a bit of a rival to the organization the past couple of years. I won't go into detail with you, but I'll say while not a member of our group, he brushes shoulders with many of our . . . esteemed clientele." Count brought her tablet back into her lap, curling her long fingers over the side. "No one does well at his casino. Many of our members have lost embarrassing amounts of money and . . . other things at his casino."

"Other things?" I questioned.

"I'm sure Mr. Michaelson saw only the lower floors during his brief visit, but Hart's is a place where people of a certain level of society can gamble much more valuable things than money. You can cash almost anything in for chips at Hart's if you're talking to the right dealers. Money, homes, secrets . . . people."

A shudder ran down my spine at that last one, and even Count looked a little uneasy adding it. A casino where you could cash in with way more than cash. Sounded like something out of a dark nightmare.

Count went on. "Some members of our organization have lost very valuable things to Mr. Hart. Usually this would be no issue. Our funds are near limitless, and resources vast. There's almost nothing that couldn't be bought back, if this were a normal casino. But Hart's doesn't play by the rules."

"Right." Mylo collapsed back into his seat. "The currency system. I almost forgot about that."

"Indeed," Count concurred.

Noelia and I exchanged an inquisitive look.

Mylo was the one to pick up the ball, though. "When you enter Hart's, it's kind of like entering a different country, if I remember correctly." He rubbed his chin, frowning at nothing but his own memory. "Not only is there security out the ass—pretty standard for casinos—but there's a different currency inside too. Hart dollars. You buy in with them, and every time you play a game, whether it's the slots or roulette or cards, you get paid out in Hart dollars. It was super weird, now that I'm thinking about it. Everything was in Harts. The souvenir shop, the drinks, even the valet fee."

"So he has people playing with his own Monopoly money inside his own little kingdom," I said. "How . . . cute?"

Count made a noncommittal sound. "Mr. Hart's *unique* currency within his building, paired with the unique way in which he allows you to buy in, is the problem." She leaned forward. "First, anyone can buy in at Hart's. However, you can only buy in with money once. After that, the only way to buy in is to trade something else for Harts. A property, information, a person. They all become a part of Hart's exclusive catalog, where the only currency to purchase something is with Hart's own currency. You can imagine the predicament someone might find themself in if they start with a ridiculous amount of money, lose it all, then decide to cash in something a little more precious. Perhaps a beloved vacation home. Then they lose that too. Then they trade something compromising about themselves, convinced they're going to win everything back. They lose again. On and on it goes."

"How exactly do you trade a secret? It's not very secret once you've told it," Noelia said.

"From what I've heard, the people who record and appraise secrets at Hart's are paid overwhelmingly well for their discretion. They also tend to disappear before they can think of cutting ties with the casino."

"Okay . . ." I shifted, leaning my elbows on my knees, thinking it all through. "So you only get to buy into Hart's with cash once; after that, it requires more. But since casinos are pretty much designed for you to lose, it's a death trap—"

Noelia snorted. "Which usually wouldn't be a problem for people who have more money than they know what to do with. It's one thing to lose a couple hundred thousand on a bad streak and a whole other to lose a scandalous tape of you and your secretary."

"Precisely," Count sighed, as if this particular issue had been irking her for quite a while. "Continuing to buy in, for several of our members, in an attempt to earn out hasn't quite worked. The only way to get back what they've lost is to win it back."

I smirked. "Or steal it."

Count matched my smile. "Yes, or that."

Count leaned back, crossing her legs. "The Hart dollars that special guests at Hart's Casino play with are worth significantly more than the current US dollar. In order to have enough to cash in for all the . . . valuables my esteemed associates have lost over the last couple of years, I'll need at least twenty million Hart dollars."

Mylo coughed. "What the hell?"

My jaw almost dropped. Twenty million in a currency that she just said was actually worth a bunch more than the average US dollar? That was . . . a bit much.

Count ignored us. "Having made a handful of . . . unsuccessful attempts to recoup this sum in the past, I'd recommend getting the job done in one visit. You need to succeed in a single night."

"Unsuccessful attempts. So who died?" I asked.

Count waved the thought away. "No one you should concern yourself with."

"Wait, so people really did die?" Mylo asked.

And as usual, Count didn't give a response. "It would appear Mr. Hart has very adept systems in place to alert him when people are attempting to cheat him or his casino. The last two infiltrations I arranged, which both were scheduled to run for a span of time, ended in failures less than three nights in. One ended the second night, after recouping less than half a million. Therefore, it's my conclusion that extending this job into anything other than a one-night affair would not be to our advantage. Not to mention, we need to succeed before Baron's team does."

Before Baron's team. How fortuitous that the organization had this little game of champions taking place. They could not only reap the winnings of one team of experts, but two. Even if neither of us managed to hit the number they wanted, but both came away with, say, ten million in wins, they'd still have what they wanted.

"Twenty million dollars' worth of special chips in one night." Noelia tucked her hair behind her ears. "How much time do we have?"

"The phase has already started," Count said. "Today is Wednesday—however, Hart's is at its busiest on Friday and Saturday nights. Those are also the only nights the casino is fully functional, and the only nights certain types of chips can be acquired. We have two days until you can enter the casino."

"A whole two days to figure out how to plan a twenty-million-plus heist at a murderous casino. You're too generous, Count." Mylo tipped an invisible hat to her.

At that, Count sighed. "I'm neither here to be generous nor to tell you how to get something done. Figure out a plan and let me know when you have. Don't forget that we all need to win this." She once-overed us like we were grade-schoolers before clicking off.

"Sooo," Mylo said, expert tension breaker, at least in his own head. "Twenty million, before Team Devroe. In Monte Carlo. One night. Don't get murdered. Any ideas?"

EIGHTEEN

WHY DON'T WE find out what Baron's team is doing, and do it first?" Noelia proposed.

"Déjà vu much?" As if she hadn't already done that exact same thing in the last Gambit.

Noelia crossed her arms. "It worked, didn't it?"

"Which is exactly why I doubt Devroe's going to let it happen to him again." I gave her a thumbs-down. She flicked my hand away.

"Mylo, I thought this was going to be your thing." I looked back his way. He was sitting crisscross in a chair, with his arms folded over the table, his head nestled inside.

"Ugh . . ." he groaned. "Look, I can give you card-counting cons all day, but I'll be real with you. I've never walked out with anywhere near twenty million in one night from a con. Not even close. And even if I had, I have a feeling Hart's isn't a place where something as simple as card counting's going to fly. We need something more . . ." He flailed his hands in the air.

"Original? Dynamic? Clever?" Noelia offered.

"Yeah. All of those."

I slumped in my bed, feeling like we'd made negative progress in the half hour since Count had logged off.

Mylo ran his hands through his hair, getting even more irritated when he remembered how short it was. "Maybe we should watch some casino heist movies. Get the ideas flowing."

Noelia looked like she could punch him.

"If you're gonna waste time with a movie marathon, I recommend *Baby Driver*." Mom flew through the med cabin door, instantly examining me. She frowned, eyeing the heating pads I was still under, though they were starting to feel more smothering than necessary. "Oh, baby girl—"

"Fine." I forced myself to sit up. Noelia snapped toward Mylo and gestured for them to leave.

Mom stopped Noelia before she got out the door, though. "That tablet is from Count?"

Noelia nodded, handing it over. Mom tapped through for a moment before giving it back. "See if you can access anything from the private chat on here. There should still be a link if this tablet was used for that before."

"Uh, why?" I asked.

"I'm curious about what kind of conversations Baron or Count may be having behind the scenes."

"I'm not a hacker," Noelia said.

"Don't you have a cousin who is? Tell her it's a favor for me." Mom flashed a devious smile. Noelia narrowed her eyes before leaving.

"You just know all the Boscherts' specialties?"

"It's good to know weak spots. Even better not to have any." Mom pressed a palm to my forehead. Ironically, I thought she felt cold. I brushed her off. "The med officer said I'm good. I'm not dying or anything."

"Good. If you did, I would have to kill that boy."

It wasn't a joke, how she said it. Fighting a shudder, I stole a look at Devroe's last message before sliding my phone away. "Mom, did you threaten Devroe's family?"

Mom scoffed. She turned away, facing the bland gray walls for a second. "What do you think I've been doing for six months, sending Diane death threats? I already told you I haven't talked to that woman in twenty years."

"That's not a no." I pushed off the heating pads and went to stand before she put her hands on my shoulders. I matched her gaze. "Don't lie to me anymore."

Mom's fingers curled into my shoulders. She seemed to be debating with herself. "I haven't threatened Diane . . . recently."

And there it was.

I stood, dragging my fingers down my face. "Okay, now, hold up," Mom said. "I was serious when I said I hadn't talked to her in, like, twenty years. But back then, she started following me, I *knew* she was. I was pregnant, and she was bitter. If she was watching me, what else was she going to do—"

"What did you do?" I asked slowly.

"Nothing!" Mom insisted. She pinched a piece of fuzz off the hospital blanket. "Nothing, really. I only broke into her apartment one night, and I left her a note . . . in her baby's crib. I told her if I ever saw her again, she would regret it."

My stomach turned. "You threatened to kill Devroe . . . as a baby?"

"Those exact words never left my lips." Mom examined her nails and swallowed hard. "And I haven't done anything to her since then, so don't think I prompted some new drama. Even back then, I was only keeping you safe. There's nothing more dangerous than a friend turned foe."

Maybe she didn't notice it, but Mom was pacing. She traced the walls, picked up my empty cup, tossed it in a sterile trash bin before huffing and turning back to me. Any ounce of regret was gone in under twenty seconds. Horrible as it was, she'd gotten what she wanted. Two decades of peace.

Rhiannon Quest wins again.

"Were you ever really friends?" I whispered, rubbing my arms. How similar were Mom and I, honestly? Even if I wanted to, did I ever have a chance of becoming the heartless victor she was?

Mom burrowed a glare into me I hadn't seen since I was a little girl and had done something particularly stupid, like trying to run a mile down the beach to meet the nearest neighbors. "Renaissance fairs, midnight movie premieres. Yes, we were 'real' friends. I loved Diane, and I loved August too. Don't ever question that."

My breath caught at August's name. August Kenzie. Devroe's dad? Mom knew him too . . . and she still let him die.

"Mama, do you love me?"

"You know I do."

"Okay, but I don't . . ." I tried to arrange my thoughts correctly.

"What makes me different from how you loved them? Are you going to let me die too one day for the sake of whatever goal you have at the moment?" I rubbed my chest, kneading at a building dread. Diane was already trying to kill me. What if someday it was someone closer to home letting my life slip away?

Mom seemed utterly gobsmacked. "Loving your friends and loving your daughter are not the same. Diane and August were something I loved. You're *everything* I love, Rossie."

What was the difference?

Mom must have read the question in my eyes. "They had each other. I only have you."

Everything . . . the only thing?

Underneath her bravado, how lonely was Mom? How . . . purposeless without me?

She blew out and reached for me, cupping my cheeks in typical Mom fashion. I could sense the pivot coming. "Don't you see why I know better than anyone not to trust 'friends'? Even that won't keep someone from carving your heart out and selling it on the black market when it matters." Mom's thumb traced my jaw. "It's better to learn from someone else's experience than work it out yourself."

A lightbulb switched on. Perhaps I was just eager not to delve into all these emotions right now, but I peeled her hands off of me, eyes wide.

I knew what we needed for the next phase.

And to get it, we needed to go to Tokyo.

NINETEEN

"ARE YOU SURE he hasn't changed his number? It's been six months."

Noelia's lip curled. "Just be grateful I didn't delete it at all." She aggressively brushed wrinkles out of her skirt, muttering something about kidnapping and honor.

For the umpteenth time, I reread the brand-new thread I'd started with the contact she forwarded me.

Opportunity available.

12PM

Ross Quest

I dropped a location too. Was it vague? Yeah. Did I sort of think that was going to make him more intrigued? Also yes. Did I debate adding my last name unnecessarily because I thought it would remind him that I was indeed Ross mother-hugging Quest and that would add a little extra clout to draw him? Definitely.

Even with all of this, I was starting to get nervous that he wasn't going to show up at all. I mean, I'd sent the message sixteen hours ago, and besides temporarily flicking on his read tags to let me know he'd seen it, there wasn't exactly a response.

If he didn't show, then we'd wasted a lot of our prep time for nothing, and still had no idea how we were going to pull off this secret casino-heist thing.

So, was I nervous?

My sweaty hands were enough of an answer to that.

"Do you think the squid ink mochi will turn my tongue black?" Mylo looked up from the digital menu that covered our low-sitting table. Everything was low-sitting here. Instead of chairs, there were cushions on the floor, taking up most of the space in our cozy private room. Individual rooms for dining parties were definitely something I thought the rest of the world should adopt in restaurants as well.

"It's bad manners to order before all guests arrive. Have you had no basic etiquette classes?" Noelia canceled his order on the digital tabletop.

"*If* he shows up," Mylo said, dropping his chin into his hands.

My gaze drifted to the time, helpfully displayed in the top corner of the menu.

11:59.

"Whatever," Noelia sighed. "Show or no show, I don't think

one person's going to increase our chances of doing the impossible that much. We might have been better off bingeing the Ocean's franchise like Mylo wanted."

Before I could mention that I'd already seen them all way too many times, the sliding door to the room slid open. We shut up. A server in a black-and-gray apron announced something in Japanese, then bowed at the waist before scurrying away. Taking his place was a boy with flawless skin, boxy glasses, the crispest wool coat I'd ever seen, and hair just as perfect as I remembered it.

Taiyō.

He actually came. Right at 12:00 too. Of course he was exactly on time.

"Oh damn," Mylo murmured beside me. I swiped a glance at him and found him looking absolutely enthralled.

What had gotten into him?

Not counting Mylo's remark, no one really knew what to say to break the ice. This was getting awkward, and I was just as much to blame as everyone else. Was I supposed to bring up the last time I saw him or . . . ?

I opened my mouth, but couldn't find anything in time.

And I guess Taiyō had had enough of the bull.

"Hello." He pushed up his glasses. With that, he slid off his coat, leaving it on the hanger next to Noelia's peacoat, and slid his shoes off, leaving them in the row alongside ours.

He took the only seat left, across from me and Mylo, next to Noelia.

He immediately tapped the call button at the bottom of the screen.

"Nice." Mylo touched the skin above his right eyebrow, to

indicate the same area above Taiyō's. True enough, Taiyō's skin wasn't quite as flawless as I remembered. There was a pale line nipping the end of his brow and climbing halfway up his forehead.

"Thanks to Ross," he said. The sliding door pulled open again, and the same server knelt in the doorway, a tablet in hand. Taiyō spoke to him in Japanese.

Mylo hit my thigh and whispered, "He has a scar now."

I gave him a quick *okay, and?* look.

"I *die* for guys with scars."

The door slid shut, and Mylo and I pulled away, ignoring Noelia's side-eye. Taiyō was just looking at me. And I mean staring hard.

Right, I guessed this was the part where I apologized.

I cleared my throat. "So . . . are you, like, okay? Besides that." I gestured at my own forehead.

"If by 'okay' you mean two bruised ribs, a fractured ankle, shattered ulna, concussion, and minor internal bleeding, then yes, I am 'okay.'"

"Hmm." Noelia gave him a sympathy-free once-over, as if that wasn't quite enough for her but pleasant to hear nonetheless.

Really not helping, Lia.

I fidgeted. Taiyō didn't.

"Sorry about that," I said. "But to be fair, you were trying to kidnap a fourteen-year-old, so, you know."

At that, he finally cracked a bit, glancing away for a second. "I was only trying to win. Nothing more."

"Weren't we all."

Another short silence. Taiyō fisted his hands in his lap. "I . . .

appreciate you phoning the ambulance. Most of my injuries were minor, but I was told that the internal bleeding would have been much more severe the more time passed. I understand you didn't have to do that."

Not really a thank-you, but if I was being honest, my apology was underwhelming too.

"Now that we're past all that," Mylo said, slapping the table. "Wanna help us rob a casino?"

"Really?" Noelia said.

"What?"

"You have no sense of subtlety."

"It's cool, I'm sure Taiyō appreciates brass tacks," I said. "We wouldn't want to waste his valuable time."

"And this impromptu casino heist itself isn't going to be a waste of my time?" Taiyō asked. He was trying to sound disinterested. But I caught a minor sparkle in his eyes. He wouldn't have been here if he wasn't already intrigued.

The waiter returned, bringing a handleless cup of what I assumed was tea for Taiyō, and said something in Japanese that was probably promising the rest of the food to come. Gosh, how I really, really hated not knowing the local language.

"You don't have to participate," Noelia said, making me snap my head toward her. But she wasn't looking at me; instead she brushed wrinkles out of the napkin in her lap. "We're only here because Ross thought you might have some insightful suggestions."

"Suggestions?" Taiyō asked.

"We're planning something . . . ambitious," I clarified. That alone seemed to capture more of his attention. "We need to do it fast. You're the person I thought would have the best chance of coming up with a plan with the highest probability of success in the shortest amount of time. Especially if someone's pulled off something like this before."

Taiyō thrummed his fingers against his cup, still not having taken a sip, though. He sighed and pressed his lips together, an action that almost made Mylo swoon next to me. I had to pinch him to get him back on track.

"What's the objective?"

"Upward of twenty million American dollars from a shady place in Monte Carlo. They also deal in secrets and other unconventional currencies," Mylo said. The more he talked about this, the more excited about this whole job he seemed to be.

Taiyō rubbed his chin. "That's significant, but not impossible—"

"In one night," I added.

Taiyō leaned back. "Ah, I see." He took a sip of his tea. "And the reason for the time constraint?"

"We're trying to win a Guinness world record," Mylo said.

Noelia rolled her eyes. "It's phase two in a new Gambit we've gotten sucked into."

"Wait, *what*?" Now, *that* got Taiyō's attention.

"It's a really long story," I said.

"Hm," Taiyō said, clearly thinking. But what was he trying to decide? Whether he wanted in on this, or was he already thinking of a plan? "And my cut is?" he finally said. "I'm assuming you're not keeping all if any of these winnings. If this is another Gambit, I'm assuming the organization will be keeping any and all additional spoils. What incentive do I have to help you?"

"You mean other than another chance to impress the organization without having to kidnap a minor and end up in an ambulance?" Noelia asked. I would've kicked her if I'd had the room.

Taiyō's eyes were sharp, unblinking. I squared my shoulders. Right, that would be the next question any one of us would have asked. Or one that I would have six months ago. Lately, I was thinking a lot less about money and cuts than I had in another life. Sometimes I forgot how being a normal player in this industry worked these days.

"I can offer you two hundred grand, American," I said, which made Mylo choke on his own tea. I mean, they weren't exactly getting paid for this themselves.

It was a big chunk of what I had left in my own personal accounts after I blew a hefty sum during my shenanigans at the end of the Gambit, and although I was technically being paid a very healthy amount of money for all the jobs Count and the organization were flying us around the world to complete, she had conveniently failed to mention that all of those payments were going to be withheld until my year's tenure with the organization was finished. Insurance, she'd called it. To make sure no one took advantage of the organization by taking their payments and running off before the year was up. Also, why would we be in need of immediate money when they were covering all of our expenses for a year?

Taiyō watched me closely, and Mylo mouthed something to Noelia. I held my breath. If he was going to barter, then I could probably get up to a million if I went begging to Auntie to empty out some of the family accounts for me, but that was far from optimal. I could also probably get Count to pitch in if I convinced her how much we really needed Taiyō.

There was also the half a billion Mom was sitting on.

I suppressed an angry tremble, clutching my hand under the table. That money existed, yes, but Mom had conveniently not brought it up the couple of times we talked. What she was doing with it, had done with it, was unknown to me. And there was something about those dollars in particular that felt like the blood money Judas sold Jesus out for. Tainted. Unsafe. I'd feel . . . unclean just thinking about touching it.

Not to mention, I'd have to ask Mom for it. If she said no, then that would be another nail in the I-hate-you coffin, and I couldn't deal with that right now.

"I don't want money," Taiyō said.

I frowned. "Uh? Can you repeat that?"

"Don't you think I could easily leverage the information you've given me to make a pretty profit myself, if that was all I cared about?"

"And add yourself to the organization's hit list? Surely you're smarter than that," Noelia said.

"Then what *do* you want?" I asked, leaning in. He hadn't left yet; we were still stealing his time, and he was letting us. He wouldn't have let us keep up this conversation for no reason.

Taiyō smirked, just a whisper of one, and it sent a ripple of unexpected nostalgia through me. I'd seen that smile before. A long time ago during a conversation about his plans for the future in a hotel in Marseille.

"Three pro bono jobs at my request," he said. "And there's no time limit as to when I can request them."

"Three?" Noelia gawked. "One for the price of three isn't exactly a fair deal, you know."

"Not from you," Taiyō said, verbally waving her off. "I only want Ross."

"Ugh!" Noelia fumed. Mylo pouted, looking like a rejected puppy.

"You couldn't even have offered us a pity request?" Mylo said. "That's cold."

Taiyō kept his focus on me. "I'd appreciate having your name to drop as an associate. Three times working together, under jobs I plan, seems like enough to make that true."

I chuckled. "So you don't just want me, you want the Quest brand recognition for your résumé?"

"Connections are everything in this industry."

Connections are everything in a lot of the world, aren't they?

"Done, then." I put up a hand. "On the condition that we succeed in this casino heist."

Maybe it was petty of me to add that last condition. What would it cost me to hold up my end of the bargain either way? But it never hurt to add that extra dash of incentive.

Taiyō's half smirk was still there. In fact, it seemed to grow by a size. Mylo was dying next to me. "Unnecessary, but I accept."

"Unnecessary?" Mylo asked.

"Yes," Taiyō said. "Because we're not going to fail. Not with my plan."

TWENTY

FOR THE THIRD time, Mylo tried to peek over Taiyō's shoulder at the notes he was taking—which he'd explicitly told Mylo not to do—and for the third time, Taiyō caught him.

He pinned Mylo to the floor with ease.

"That's three," Taiyō said.

"Does that mean I struck out?" Mylo asked, his face still pressed to the carpet. If anyone could flirt while their face was on the carpet, it was certainly Mylo.

I watched this exchange from the upper floor of the loft Count had booked for us. Our plane from Tokyo had taken us straight to Nice. Tomorrow we'd head into Monte Carlo. According to Count, although she hadn't been able to prove it yet, she suspected that Quinton Hart had some sort of connection at

Monte Carlo's immigration office. It looked like someone working at Hart's had cross-referenced the faces of Count's old goons with the mismatched passports they used when landing in France. Lesson learned? If we were going in using aliases, which was the smart way to do things, we needed to enter the country with new passports for our aliases too. Count arranged to have all of that done by tomorrow morning.

The more I learned about this mysterious Quinton Hart, the more precarious I suspected trying to rob him was going to be. Here's hoping Taiyō was going to pull out the real big brain stuff for this one.

"I think he's enjoying this," Noelia said. I folded my arms over the loft balcony. Behind me, my toe grazed the bag from my shopping excursion. In the middle of another Gambit wasn't the optimal time for shopping, but now that Taiyō was aboard, there was something I needed to get. It also gave me a way to ditch Mom. When I said I was dipping out for an hour to shop, per usual she wanted to go too. I was in and out of the boardwalk mall within fifteen minutes. Two hours later, she was still out.

"Which one of them?" I answered, noting how Taiyō didn't appear to be trying that hard to shoo Mylo away.

Noelia's phone buzzed. She glanced at it, grimaced, then tucked it away.

"Who's that?" I asked.

She shook her head. "Just Nicky completing his daily quota of calling me Witch Bitch."

"Ah." I traced the edge of the balcony. "What's that like? Having a sibling?"

"I despise him, and he despises me. But I also wouldn't want to be in this family if he wasn't in it too." She shrugged. "I don't know. Do you wish you had one?"

"Maybe, maybe not. Could just be another person to compare myself to."

"Hmm," Noelia said. "I didn't know if I should bring this up, but you really lost yourself at the lab for a second there."

"Hypothermia does that to a girl."

"Before that. When you were about to pincushion a scientist with my sedative gun."

"It's what my mom would've done."

"What does that have to do with you?"

The sound of feet on the stairs put an end to any would-be hard truths we were about to share. Noelia gave me a look that made me think she'd want to talk about this later. We'd see about that.

Taiyō trotted the last handful of steps into the loft, and Mylo wasn't that far behind.

"He's finally ready to grace us with his brilliant plan," Mylo said, hopping up to sit on the balcony before Taiyō snapped and pointed to a sectional instead. "Is he telling us to sit down and listen?" Mylo whispered.

"Just do what he wants." Mylo and I took one side of the couch while Noelia perched petulantly on the sofa's arm. It was going to take more than a few hours for her to get over the kidnapping-her-brother thing.

"*Twenty-One*," Taiyō announced. "Who's seen the movie?"

Not ringing any bells.

"Oh!" Mylo raised his hand like we were in an actual classroom. "I knew you were going to go that route."

"*Twenty-One*?" Noelia repeated.

"It's this flick from the early 2000s," Mylo said. "A bunch of college kids counting cards, clearing out some of the biggest casinos in the country with the help of their math professor." He cut a knowing grin at Taiyō. "So that's the plan, eh? Good old-fashioned card counting."

"No, don't be ridiculous."

Mylo's smile dropped.

"The film is based on real events," Taiyō continued. "Which brought card counting into the public consciousness. Card counting attempts increased notably after the scandal, if you want to call it that, was revealed. An ingenious concept for its time, but casinos will be extra vigilant about looking for that these days. Keep it dog-eared in your memory, though.

"Now, what about the 2006 Harrah's chip forgery case?"

Mylo opened his mouth, but closed it a second later.

"Slot machine rigging?"

Silence.

"What about the pool-hustling gang out of Montana?"

Noelia yawned.

"Were these all twenty-year-old movies only Mylo would have watched?" I asked.

"Not at all," Taiyō said. "But they were all smaller heists that took place at casinos."

"Fascinating," Noelia said. "But not really seeing the relevance here."

I straightened, locking eyes with Taiyō. "So this *Twenty-One* thing was a big heist that the casinos fell for before and a lot of people knew about it, and the others are smaller heists that no one has really heard of."

I thought I knew where he was going.

Taiyō smirked, pushing up his glasses.

Yes, yes, I did.

"I suspect Ross is the only one up to speed, so I'll be blunt. We're going to do them all."

Mylo belly laughed. "This is a joke, right? Why would we do all of those? Didn't the *Twenty-One* heist rake in a hell of a lot of money on its own? And didn't you just ream me, like, thirty seconds ago when I asked if we were going to do the *Twenty-One* heist?"

"I'm seconding Mylo's thoughts," Noelia added. I think she might have agreed to anything that was anti-Taiyō at the moment. Quite the grudge she could hold when she wanted to.

"The *Twenty-One* con is a decoy," I explained. "It's so notable the casino probably knows how to peg it. It's perfect as a distraction. Some of us are going to fake the *Twenty-One* con, while the others are efficiently and subtly pulling off these smaller cons, racking our way up to twenty mil one mini heist at a time." I tilted my chin up. "Am I right?"

"Lacking some specifics, but yes. That's the plan," Taiyō said. I'd say he was looking awfully proud of himself, but real deal, he deserved to be. Concocting a plan that utilized not only one major heist but probably at least a dozen. It could be . . . well . . . extraordinary.

"You asked him to plan one job, and my man comes back to you with a heist buffet. You really like to flex, don't you, Taiyō?" Mylo cocked a brow at him, and maybe I was hallucinating, but I thought Taiyō was blushing under the praise.

"It sounds clever in theory," Noelia said. "But can we execute? This is a heavy workload, and there's only four of us."

"Did they make you skip primary school back at Boschert HQ?" Mom stepped into the loft with a distinct lack of shopping bags dangling from her hands. If she hadn't bought anything, what had she been doing all this time?

Mom pointed at each of us, counting. "One, two, three, four—" And last she pointed at herself. "Look at that, five."

Noelia soured. Biting her tongue, I'm sure.

"There's no use in counting you if you're just going to be *running coms*," I said, resisting the urge to do air quotes.

"I'll be on the floor."

I narrowed my eyes on her. "Even if you know who is—"

"I said I'll be there," she insisted. "Wouldn't miss it for the world."

"Good. Five is stronger than four," Taiyō said. He checked his smartwatch, a tiny gesture that seemed to make Mylo almost melt next to me. "We have twenty hours until the assignment commences. That's how much time to learn all the tricks necessary to pull this off flawlessly, and for two of us to learn how to cheat expertly at Hart's Bluff."

"Hart's Bluff? Are you talking about the card table decoy? I thought we were using twenty-one as the distraction game." Noelia looked so exasperated she could collapse. Or punch someone.

"I was only using twenty-one as an example. The students who ran that con were advanced mathematics undergraduates. Are you saying you think any of us already have that level of probability and statistics skill to be able to make snap judgments in under a second?"

"Yes," Mylo answered for all of us, before Noelia jumped in.

"Not all of us frequent casinos like movie theaters." Noelia cocked a brow at me.

"Don't look at me—they didn't cover that in my homeschool curriculum," I said, not acknowledging Mom.

Noelia dropped her head into her hands.

"Hart's Bluff will be easier to learn, and easier to con. In an obvious way, of course." Taiyō knelt, finding a palm-sized leather-bound notebook in his pocket and a pen. Because of course he just carried a notebook around with him.

"What else do you have in there?" Mylo asked. I stepped on his toe.

Taiyō started scribbling lines as he spoke. "It's Hart's Casino's signature card game. Crafted in-house."

What was up with this casino and its overwhelming exclusivity? Maybe that was part of the appeal. Not just prizes, but games you could only get there. "The game isn't listed on the website, so I'm guessing it's a game you can only play with victor chips. I had some contacts slip the rules to me."

"Which contacts?" Who else out there in our industry had been losing their life savings—or more—at Hart's lately?

"More importantly, how much did you have to pay to get your own rundown of the rules to this secret card game?" Mylo asked.

"I reached out to a number of people, and none of them requested any payment." His gaze flicked up to Mom. "None of them asked for anything after I mentioned I was working with Rhiannon Quest. It would appear there's a certain number of people who wouldn't mind throwing away a sliver of information for free to stay off your mother's bad side."

I glanced at Mom. The barest hint of a grin sat on her lips. How long had she had this reputation for being such a gangster? My whole life, and I just didn't know it.

I guess when word gets around about you betraying best friends, manipulating your daughter into death games, and letting your own sister get kidnapped in exchange for half a billion dollars, people decide they don't want to screw with you.

"The game is simple," Taiyō went on. "Part luck, part memorization."

"Like Uno!" Mylo said.

"No. Well . . . kind of. The dealer divvies up five cards for each player and keeps five for themself. They show their five cards to the players to memorize. From there, it becomes like a game of find the lady. The dealer shuffles those five cards facedown, usually in a confusing way, before selecting one. If the player is lucky, they'll have kept an eye on all the cards and will know what card the dealer has facedown. The player's goal is to pick a card from their hand that will beat the card the dealer has facedown."

"So, you just have to remember what cards the dealer has and play a higher card. That's basic," Mylo said.

"Not quite," Taiyō said. "In Hart's Bluff the color of the suit determines what cards 'beat' others. If the dealer plays a black card, you only win by playing a higher card. If it's red, you have to play a lower value. And then there are jokers. If the dealer plays one of those, the only way for the player to win is to call it a zero and play nothing."

Noelia scoffed. "What a ridiculously simple card game."

"Probably why it's popular." Mylo rubbed his chin. "So if

you're gonna cheat, with someone spying on what card the dealer's playing and signaling the player, then they'd have to signal not just the card's number but what color the suit is."

"Still, it should be pretty easy to actually con this game," Noelia said.

"Too easy," Mom said.

"Luckily for us, that's the point," Taiyō said. I reached for the notebook to see what he'd written, but he snatched it back and ripped the paper out instead. "No one opens my notebook but me."

"Oooh, mysterious." Mylo took the paper eagerly, and I peered at the lines of text myself. It looked like he'd written the rules of the game down. The surprisingly jagged and lopsided handwriting made me do a double take.

"I write more tidily in Japanese," Taiyō promised.

"I hope not. People with messy handwriting are statistically the most brilliant," Mylo said, still scanning the paper.

Taiyō flushed.

"Whatever. Let's figure this out." Noelia stood. "One decoy con and, like, fifty others. Sounds like we've got a night of cramming."

TWENTY-ONE

8:00pm, 0 victor chips accumulated.

That was the newest message dropped in the encrypted chat app Taiyō'd had us all download. Zero, depending on the context, is the most intimidating number. But at least I wasn't staring it down alone, even if Taiyō's plan *technically* had me venturing into this nightmare of a casino solo.

Hart's was reminiscent of a haunted mansion from some gothic novel, trying to camouflage its ominous nature with glowing lights and a come-hither spirit. But I knew better than to be seduced.

On the southern tip of Monte Carlo, sitting on prime ocean-front property, the casino might have climbed out of the waves. The flat stone design with curving balconies, arched windows, and larger-than-life crown molding made me think of a summer palace, one that would sit large and echoing and empty for most of the year while waiting for some faraway prince or princess to return on a whim. It didn't, however, look much like a casino. Only the endless parade of brake lights and people headed toward the gates hinted there was something going on inside. That, and the classy albeit understated Hart's logo protruding from the corner of the roof. A heart lying on its side. The left half was black, and the right a maroon red.

Entering the casino was something like entering a lush devil's wonderland. After a short line, on a red carpet no less, and a flash of my fake ID, I was in. As the bouncer waved me through the gilded doors, I was almost reminded of being back in Cairo, entering a certain auction.

Jittery as hell, I pulled my arms apart just a few seconds after folding them. Tonight's outfit was a departure from the usual ritzy cocktail dresses. Instead, I found myself in a chic white blazer with black satin trim and piping—the fabric was stiff, and since I didn't wear this sort of thing often, I had to walk circles around for half an hour just to break it in—paired with wide-legged black shorts and a fashionable crop top. Not gonna lie, I was really liking the look, especially the sheer leggings and the black suede booties and the high ponytail Noelia helped me wrangle my braids into. Even in the occasional designer—or high-quality knockoff—evening gown, I'd never felt like I walked off a high-fashion runway until now.

Music unlike anything else on earth wrapped around me: upbeat disco-pop in the background; yelps, laughter, giggles, and squeals; and the constant ring of clattering coins, the whir of shuffling cards, the chime of slot machine levers, the skim of balls over roulette tables, and the stacking of poker chips. Add it all together, and you got an intoxicating and exhilarating song. I think I was finally starting to understand the death grip casinos had on Mylo's heart. It was two hundred thousand square feet of booze, luck, loss, and temptation.

Two hundred thousand square feet of secrets, hidden currency, and danger. I was about to dive into the deep end.

"No funny shoes tonight?" I recognized the voice and stopped. Slowly, I followed it to find Baron sipping a fruity margarita, legs crossed on a suede bench. Dissatisfied, he added something from a flask in his jacket, which turned the concoction a shady gray, before taking another sip.

"No bodyguards tonight?" I countered.

He nodded to the side, where the man I'd come to know as Marc was holding his own suspiciously colored cocktail. He didn't seem inclined to finish it, but winced and took a gulp once he realized Baron was looking his way.

"I'm here in good faith." Baron gestured for me to sit. I ignored him. "Hart's is a hell of an undertaking. You really think you can hack it?"

"Do you think your team can?" Why the hell was he here? We hadn't accounted for the possibility of Baron inserting himself into the game.

"I think the odds are in my favor. But I'd feel a lot better if you and your mummy agreed to jump ship."

I scoffed. "Jump ship right into Diane's shark-infested waters?"

"Don't pretend that's my fault. Can you blame a downtrodden woman like Ms. Abara for wanting to protect her baby boy from a vicious heart eater like Rhiannon Quest?" Baron took a sip, the shadow of a grin on his lips. He was hiding something, but the chances of me getting it out of him were minimal.

"I'd dump her for you in a heartbeat," he said. "*If* you brought your mom with you."

My nails dug into my palms. For Mom. Notorious, efficient, brilliant Mom. That was why he was here. Mom knew better than to side with something as slimy as him from the get-go, but if I switched up now, then she'd come with.

As pretentious and pathetic as Baron was, why did it twist a knife in my chest to know even he thought she was still leagues more valuable than me?

"Screw off," I said, turning on my heel. After two steps, Baron caught me by the shoulder.

"With or without you, I'm still going to win." His breath was scalding on my ear. "You know, Diane didn't specify how she wants all of you to die. Some members and I have been betting on the most creative ways to get the job done. I'd share some with you, but I guess you'll find out soon enough."

With that, he strode away.

I ONLY GAVE myself a minute to shake Baron off. There was work to do.

"Excuse me." I approached a row of cocktail waiters with placid smiles and complimentary champagne. "Where can I cash in?"

A man, tanned and twentysomething, gestured with a smile into the wide-open doors leading into the first floor, as if they weren't already beckoning everyone in. "Cashier's booths are inside on both walls. You can only use Hart's currency inside the building. They can cash in any amount of money you'd like and convert it out when you're ready to leave."

"Thank you," I said. My next words were important. Count had told us that they had to be said verbatim. No paraphrasing. No stuttering. No second chances. "I'm feeling blue tonight. Can you lend a hand to a dealer's friend?"

The waiter gave nothing away. "Are you an old friend or a new friend?"

"A new friend."

He looked me up and down before gesturing to the side. An empty-handed waitress scurried up, and he handed his champagne platter off to her. During the handoff, I noted bruises on his knuckles. The waitress had the same. A quick glance down, and I caught a pinkish rash under her knees. Rashes from hand wraps and shin guards, bruises from training. They weren't just waiters—they were fighters. Something told me that staff training at Hart's comprised a lot more than watching outdated HR videos.

The waiter led me away from the tiled lobby to a nook with a row of golden elevators. I followed him into the last elevator. He pressed his thumb to the down button long enough for me to know his print was being scanned. After the elevator doors closed, he turned to face the back of the car, only for it to completely slide away, revealing a windowless velvety blue room. A trio of cashier's booths were nestled into the left wall, each with a line of three or four people.

"Have a dazzling night, new friend," the waiter told me before retreating back into the fake elevator. The door shut behind him.

As I waited my turn in line, I watched one man cash in four million dollars; another slid the deed for a house under the teller's window, a woman handed in a cooler with god knew what inside, and the man in front of me, at least four times my age, just wrote something down on a paper, his hand trembling. He swatted a tear off his cheek as he folded the note and handed it over.

This place was a death trap dressed as a playground, and I was suddenly very grateful that this was the last time I'd ever be cashing in here. Hopefully.

"Hi, there," the teller said. She wore shoulder-length box braids that reminded me of my own. "You're a new friend?"

"I am." I handed over my forged American passport.

She closed the curtains of her booth, returning about a minute later. "What would you like to cash in tonight, Ms. Nolan?"

I took my passport back, not knowing what she'd done with it.

"Currency. Five hundred thousand US dollars." As I stashed my passport back into my white leather purse, I found the cashier's check. Made out to Hart's, as ordered by Count.

"Excellent." She swiped the check out of my hand so fast it almost gave me a paper cut. "This is the last time you'll be able to use any form of monetary currency to cash in for blue chips. Should you need to cash in again, we'll require another form of payment."

"I understand."

She disappeared behind her curtain again, and when she came back, her glass window slid aside. She pushed a short box over the counter, then opened it for me. Inside were four rows of shimmering blue chips. I picked one out. Identical to the other Hart's chips Taiyō had us research, aside from the sparkling sheen and the midnight-blue shade.

"Five hundred thousand buys you fifty chips. These, the blue, are game chips. You can use them to play any game in the casino. Win a game, and you'll be paid out in victor chips." She held a shimmering black chip with gold trim up for me to see. "If you win using these, you'll be given four times however many victor chips you wagered. You can also use victor chips to shop from our *exclusive* catalog. Victor chips are the only currency accepted for the catalog."

Their catalog of curiosities, the former possessions of desperate people who cashed in more than they could afford. Things even the organization couldn't buy back. I looked down at my new collection of game chips. They were worthless now unless I turned them into victor chips. Just like that, Hart's had me invested.

"Have a dazzling night," the teller said.

I tucked the box of chips into my bag. "I intend to."

TWENTY-TWO

8:20pm, 5 of 2,000 victor chips accumulated.

Mom *would* be the first one to win some victor chips. I was surprised she didn't send some self-congratulatory emoji along with being the first one to update the "grand total" twidget Taiyō had pinned to the top of our encrypted chat.

As I entered the main floor of the casino for the first time, I took a moment to spot my team. Mylo and Noelia were a no-go, but that was to be expected. According to the plan, they were at the high-end poker tables. At the back of the first-floor balcony, I could see the first row of pool tables, where Mom was supposed to be hustling. Taiyō's schedule had her set to rake up at least fifteen victor chips, so she still had some work to do. I thought I spied her glittery leggings, but no way to be sure.

Where was Taiyō again—around the pachinko machines

right now? I kept a subtle eye out for him as I passed that area, but a familiar stride caught my eye. Was that . . . Devroe?

He was a vision in snug black jeans, a white button-down open just a button more than necessary, and a muscle-hugging navy-blue blazer. He didn't appear to be doing much, just chatting it up with a stranger while he watched someone else play roulette.

What was he up to?

I was supposed to be at my first station in a couple minutes, eight thirty according to Taiyō's schedule, but I couldn't ignore the urge to snoop. I headed his way as covertly as I could. But when I got to the roulette tables, he was nowhere to be found. Until I did another scan. He was by one of the many bars, his attention undeniably on me. He nodded me his way.

Was he saying he wanted to talk to me?

It was probably a trap. But maybe it would be useful to see what he had to say . . .

I might have been about to take a step that way, but a gaggle of guests blew past me, and in the temporary chaos, a hand grabbed my arm, spinning me around. Taiyō had me walking the other way in under a second. "Ignore him," he said.

"I wasn't . . . Yeah, okay, sorry."

"He's not the only one here. I saw Kyung-soon enter from the lobby a few minutes ago. Run-ins might be inevitable, but you can't let him or anyone else distract you, no matter your emotions."

I took my arm back, rubbing it despite not being hurt. "I don't have any emotions about any of this."

"A wise word—denial never worked out in anyone's favor in

the long run," Taiyō said. He was rocking a crisp three-piece dark-blue suit with a faint plaid design, complete with a waistcoat and an actual silver pocket watch, connected by a shimmering chain stretching from his pants to his coat pocket.

Taiyō reserved a spot at the nearest roulette table, and I did the same. My first job of the night was a two-person. We'd "luck" our way into about a hundred thousand together, then dip out. As expected, security was already distracted. Probably just having been alerted about possible suspicious activity at one of the blackjack tables.

Taiyō and I were already set up for success.

I looked up to the floor above. One of the bouncers outside the private card table area where Noelia and Mylo were located was frowning, talking into an earpiece.

Just starting to draw suspicion—we were on schedule.

"Emotions are not inherently a bad thing," Taiyō said quietly. "But they can be pricey. You should decide if that's a risk you want to take."

Not inherently a bad thing. That was a take I hadn't heard before. I wanted him to say more, but the dealer interrupted.

"Next, please." The dealer waved us into the fray with a sweeping arm and a dangerous smile. A second before I moved, my phone dinged. Taiyō checked his smartwatch.

8:25pm, 10 of 2,000 victor chips accumulated.

Over my shoulder, I caught Devroe on his way to his next hit.

And of course, feeling my gaze, he turned my way. My head snapped back around.

Taiyō was right—this was risky indeed.

. . .

9:09pm, 92 of 2,000 victor chips accumulated.

This might have been the most brilliant job I'd ever pulled off. Scratch that: that *we'd* ever pulled off.

Taiyō's plan was unfolding like clockwork. It may have been tempting fate maybe to say that only an hour in, but things really were going just that well. The bubbly high of "winning" more victor chips at one of the slot machines certainly didn't hurt. I might have been more of a gambler at heart than I ever realized, because the cherries lining, the cheerful dings of the machine, and the overwhelming clatter of the chips sliding into the dispenser were among the most breathless things I'd ever experienced. For the first time in a few months, I felt like the luckiest girl in the world. So much so that I had to remind myself, no, there was no luck involved.

I dropped the new black chips into my bag and spun around on my red leather stool, tossing a quick glance at Taiyō, who was across the aisle perched at his own slot machine. Though his back was to me, I felt his gaze in the reflective surface of his machine. Him and his carefully made remote. Slot machines, the computerized ones, have a certain code that makes the cherries line up. How else would they know to trigger the coin release? Getting the code to line up was fairly easy with the right device. Courtesy of a married computer science couple who lost their savings in the '08 crash. They decided to put their computer skills to work and almost got away with winning a million from slot machines—until one of them was caught red-handed with their magic device. Luckily, unlike the original couple, none of us had shaky arthritic hands that made constantly pressing a remote as obvious as it was for them.

This also went down in middle-of-nowhere Alaska over fifteen years ago, and never quite hit mainstream infamy. Niche enough that very few casinos had thought to correct the issue.

Hauling my white leather purse full of chips over my shoulder, I quickly updated the stats.

120 of 2,000 victor chips accumulated.

You eat an elephant one bite at a time.

I passed Taiyō right as he was heading toward his next area of attack. According to the schedule, Taiyō would be off to earn at least thirty chips in rummy right now. I was heading to the row of higher-jackpot slot machines for the next twenty minutes, to win at least ten more victor chips. The second row of machines was more packed than I would have liked, with a velvet rope anticipating a line, though I didn't encounter one. Still, there was only one seat for me to take toward the middle.

Wagering a blue game chip, I won four victor chips on my first pull.

Using the remote was easy. Small and compact, it fit perfectly up my sleeve. Before I pulled the oversized lever on the side, I propped my elbow on the machine and my chin in my hand. It was all too easy to slip my hand inside and press the button I needed. The digital slots rolled for an eternity, but when they stopped, they landed in a matching set.

Virtual confetti exploded on the screen, and a single victor chip fell into the dispenser.

"Congratulations!" a woman with a bridesmaid sash slurred in my direction, almost tripping over herself. I gave her a smile as her giggling friends pulled her away. Behind them, one of the cocktail waitresses, this one with the same telltale martial arts bruises, held an empty platter behind her back as she patrolled. I skipped using the button on the next spin, earning a *womp-womp* from the machine. Satisfied, she moved on.

So it wasn't just the bouncers to look out for. Seemed like the waiters and waitresses were trained to be on guard for suspicious activity too.

"Hey, lucky girl!" A hand grabbed my shoulder and spun me around on the stool. Another sloshed bridesmaid from the same party. She and about four other women and a guy in identical sashes were crowded around the machine directly behind me, where three uneven cherries were lined up. "Take a picture of us, pleeease?"

I wanted to say no, but the woman was already dropping her bedazzled phone in my hand. Fine, two seconds. I picked up my purse, because you never knew what thieves were lurking around, and took a step into the aisle as they waved me in. After spamming the photo button, I handed it back.

"You're awesome," she told me, and they all meandered away arm in arm.

I turned to my seat, only to find a hefty man in a black denim jacket and a fedora sitting in it.

"Uh . . ." Oh right, I had picked up my bag. The seat had probably looked empty.

Back to the machine the bridal party just left—

Taken by a supermodel-tall woman with a pixie cut. How the hell'd she get there so fast?

There had to be another machine somewhere. I still needed to earn another twenty chips here . . .

Taken. Taken. Taken.

Well, crap.

"Hi, miss, please don't stand in the aisle. There's a line for the slots forming over there, okay?" The same suspicious cocktail waitress from before touched my shoulder, silently pointing me to a line behind the velvet rope that hadn't existed five minutes ago.

I pushed the remote higher up my sleeve, sweat starting to build in my hands. Taiyō had been pretty serious about not messing up his schedule. But what was the alternative to getting back in line? Throwing a fit and getting rewarded with another machine?

"Miss?" The expression on the waitress's face was souring. Translation: *Go get in line, or else.* Attention wasn't exactly what we needed either, and I was starting to draw it.

An arm snaked around my waist. Before I could comprehend what was happening, I landed with a little bounce in someone's lap.

"No trouble. She was sitting with me." Devroe's voice was so near, I could feel the heat of his breath against my cheek, feel him smile at the woman.

It was a split-second decision. Go with it or ditch him, lose my spot, and probably draw even more attention.

Before I could think about it, I threw my arm around Devroe's neck and—god help me—snuggled myself into the warmth of his chest, keeping my other hand covering the remote.

It took everything to keep my breath from hitching. God, he was firm, and smelled like mint and spice and everything right, and all of my dips and curves seemed to slot so perfectly into him.

The woman, satisfied, gave us a quick polite smile before moving on to another disturbance at the other end of the aisle. Devroe spun us around to the screen. I felt something like a chuckle in his chest.

"Don't say anything," I warned.

"I think it'd be weirder if we just sat here in silence." He put his hand on the lever. "I was trying to get your attention earlier."

"I didn't see you."

"Liar."

He pulled. Another *womp-womp* from the machine.

"I was going to make a joke about you being my lucky charm, but I see that's not the case."

I scoffed, and inadvertently squirmed a little in his lap. Oh gosh, just thinking that. I was in Devroe's *lap*.

As soon as another machine opened up, I would zip away, even if I had to kick someone out of the way to get to it.

"I see you've invited Taiyō onto your team."

His leg moved just the slightest, and I made myself answer if only because talking was the best way to distract myself from this position, whether I wanted to chat or not.

"It's not my team, it's Count's. And no one said we couldn't invite a new member onto the team."

"No, they didn't." He inserted another chip—curiously, a regular game chip—and pulled the lever again. Two cherries lined up, but the third fell short.

"What's Team Baron's plan for the game, then?" I asked. Devroe's arm was still around my waist. "If you want to swipe something off of me this time, you're going to have to actually commit and kill me." My free hand had a death grip on the top of my purse. I'd be damned if I was going to let that happen again.

Devroe tensed at the word *kill*.

"My mum isn't on the premises right now," he said. "That's why I wanted to talk to you. I think you should forfeit the game."

I genuinely laughed. Reaching to hold on to something that wasn't him, I pulled the lever next and managed to win three regular chips. Not much of a return, seeing as he'd deposited at least five since I . . . uh . . . sat down.

"Despite my antics, I'm not suicidal." In pettiness, I stole the plain chips, which I had little use for. He didn't stop me, but his arms suddenly felt snugger around my waist.

"Ross, I'm serious." He turned my face to his. Him and his suddenly gentle eyes and furrowed brow and cinnamon-spice scent that I really wished I could forget about. "I'm trying to help. I don't want to see anything happen to you."

"If you care so much, then why did you join Team Baron? Why don't *you* quit, and then we can talk."

"I couldn't just . . ." He sighed, deflating as he watched the slots for a second. "She's my mum, Ross. I can't just abandon her. I have to prove to her that I care. I feel . . . not good about all of this."

"Boo-hoo for you and your guilt-ridden soul."

"This is all she has left. It's all she wants. My whole life, all she could talk about is Dad and how he deserves justice. If I didn't help her now, she would know . . . she would *think* . . ." He paused. "I have to value Dad as much as she does, Ross."

For a second it was just the music of the casino around us. Chimes and clinking glasses and laughter and cries and the clatter of chips.

"So I should just roll over and accept my fate, then. Make it easier for you by quitting." My hand dug into his knee with each word; it must have stung, but he didn't complain.

"I'm going to protect you."

I matched his gaze, looking for the spark of a lie, a game. I didn't find one, but I'd never been good at seeing those before, had I? You just had to assume the lies were there even if you couldn't see them.

"Oh?" was all I could say.

"I talked to Baron. After we win, he's agreed to grant me a wish too." I held my breath. He went on. "When Mum wins, I'm going to make sure she can't do anything to you. I swear."

"And the rest of the Quests?"

"He's only offered to let me wish one person out of harm."

Just me. And Auntie, my grandparents, even Mum, they would still be as screwed as ever. Who the hell would make a trade like that?

"You must think I hate my family," I said. "Believe it or not, estranged or whatever, I'm not keen to put them in front of your mum's firing squad only to hide in your arms while it happens. Excellent pitch, by the way. Is the scare tactic one of the chapters in your playbook, or is this just right off the cuff?"

He stiffened. "That wasn't what I was doing, and you know it. I'm just trying to protect you from the bloody inevitable, and this is the only play I've got."

"If you really wanted to save me, you would've used the wish you already banked to stop this."

"You think I haven't tried that?" He yanked the lever. "I can't use that until after this interim Gambit is over. I'm sure the organization doesn't want me spoiling their fun."

"You had a whole six months before to use it—"

"And wish for what? I didn't know what Mum was doing, so it's not like I could've wished to stop her." He took a breath. "This new deal is the only option we have."

"Well, thanks, but I think I'll pass and put some cards on beating your mum. I know you think she's infallible, but don't forget we were the ones who came out on top after Antarctica. Take your arm off me."

Schedule or no schedule, I wanted to get the hell away from him right now. I'd find another way to recoup those victor chips. Taiyō could ream me for it later.

Devroe reluctantly peeled his arm away, and I slid off his lap. But that left a breath of a second in which I was acutely aware of all the places we were and had been touching, and my body rebelled at the thought of leaving him.

He watched me with sad eyes, and I wanted to melt. God, why was he so beautiful? Everything about him was so flawless. His skin, his eyes, those lashes.

"That was the worst moment of my life," he said, fiddling with his cuff. "When I pulled you out of the water. I thought you were . . ." He cleared his throat. "I won't let that happen again. You can hate me for the rest of your life afterward, but I'm going to make sure you're okay, even if I have to beat you to do it."

He stood. We watched each other, eye to eye, for a long moment before he disappeared into the crowd.

I rubbed my chest, trying to tame my wild heart.

Even if it was real, if Devroe Kenzie wanted to save me, what did it matter? I had every intention of saving myself. I was the only person I could trust to do it.

TWENTY-THREE

10:15pm, 304 of 2,000 victor chips accumulated.

Thirty minutes later, and I was still thinking about Devroe as furiously as I had been a minute after he walked away. At least his departure left me with a slot machine to work with. I racked up the thirty or so victor chips I needed, filling my quota for Taiyō's schedule. That plus the chips he and Mom had won crunched us up to over a hundred fifty thousand in an hour. Honestly, I wouldn't have minded hitting the slots all night, but according to the book Taiyō got this con from, about an hour and twenty minutes in was when the house started noticing the uncanny lucky pulls that got the original couple caught. I was supposed to dip long before that. Thankfully, my next assignment involved a touch of cardio, so maybe a long stroll around the casino was going to be good for my thought process.

With my leather bag on my arm, I took a glass from one

of the servers and started teetering through the first floor. My steps wobbled just the subtlest bit, feigning tipsiness. Just enough to blend in, and to give myself an excuse when I walked a little too close to people or brushed past them. Mini con number seven—forged chips. Or rather, swapping real chips with my forged ones.

I dug into my bag, feeling for the hidden compartment inside. With the help of a contact Count had, we were able to get our hands on a last-minute collection of forged victor chips. Apparently, fake chips were a route a lot of people went when they were desperate to earn something back from Hart's exclusive catalog. It never worked; the forgery attempts were always caught by the cashiers. And the people who tried to cash them in one too many times, well, there was more than one case of such people coincidentally swan-diving off the roof into the ocean below. We weren't going to risk trying to cash them in ourselves, obviously. But just because the cashiers' vetting machines were excellent at telling the reals from the forgeries, that didn't mean that the average casinogoer was. Chances were, if I switched a few forgeries with real ones I found around here, no one would know until they were attempting to cash them in. Hopefully the people who were cashing them in one by one wouldn't be facing too harsh of consequences . . .

I brushed past a group hurrahing around a roulette table, one where Taiyō was currently on an astounding winning streak, keeping an eye out for any iridescent black chips. The rare black chips weren't the easiest to spot, but they were there. I'd say about one out of every ten players was using the special chips. Once I spotted one, it was almost too easy. With a little sleight of hand and an occasional apology for bumping into someone, I swiped chips here and there, sliding in my own replacements. The first thing everyone did if they noticed me stumbling a little too close was glance down at their stack of chips, but noting that they were all still apparently there, no one was that worried.

Passing through the first-floor card tables, I managed to swipe eight victor chips from a woman who'd been messaging someone on her phone, leaving her chips in a Tower of Pisa–like stack at the corner of a blackjack table. I may have inadvertently toppled her tower, but she didn't care too much when I stacked them back for her.

I weighed the chips inside the purse swaying at my side. Electricity crackled at my fingertips. Ten thousand dollars. I'd just swiped ten thousand dollars in less than ten seconds. In total, there was at least a hundred thousand's worth in my purse, and I still had fake chips to switch out. This was freaking genius. We were on track to rake up around a million from this mini con alone.

Looking over the rim of my glass, I eyed the higher-stakes card tables one floor up. Mylo pumped a fist in the air, apparently getting another "lucky" hand, and behind him security was circling like vultures. He'd leveled up from curiosity to person of interest. Just as planned. All he had to do was keep it up for a few more hours, but if I could read Mylo at all, he was having the time of his life up there. Could I blame him? We were all on fire. It was like this pulsing, addictive thing lighting us all up.

We were really doing this. It felt impossible a couple of days ago, but we were doing it. Piece by piece, we were working our way up to twenty million. One hour, one minute at a time.

I kept going, feeling drunk on something that wasn't alcohol. One thousand in chips here, two thousand there, four thousand next. The whistles and bells and jackpots and clattering chips around me fueled my zeal. More, I needed more and more. So I kept going, and I'd go on and on until this hour was up and I had the fifty black chips Taiyō wanted me to get during this mini job.

"'Scuse me," I slurred, pushing into my next target. A young man in a well-tailored, honest-to-god moonlight-silver waistcoat was lazily flipping a particularly shimmery black chip with one hand and taking a dab of a vape pen with his other. He had a careless ease about him.

An easy grab.

My elbow hit his, knocking the chip off course. It skidded a foot or so over the carpet. Simultaneously, I dropped one of my own, letting it air-hockey across the floor to land right next to his. In an apologetic scramble, I swiped up both, then pressed the fake one into his hand. "So sorry." I pointed to my heeled boots. "Still breaking them in." I turned to keep walking, but a hand clasped onto my shoulder.

"Excuse me," he said, his voice not particularly loud, but with an unquestionable authority to it. "That one's mine."

I turned around, feeling more focused than I had just a few seconds ago.

The boy blew out, and a wave of cherry-flavored mist hit me. Was he European? Middle Eastern? Asian? Maybe all of those. His wavy brown hair, cut right above his pressed collar, was a little too textured to just be white. I really needed to break my habit of using hair as a way to judge someone's ethnicity.

He gave me a well-practiced sideways smile, nodded once to my hand that was currently clutching the chip that, well, had once been his. His palm was open, as if he just expected me to drop it in. Maybe I should have.

I pulled my hand to my chest. "Why does it matter?"

"Because . . ." He held up the other chip between two middle fingers. "This one's a fake. I should know. This is my casino."

TWENTY-FOUR

10:50pm, 341 of 2,000 victor chips accumulated.

"I don't believe you."

It was the first thing that came out of my mouth, and whether that was part of my cover or my genuine thought, who knew. Maybe the more accurate statement would have been that I didn't *want* to believe him. Count hadn't had much information to share on the elusive Quinton Hart. Apparently a man who banked secrets was good at keeping a low profile. But I was sure Count would have mentioned if he was a freaking teenager.

He didn't laugh, but his lips tilted into a smirk that felt like his version of a laugh. "Do I look like a liar?"

"You look like someone who's too young to sign a lease without a guarantor, let alone own this place."

He couldn't have been that much older than me. In fact, I

would've bet he'd gotten in with a fake ID too if I'd had to put money on it.

"Well, if you want to get technical, it's my great-uncle's. But he's one coronary away from a dirt nap, and since I'm the only family member he doesn't wish he could drag to hell with him, it's practically mine." He extended his hand. "Kiah Hart."

Hart. Like the name outside the building. He was serious.

It'd be best if I just gave him the chip back and left. Just shake his hand and go on my merry way.

I extended my hand in return, but instead of shaking it, he pulled me into motion, stumbling behind him.

I tensed. Did I screw it up? Was I getting kicked out?

"Where are we going?" I kept any panic as far back as I could.

"I've never seen you before." He ignored my question. I wanted so desperately to yank my hand away from him, but something told me that might make whatever this situation was worse. "How interesting."

"I'd think new visitors would make up at least half of your guests." He tugged me past the pool tables and around to the edges of the first floor. Where was Taiyō? Mom? Did I want them to do something? That might have made things worse too. For all I knew, I'd just been compromised, and it'd be a foolish thing to drag anyone down with me.

"Most people with these chips are repeat customers." He skipped the forged black chip between his knuckles and peered into my open purse, which I quickly closed. "My, how many chips you have."

A quick glance around, and I realized at least half a dozen

waiters and bouncers were watching us. Waiting for some kind of signal. One they might get if I decided not to play along.

Steeling myself, I let Kiah lead me through the lobby and the secret elevator and into the private teller room. The bouncers by the entrance, as well as the tellers behind their glass walls, postured when we entered.

The cashier at the first booth held a halting hand out to the guest she was about to help and made eye contact with Kiah. He waved her off and guided me to the back of the short line instead.

My heart was hammering. Was he making me cash out early? Granted, that was better than what Count implied would be the punishment for being caught cheating, but still disastrous. How was I supposed to finish my third of the mini cons?

"I hope you're not making me cash out. *I* was actually having a good time." I folded my arms, trying to play it at least a smidge cooler than I felt.

"I bet you were." His gaze returned to my purse. "Having a lucky night?"

"And if I am?"

He flipped the forged chip high in the air, catching it with practiced ease. "Want to know how I knew this was a forgery?"

Pettiness made me want to snap no, but honestly, yeah, I kinda did. "Tell me."

Satisfied with my curiosity, Kiah opened his palm to reveal the chip. He pointed to the tiniest string of numbers running alongside one of the inner curves. Twelve, maybe thirteen or so characters long. "The first number here is 101."

I fished a handful of the *real* chips I'd swiped out of my

purse. Of the four I held in my palm, three of the serial numbers didn't start with 101, but lo and behold, the fourth one did.

"So is this a fake too?" I asked, holding up the very real chip. Maybe we weren't the only ones running this scam tonight.

"No, but see this?" He took mine and compared the fake and real chip side by side. "The trim on the edges of yours is maroon, not burgundy. It's a newer design. This fake has a darker shade of red around the rim. The serial numbers for this printing of chips didn't happen until after the redesign and the shade change. This combination of color and serial number should be"—he curled his fingers over the chip—"*impossible.*"

It was a meticulous, obsessive attention to detail. And it had taken Kiah only a couple of seconds with the chip to realize it.

"Remind me what your name is?"

He knew damn well I hadn't given him my name yet.

"Kennedy," I said.

The corner of his mouth twitched, like he could taste the lie. He scrolled through his smartwatch. I tried not to make my leering at it obvious, but I was too close not to notice the scan of the passport I'd used to check in, and a scan of what looked like the fake passport I used when we landed in France. Thank god Count had warned us about that.

He clicked his watch to black, a shade of disappointment on his face. *Sorry, I won't be that easy to catch.*

"You wouldn't happen to remember where you picked up this chip? It was in your hand when you accidentally ran into me. You must have gotten it recently."

I shrugged. "Couldn't tell you. Do you remember where you got *your* chip?"

A razor-sharp silence sliced between us. I bit the inside of my cheek, waiting. "Guess not."

The guest ahead of us collected his chips and moved on. The teller behind the glass beamed too wide. "Good evening, sir. What can I do for you?"

Barely sparing the employee a glance, Kiah slid the chip under the glass. "Get me a replacement. This one is a forgery."

The young man nodded and disappeared for a moment.

"Since I graduated high school, I've spent most of my nights here," Kiah said, resting his weight on the counter. "You know why?"

"Because they don't charge you for drinks?"

"I'm actually not very fond of casinos, in and of themselves." He kept on as if I hadn't spoken. "Once you know all the games and machines and tables, it can get kind of stale. But you know what never gets old? What always keeps me coming back?"

He leaned in, and like the most stubborn little mouse, I held my ground, glaring back. "Cheaters," he said. "They're always evolving. Always trying something different. Always so confident they're going to get away with it. Plucking them out is like . . . popping my knuckles or cracking my neck, you get it? It's just so satisfying. I stay thrilled to come back every night, desperate to get my fix."

I swallowed. Our eyes stayed locked. "So what are you trying to say?" I started. "You think I'm a cheater?"

"I hope so." The teller returned with my new chip. Kiah pressed it into my palm, grasping my hand with both of his. His pulse thrummed with exhilaration. "Weeding out cheaters is satisfying, but getting to *punish* them is like . . ." He blew out, breathless for a moment. "Well, I'll let you fill in the blank."

His eyes were practically glowing with a ravenous bloodlust. I swallowed a shudder, suddenly feeling not quite like a lamb in front of a tiger, but a tiger careless enough to hunt in a dragon's lair.

Despite the overwhelming anxiety, a little bit of that electricity from earlier started teasing up my spine once more. He hadn't called me out, which meant Kiah hadn't won yet. This match was just getting started.

Game on, Kiah Hart.

TWENTY-FIVE

11:01pm, 360 of 2,000 victor chips accumulated.

Where are you?

I tried to respond to Taiyō's message as stealthily as I could. He sent another before I could even get mine off. I hadn't even noticed the dots dancing. How fast did this guy type?

You were supposed to be at baccarat two minutes ago.

Caught up in a thing.

Quite the annoying thing. Kiah just had to poke around and ask what game I'd won my chips in. I replied that I had only played the slot machines, because I really didn't need him asking around and finding out that I hadn't actually won these chips at any tables, so then that gave him the perfect opening to invite me to play a game with him. Great.

Dots danced across the screen. Maybe Taiyō would have an out for me—

"Kennedy." My head snapped up. Kiah's line of sight flicked to my phone. I slid it into my jacket pocket, ignoring the string of vibrations. "What game do you want to play?"

"Are you sure you want to play with me? It might make it harder to catch me in the act if you're trying to win too."

"You don't get a better view than when you're at the table. And I don't mind multitasking."

At least he was letting me pick where we went. *I* might be screwed, but I could make sure he stayed away from Taiyō and Mom.

Actually, maybe this was perfect. If Kiah wanted a cheater to catch, I had two I could deliver right to him. Noelia and Mylo's whole shtick tonight was drawing in suspicion. If I could redirect Kiah's attention to them, it might just be my salvation. Or at least, the assignment's.

"A card game," I decided, glancing up at the tables that I knew Mylo and Noelia were at. "Something high stakes."

Kiah seemed pleased. "As you wish."

Instead of the glass elevators, he opted for the curving glass staircase, much to the woe of my feet, dying inside these heeled boots. The bastard probably did so on purpose.

I scanned the first floor as we climbed the steps, looking over the black-and-green floor, pool tables, blinking neon machines, and sea of people. It reminded me of Wonderland, but with more gambling addicts. Guess I forgot the part of that story in which Wonderland was just as deadly as it was magical.

It took a moment, but I finally spotted Taiyō, and subsequently Mom coming up to meet him. Both were looking at me. Taiyō was as still as a corpse, probably trying to figure out how I managed to ruin his plan before we even got to the halfway mark. Something told me he knew exactly who I was walking behind.

No matter what, it was going to be hard for me to go back to being an inconspicuous rando, so me racking up more little thefts was probably over.

My stomach knotted. Even if I wasn't officially busted yet, I might have really screwed us.

A sense of polite quiet enveloped the second level of the casino. There was a clear divide between up here and down there. A preppier general dress code, softer music, more tastefully dressed cocktail waitresses, and a lot more bouncers. Various game tables were organized around the space. Small lights glowed along the edges, setting the rest of the floor in a shadowy dimness reminiscent of a club.

Two bouncers stood sentinel in front of a velvet rope, keeping out anyone who hadn't paid for their two-hundred-dollar exclusive entrance chip. For me and Kiah, however, the bouncers stepped aside.

"Which game?" Kiah asked.

"Which do you want me to pick?" It might seem too obvious if I picked Hart's Bluff myself. I was trying to distract him with Mylo and Noelia, but I couldn't have him thinking I was in on anything with them. It'd be better if he thought he picked the game himself, and my gut told me he'd go for the one with his name in the title.

"Hm . . ." He started nudging me in a certain direction. "Ever played Hart's Bluff?"

Typical narcissist.

"Nope."

He was practically shaking suddenly. Not a nervous kind of shiver, but an excited, anticipatory shake.

"It's a house original."

"I could tell by the name."

"My favorite game in the whole casino. We're going to have such fun playing together," he said, an unspoken threat in his words. I hadn't even said I wanted to play.

"Not like I had much of a choice," I mumbled.

With his annoying hand on my back, Kiah guided me toward the Hart's Bluff table. There was only one on this floor, and it was flocked with people. One of the bouncers stepped in to nudge a path for us. We arrived just after the latest hand, in time to watch an older Black man with graying dreads slam his fist against the table and throw his cards down before storming away. Mylo raked in a new collection of chips to add to his obscenely growing pile.

"I'm on fire," Mylo announced, eliciting a scowl from the pair of security guards lurking at the edges of the crowd. Noelia should have just been starting to make her signaling a touch more obvious too.

I caught her mingling with the crowd, wearing a gleaming smile and whispering with a man I'd never seen before.

Her smile faltered when she noticed me. I pinched my lips,

wondering if I could convey all the things in just one inconspicuous look.

"Mr. Hart, we were just about to call you." A man in a too-tight-for-comfort jacket with an earpiece spindling from his ear leaned into Kiah, whispering. The angle wasn't in my favor, so I couldn't read his lips, but I assumed he was filling Kiah in on the possible suspicious activity going on up here.

Great. Just what I needed.

"Feel free to back off some," Kiah interrupted, putting a dismissive hand up. "My new friend and I are on the case." He slapped my shoulder, and I really, really had to refrain from twisting his hand into a wrist-shattering lock.

"What a coincidence," Kiah said, to me this time. "I've just heard that there's some uneasy antics going on up here too."

"Sounds like a dream come true for you," I said.

Another couple of people left the table, and a convenient two chairs opened up, with only one pantsuited woman between the new seats and Mylo. The dealer shooed away an incoming pair, who might have been waiting for their shot at the table for who knew how long before Kiah and I stole their seats. Kiah held mine out for me, the one farthest from Mylo but closer to where Noelia was standing with the rest of the curious onlookers.

As I sat down, I made eye contact with Mylo. Bow tie unraveled, he played with one of his chips and gave me a what's-up sort of nod, as casually as he might have any new player. But past that, I couldn't help but read what he was actually thinking.

"Whenever you're ready, Mr. Hart," the dealer said.

"Did he say Hart?" Mylo asked as Kiah took the seat next to

mine. Whispers brewed around us. "As in, *this* Hart?" Mylo held up one of the chips, flashing the Hart's logo in the center.

"And if I am?"

Mylo shrugged, dropping the chip with a delightful clatter. "Just want to know who's financing my next vacation." He slapped the top of his pile of chips, drawing just as much laughter from the crowd as skepticism.

The dealer eyed Kiah, a little flinch in his eyes. Kiah nodded at him, and he started to deal.

"Vacation? Won't you be missing a semester of school?" Kiah teased.

"You're one to talk," I sneered. "Are you taking a gap year, or is inheriting a major casino empire, being a skeptic, and having a haughty attitude all you want to do in life?"

"Yes, actually," he said. "And tell me, did you skip out on college to pursue the con thing?"

I didn't say anything.

"I feel like I'm missing out on the joke," Mylo interjected.

"It's nothing," Kiah assured him. "I'm just so amazed to see so many people my age in the house tonight." His steepled his fingers, looking between the two of us. "Isn't that bizarre?"

We all took our first set of cards. Mylo and the other woman at the table eyed theirs, but I was far more interested in keeping an eye on Kiah.

"You're not even paying attention to me," I said to him. "How are you gonna catch me cheating like that?"

"Cheating?" Mylo repeated. "That's what you're doing here, trying to weasel out hacks?" He laid down a card. "Can't you just accept that some people are luckier than others? Maybe I brought my rabbit's foot with me."

"The only rabbit's feet I like to see are the ones in the gift shop. They come with a little Hart's logo clipped to the side."

"Classy," I said, folding.

Maybe this wasn't so bad. Well, not as bad as it could be. Perhaps if Mylo stole enough of Kiah's suspicion, he'd let me go. We'd be behind schedule, but I could get back to my side of things, even if I had to deal with Kiah's hawk eyes on me.

That had to be what Mylo was doing. But would it work?

Mylo pressed some more, reeling in another win, and another, each time making Kiah's stare linger longer on him.

Quietly, I stood while the woman across the table filtered out as well. He wanted his thief to catch? He could have him. That was what Mylo was here for—

A hand grabbed my wrist. I froze.

"Where are you going?" Kiah asked.

"She's quitting," Mylo said, as loudly as possible. "I'd quit if I had to play next to me too. I'm just so infuriatingly lucky, am I right?"

"I'm done playing with you," I said. "Just because someone slipped me a forged chip doesn't mean you get to label me a con. I'm out."

"Only one?" He laughed and let me go, but lifted a handful of chips in his other hand. My purse. I'd set it on the ground between us. When had he gotten his hand in it?

"Fake, fake, fake." He thumbed through them one by one, letting them fall to the floor. "So many forgeries in one stockpile. Where'd you get 'em?"

"Your tellers gave them to me. Guess they're not as good at recognizing frauds as you are."

"Few people are." He let the last chip fall to the floor. "You know, my uncle isn't very good at identifying frauds himself. Back in his heyday, he says he used to just chuck anyone he thought might be conning him over the rocks." He let the implication sit. I swallowed. If he was trying to intimidate me, it was working.

Kiah stood and leaned in, whispering to me and me alone, "I only do that when I know someone's screwing us over. It's not fun otherwise. So no, you're not going anywhere, *Kennedy*. Not until I can decide whether you're guilty or not." He pulled back, a soft smile on.

I wasn't getting away from this. And when he found what he was looking for . . .

I shuddered.

This wasn't good.

TWENTY-SIX

I'M GOING TO the bathroom."

Kiah was at least "kind" enough to allow me that. Between rounds, the dealer held the game for me, and one of the bouncers escorted me to the second-floor restroom.

Passing the inner powder room, I found myself in an overwhelmingly maroon-and-red bathroom that reminded me of something out of *The Shining* in the worst ways right now. Noelia was primping her hair in front of the mirror at the farthest end. She probably figured I needed more help than Mylo at the moment. I made my way to the sink next to her.

"Didn't expect to see you up here," she said, the reflection of her eyes flicking to me.

"Things got twisted," I said. "I just ran into him. I'm not going to be able to finish downstairs now—"

"Oh, you don't say?" She whispered something to herself in French about me and chaos running into each other.

"I don't ask for this stuff to happen," I snapped back in English, which seemed to surprise her.

"Can your mom and Taiyō handle the rest of the mini jobs without you?" she asked, applying some mascara.

"I don't think so," I admitted, lathering up my hands with a seafoam-scented soap. "Taiyō planned things so meticulously. Take out a cog and—"

"We're screwed." She twisted the mascara cap on a little too tightly. "I can go. You and Mylo already have the distraction thing covered."

"Do you know how to place the remotes on the slot machines?" I asked. "Or apply the magnets Taiyō brought to the roulette table? Or jimmy the high-stakes pinball machines?"

Noelia's lips drew into a straight line. Me, Mom, and Taiyō had spent the last twenty or so hours learning and polishing those skills. She wasn't prepared to execute that side of the job.

She thrummed her nails over the sink. "Mylo would be able to catch on."

He would. If someone had to trade with me, Mylo was the ideal choice.

"He can't just leave, though," I said. "Hart's, like, this close to having me taken out back and shot or whatever. He already hinted that he thinks it's sus we're close to the same age. He wants to keep an eye on both of us. If Mylo cashes out now and leaves, I have a feeling he'll be tagged for the rest of the night."

"What if he just abandoned his winnings?"

"Who the hell would do that? It'd be even more sus."

"He could start losing?"

"As soon as we need him to? That's just as bad."

Noelia laced her hands behind her back. "Such a Catch-22," she decided. "So we need a way for Mylo to be able to leave without taking the money, which is a very weird thing to do, but without drawing suspicion if he takes your spot downstairs." She cocked a brow at me.

Oh, she was expecting me to have figured it out already.

"I don't freaking know!"

She checked her phone again. "It's been a while. Go back, I'll text Taiyō. Maybe there's a previous protocol for this we didn't know about."

Honestly, if someone had already lived through this exact situation and come out on top right now, I was quitting the organization and going to work for them.

With a feeling of urgency, desperation, and all the other worst feelings in the world, I headed out of the bathroom. My security escort was on my heels until I was safely seated again at Kiah's side.

"I was starting to think you weren't coming back," he said.

"There weren't any windows for me to shimmy out of."

He smirked, like he might say something else threatening or smart, but I was not here for it. "Can we start the next round?" I asked the dealer, who, frustratingly, turned the question to Kiah. Only then did we get the okay to play.

A familiar figure over the edge of Kiah's shoulder caught my eye. My gaze narrowed, but I tried not to draw attention to it. I might not have noticed at all if Noelia hadn't given him a noticeable once-over.

Oh god, as if things couldn't get any worse. Now Devroe was hovering on the floor. Was he spying on me now too?

Ignore him. You have work to do.

The first card felt slippery between my fingers. Not gonna lie, if I hadn't been so well trained, my hands might have been shaking. Failure was starting to unfold oh-so clearly in front of me. No win, and the cherry on top would be having to fight my way out of a back-alley brawl, if I could.

How cringey would it be to admit this failure to Mom?

Of all the things in the world, why was that on my mind?

I checked my watch. Past midnight now. Half the night was gone, and for all I knew, this hiccup was going to eat up the rest for me and, at the moment, the more valuable Mylo.

"What are you doing?"

Taiyō, speaking louder than I thought I'd ever heard him speak before, was standing behind Mylo. He'd somehow shouldered through the people behind us and approached the table with a certain authoritative swagger. Through his glasses, his gaze was leveled solely on Mylo. I swallowed a gasp. What was going on here?

Mylo cleared his throat. "Um, I . . ." He squirmed. Whatever Taiyō was doing, we were off script.

"You've been gone for three hours," Taiyō continued, gesturing his hand in an expert display of controlled exacerbation. "And you haven't been answering your phone or texts."

"I—" It clicked, and Mylo relaxed into the role in the flash of a moment, even faster than I put it together. "I told you I was going to the tables, babe."

"Not the second floor. I was running around the first-floor tables looking for you like a fool for the past hour! What the hell?" Taiyō bit the inside of his cheek and huffed; it was on point and flustered and angry and a little adorable. So much so that I almost believed it for a second, and watched carefully. Just as Kiah was.

Taiyō dropped his voice to a whisper, but one of those that everyone around you can still hear. But maybe you want them to hear because you're the kind of person who doesn't mind making a scene when you're pissed. "You said I was going to be the priority tonight."

"You're always the priority!" Mylo insisted, nailing this soap opera perfectly. Taiyō narrowed his eyes doubtfully. "Look, um, I'm gonna finish this game and then we'll—"

Taiyō closed the distance between them, pressing his lips to Mylo's. The crowd gasped; this was the turning point in the drama, and they seemed addicted. Mylo melted into it instantly, grabbed the lapels of Taiyō's jacket, while Taiyō cupped his face. Even to me, for that moment, it didn't look like either of them were acting. And when Taiyō pulled back and straightened his glasses, Mylo's kiss-flushed face sold it all.

"I'm tired of the games. Pick one." With that, Taiyō strode away, leaving all of us, Mylo in particular, to watch him go.

Mylo jumped up so fast, he almost knocked his chair over. "I . . . um . . . I'm out." He ran a hand through his hair, still flustered and looking more boyish than I'd ever seen him. He took off after Taiyō.

"Sir!" the dealer called, slowing him down for a second. "You can't leave your chips like this. Are you forfeiting?"

Mylo glanced at the chips, then back Taiyō's direction. "Keep them!" And he was gone.

Well, that was one way to get us out of that situation.

TWENTY-SEVEN

I COULD'VE LAUGHED WITH delight. We were saved, sort of. The point was, we could be back on track to actually get this job done.

"What's so ticklish?" Kiah asked, jerking me back to reality.

Oh right, the reality that I might maybe still be on track to get thrown into the sea. But if it got us the chips we needed and secured the win that would keep my family from being destroyed, maybe that was a fair trade.

"Just you and your skepticism." I flicked my single card as the dealer flipped over their first one. I played a card, not thinking about it nearly as much as I was about the look on Kiah's face.

"Oh, is it just totally killing your vibe that you haven't

proved anyone at this table is a high-rolling con artist?" I pressed a hand to my chest. "I feel for you."

"You win some, you lose some." Kiah clicked his tongue. "I'll have to catch that guy the next time. Him and whoever I assume was helping him count cards." He sighed, leaning back in his chair. "Such a disappointment. I would've loved to catch two cons tonight." The dealer was busy resetting, and I noticed that the table was empty. There was still an audience watching from a respectable distance, but the bouncers must have been keeping them back.

When did he order that to happen?

Kiah thrummed his fingers over his thigh, watching two of the cocktail waitresses reeling in all the chips Mylo left behind.

"It doesn't make any sense to me," he said. "So frustrating. If you two were part of the same gang or something, how do any of you benefit by leaving all your winnings behind?"

We were far from home free. He was sharp, and still trying to puzzle this out.

We didn't allay any suspicion; we just deprived him of the chance to get that elusive proof he wanted so badly.

"I don't know that guy," I insisted, not that it was helping at this point.

"So you don't mind that I had them kicked out?"

It took all my training not to react. He was bluffing. When had he done that? I'd been sitting next to him the entire time. This had to be him just testing me to see how I'd react.

"I'm not a fan of the crowbar treatment for anyone, strangers included," I said.

He chuckled. "I told you, only those found guilty get that

treatment. But it's no fun having cheaters around if I can't keep an eye on them myself. I had those other fellows escorted out."

"Seems like bad business to kick people out just because of a theory." What if he wasn't joking? If Taiyō and Mylo were out of the game, then it was even worse than before.

"Do you wanna know exactly what my theory is?" he teased.

"I have a feeling you want to tell me."

"I think you're a decoy. Somehow you and your friend knew about my fascination with forgeries and cheaters. So you were supposed to distract me with your admittedly forged chips, while your associate handled the real con upstairs. Am I right?"

Quite the opposite, actually. But I figured it was better than Kiah guessing the whole truth.

"And then, what, my 'associate' just got spooked and left when you decided to come up here?"

"Maybe."

"Sounds like you haven't actually figured out anything." An idea, a weak one, was starting to bloom. "And if you were right, hypothetically, exactly how was my 'associate' managing to rig the Hart's Bluff table in the first place?"

At this, he flinched. "There are dozens of ways to cheat at table games."

"Prove it. How?"

"I can't prove anything now that his boyfriend conveniently took him away before I could."

I took a breath. "What if I played for him? If he was, again, hypothetically, on my team or whatever, wouldn't I be able to slide right into his place?" No, no, it was really not the case, but it was all I had.

Mylo had won a lot of chips tonight. We never expected to actually count any of those chips in our grand total; he was always supposed to get caught and taken away. *But*, if one of us could actually make out with that decoy sum, then we might just surpass our two-thousand-victor-chip benchmark.

I gave Kiah a haughty grin. "You're right, Kiah Hart. I am a con artist, and my friends and I came here tonight to walk away with a lot of your money. I want the chips you spooked my associate away from. So you're gonna let me play, and cheat, just like he was. And when you can't prove how I'm doing it, I want you to let me keep it."

His eyes were alight with the challenge, and I fed it. "No more kiddie games. Let's play for real, yeah?" He leaned closer to me. "And when I call you out, it won't just be your last night in my casino, it'll be your last night anywhere."

He snapped his fingers, summoning the waitresses who were carrying away Mylo's chips. "Bring those back, please. Dealer, new game. One player. Clear out this floor too. I don't want anyone from this crowd here for next game." He stood. "Good luck."

THE DEALER DIDN'T just rake in the cards, he brushed down the table, unpackaged a fresh new deck, and counted the cards out, all fifty-two of them, for Kiah to see. The staff restacked Mylo's chips, freaking one hundred thousand dollars' worth of victor chips, in neat towers along the edge of the game table. Maybe it was meant to be an intimidation tactic, but I was grateful it gave me a few minutes to get myself together. This was my last-minute, last-chance foolish little idea, but there was one problem.

Kiah banned everyone who'd been on the floor when Mylo was playing. Noelia had been ushered out along with Devroe and everyone else. While new people were already filtering in, none of them were here to help me. Even if Noelia had been able to stay, it wasn't like I knew any of the hand signals or calls. I was alone. I didn't even have one of those stupid Hart's rabbit feet for luck.

One bust, and I was out.

One suspicious move, and I might be dead.

Kiah, done examining the playing field, prowled the perimeter of his game floor. His anticipation was toxic, like acid on the skin.

"Ready, player?" the dealer said. I swallowed and nodded. He shuffled the fresh cards, drawing them into an arc, then a rainbow spread on the table before gathering them with one swipe of his palm and flicking out five into a tidy pile in front of me. Slowly, savoring the seconds I could, I pulled my hand in.

Lord Jesus, I know you don't like the thieving thing, but give me the cards I need, and I swear I'll start going to church with Auntie again when I go home. I won't even swipe anything from the tithing plate.

Quickly, I committed my cards to memory. Black ace of clubs, black two, black seven, red king, red five.

The dealer dealt himself five cards, taking his time to hear the *fwip* of the cards as he piled them. Whispers and curious conversations surrounded me. What was the odd game going on, with only one player at a table by herself?

Even with a packed audience, Kiah made sure to keep a careful eye. He watched unblinkingly as the dealer revealed his own hand of five for me to memorize.

Red two. Black seven. Black queen. Red four, black ace—

He swiped his cards away, not giving me more than three or so seconds to get a good look. I was sure that when I saw Mylo playing, the table had gotten at least five or six seconds to ogle the dealer's cards.

Kiah was smirking.

Like a street magician, the dealer slid and shifted his five cards over the felt tabletop. He was dizzyingly fast, pushing one card over the next, then another up, another to the side. I tried to remember which card was which, what went where, but keeping track of one card would have been near impossible, let alone all five.

Finally, he drew the five facedown cards back into a tidy row. His fingers danced over the set, teasing the second one from the left, before sliding the first one toward the center of the table, still facedown. He stole a quick peek at it before returning it to its place.

I thrummed the table, my own cards sweaty in my grasp. Okay, if I had to guess, I felt like that card was the red four he had? Yeah, that seemed right. If it was a red card, then I needed to place a card that had a value *less* than his to win. I eyed my hand again, specifically my ace and my two. Either of those would be a win if my hunch about his card being that red four was correct.

But *was* it correct?

The dealer slid a low-lidded glance at Kiah, who nodded.

"Three hundred chips." The dealer retrieved ten neat stacks of black chips from his table. "Match it or raise it, please."

I pushed a cluster of what used to be Mylo's stacks toward the center of the table. Three hundred chips? That was a quarter of what Mylo had won, at least. I told Kiah I would play until I completely busted. If I screwed this up, I'd be taking a major blow.

"Your move," the dealer nudged.

What would Mylo say? Probably something like follow your gut. My gut said his card was that red four.

I made to grab my ace.

Then I switched at the last second, grabbing my queen instead. I practically slammed it on the table, drawing a slight jump from a fellow nearby.

The dealer flipped his card over.

Red, four of diamonds.

"Your loss." He didn't show an ounce of sympathy as he raked in my chips. Over three hundred black chips. Gone. I clenched my jaw, almost shaking. Why didn't I trust myself?

"Four rounds remaining." The dealer plucked two new cards from the top of the deck, one for me and one for him. He flashed his to me, a red nine, before adding it to his hand and beginning his disorienting street-magician-style shuffle again. I tried to keep up with the cards, at least the new one. It looked like when he evened the row out again that card was in the very center. Unless it was just an optical illusion.

But then he picked that center card. Was I getting lucky? The one card I actually thought I'd managed to keep an eye on was the one he selected. Maybe it was a bluff, he was toying with me, but I ignored my gut last time—look where it got me.

I'd assume it was the red seven.

"Two hundred chips," the dealer said. With no choice, I matched. The remainder of Mylo's pile was looking exceptionally diminished. Kiah had a crestfallen look. I'd promised him the chance to catch me in the act, and I was failing spectacularly.

How would he react if he thought I was losing on purpose to try and save my skin? Something told me Kiah wouldn't take that well at all . . .

"Your move," the dealer said.

Just play less than a seven. It's fine.

I reached for my five.

"No way." A familiar voice stopped me in my tracks. It wasn't speaking to me, just another voice in the growing crowd around me. But familiar voices cut through background noise like a hot knife through butter, even if no one else noticed. And especially when they're coming at you in a language you weren't quite expecting to hear in the middle of Monte Carlo.

She continued, making giggle small talk in Korean. Pretending to take a nervous breath, I took in the crowd, following the words until I caught a glimpse of Kyung-soon, looking absolutely disco chic in a sequined minidress. She was sitting at a high table behind where the dealer stood, smiling as she spoke into her phone and playing with the candied rim of a glass. She truly was a master of not looking like she was paying a lick of attention to what was going on around her. I might have bought it too . . . if she hadn't happened to be in the perfect position to sneak a peek at the dealer's cards.

She went on, and I focused on her voice. In Korean. "I *love*

Wistful Thinking. You would not believe me if I told you how many times I've rewatched that show."

Wistful Thinking . . . We'd had this conversation before—that was one of Kyung-soon's favorite dramas.

Ten times. She's rewatched it ten times.

I bypassed the five I was going for and picked my king instead, giving the dealer and by proxy Kiah a sure look.

The dealer bit his lip, but flipped the card.

A black ten.

"Your win. Three rounds remaining."

I almost hugged the chips back to me. The focus in Kiah's eyes was smoldering.

The dealer selected one new card for each of us. I paid careful attention to memorize the value and color. As long as I remembered the color of the card, if someone was telling me the number, then I'd know what to play.

"Your wager—"

"Five hundred." I pushed an embarrassment of chips to the center of the table, toppling some precariously stacked towers in the process. A few gasps ran through the floor. Kiah looked like he might have an aneurysm.

"Matched," the dealer said, and began his party trick.

If I thought he had supersonic hands before, then this was way past light speed. I had whiplash by the time he finally picked a card, stole his peek at it, and put it back facedown. Kiah's gaze was ravenous over the crowd. Clearly, he suspected someone was calling for me; that was why he set this game up this way.

"I went to Jeju once, but it's been forever . . ." Kyung-soon said to the imaginary person on the other end.

Jeju, Jeju. An island in South Korea. Oh my god, she mentioned this. Her family took her there for one of her birthdays. But was it four or five? The dealer had both, black four and red five.

I played my five. Worse-case scenario it would be a tie.

The dealer flipped, revealing his red five. "Even. No chip exchange. Two rounds left. Your wager."

I let out a breath. Okay, no win, but no loss. "I wager five hundred again." The dealer nodded. Apparently my tie hadn't done much to ease Kiah's nerves. As the dealer reshuffled, Kiah completed a full pace around the room, eyeing the cluster of people behind the dealer, the bridesmaids, the high roller with a barely legal girl on each arm, the plastered guy with sunglasses on inside, the Korean girl chatting away on her phone. Apparently, Kiah was unable to decide who was most suspicious. He angrily muttered something into his smartwatch. Oh god, was he calling some of his lackeys to get ready to drag me out after I lost?

The dealer put his card down. "Your move."

"I think I'm going to dye my hair blue again," Kyung-soon said carelessly.

I racked my brain for any conversations we'd had. I thought I remembered, during a weird late-night group chat session in which Mylo was discussing all the different hairstyles he'd had, Kyung-soon mentioning that she'd dyed her hair a shade of aquamarine not too many years ago. But she couldn't have been any younger than, what, fourteen or fifteen when that happened? Neither of those numbers were viable in this situation. Was she trying to say one, as in she'd only done that once?

Just as I shakily started to pluck out my ace, at the worst

drawing another tie, she spoke again. "Oh yeah, Madame did not like that at all."

It clicked. The rest of her story. Mylo had asked how long she rocked it, and Kyung-soon said she didn't get more than six hours before her mentor came back home; they were doing a long con that involved a certain amount of propriety. Her mentor had dyed it back to its original shade herself.

Six. The dealer's six was black. I played my seven.

Win.

Applause wrapped around me. "She's got a good eye for keeping track of them cards," I heard someone say.

"Just dumb luck," someone answered.

"One round remaining," the dealer said. He hesitated pulling new cards for us, though, and I didn't realize why until Kiah was slipping his way back into the crowd, now with one of his employees in tow.

A nervous-looking woman in a pencil skirt and a red vest—the teller that had cashed me in. I thought she looked Blasian. Wait, was she Korean?

The woman wrung her hands as she stopped next to Kiah, both of them within listening distance of Kyung-soon. Clearly he suspected she was calling the cards for me, but he couldn't quite prove how.

Relax, Ross. Kiah wouldn't act unless he could prove how she was signaling me. That was the fun for him.

The teller whispered into Kiah's ear while Kyung-soon was now fake gossiping about some girl she was frenemies with at a country club I was sure didn't really exist.

This was it, then, the last play. The one Kiah thought he was really going to call me out with.

Well, go big or go home.

I pushed all my chips into the center of the table, drawing an audible gasp from the collective new fans around me. "All in."

The dealer, leaning back a little as if he might topple over, shot a questioning glance at Kiah. Was he really allowed to do this?

I cocked a brow at Kiah myself. He folded his arms, looking from me to Kyung-soon, then gestured for the dealer to get on with it.

"All right . . ." The dealer tugged at his collar. "Matched."

The dealer made an extra show of shuffling this time around. Spinning and spiraling and shifting the cards in the most hypnotizing way possible. I gripped the underside of the table in anticipation. All this pageantry didn't matter, just so long as I still had the assist.

And she didn't get caught.

Finally, the dealer selected a card, did his mandatory peek, then slid it facedown between us.

The room was white noise. Everything that wasn't Kyung-soon's voice.

She sighed into the phone, then finished her drink and started collecting her things. "Maybe she deserved it, but do friends let you down when it matters?"

My heart froze, and I felt like the sappy but true answer was obvious. It took everything in me not to smile.

Never.

But what did that mean? One? Ace?

Or nothing.

He was playing a joker.

I put my cards facedown on the table. "Nothing," I said.

The dealer swallowed hard, looking like he would do anything in his power not to flip the card. But with the audience around us, and the rules of the game, what choice did he, or Kiah, have?

He flipped the card. Joker, baby.

I freaking won.

TWENTY-EIGHT

I SWEAR KIAH DIDN'T blink once as he watched me deposit my chips downstairs. One thousand eight hundred and one victor chip credits were deposited to Kennedy Nolan's account at Hart's. As planned, I was to cash them out for a few choice items in Hart's exclusive catalog and, according to Count, ask no questions *ever* about the things I was recovering.

At least, those final steps were set to happen at some point within the next few minutes. Kiah, petty mother-hugger, insisted on rewatching some security footage just one or two more times before I was actually allowed to place some orders with my newly acquired black chip fortune. At least, I was, like, 90 percent sure that's what he was up to. He'd more or less dumped me in a fury at one of the cashiers before mumbling something about being right back and disappearing through a hidden door.

The teller, the very same one Kiah had ushered upstairs, gave me a nervous little smile after she accepted my intake of chips. She leaned into the speaker in the glass.

"Um, do you speak Korean?" she asked, in that language. One last attempt from Kiah to have me slip up, I'm sure.

"Huh?" I frowned.

She flushed as she pulled back. "Nothing. Congratulations. You can wait in the lounge." She pointed behind me, down a snug hallway where a secluded sitting space was waiting for me.

I all but collapsed into a settee. Coming down from adrenaline was like coming off a high. Tiring and draining and ugh. Not that I would know what coming off a literal high felt like.

I heard the sound of featherlight steps coming my way. Dead exhausted or not, letting someone get the jump on me was not how we did things.

I peered over my shoulder. Kyung-soon, still shimmering in her flapper dress despite the unenthusiastic lighting, stopped a couple of steps from me.

"Hi," she said.

I held my breath, my gaze instantly skirting to the corners of the room where a camera dome would be hidden. After all that work to barely get one past Kiah, getting caught talking to Kyung-soon here would be too much of a coincidence to brush off.

"Don't worry, there aren't any cameras in these lounge rooms. Apparently one of the things you can buy from the

Hart's catalog is an hour or so of, uh, intimate interaction with some of the employees. Hence all the comfortable furniture."

Oh. Now that she mentioned it, there was a distinct lack of chairs and an abundance of settees and oversized couches back here.

I flushed. "Oh . . . interesting."

Not really knowing what else to say for a second, I scooted back so she could share the settee—which I prayed Hart's was replacing regularly—with me, if she wanted. But that wasn't enough. I did need to say something. She'd saved my skin back there. Even when I was on the opposite team.

She hesitated for a second before flopping backward onto the sofa, letting her hair hang down freely under her.

"So—"

"I'm sorry."

I felt like my apology eclipsed whatever she was about to say, but in case that wasn't enough, I pushed myself to say more. "I mean, I feel like I shouldn't be sorry for being angry about you joining my archenemy's team, but I kinda *do* feel sorry for that, but mostly I'm sorry about the pretending not to know Korean thing. It was petty and inappropriate and kinda racist, so I'm, like . . . extra sorry for that."

Oh god, did I just apologize for being a racist? Somebody kill me now.

Kyung-soon just looked at me, brow furrowed. She opened her mouth, but I started word-vomiting again. "Not that I'm saying this because you *have* to forgive me, because, you know, no one should have to forgive anyone if they don't want to because being angry is your right and my right and everyone's right, but you still put your neck out for me, so you deserve to hear a thank-you. Which I just realize I didn't give you yet. So, uh, thanks. Also."

If shutting up and letting her talk now didn't work, I was going to staple my mouth closed.

Kyung-soon took a heavy breath and breathed it out slowly. She picked some strands of hair and twirled them around her fingers. "Just because we had a fight doesn't mean I want you to get beat up with brass knuckles and tossed into the Mediterranean Sea," she said. "Of course I was going to show up and save you. You're just lucky you actually *did* know Korean."

I nodded, until . . . "Wait, how did you know—"

"We'll get to that," she said, putting a hand up. "It really bothered me, though, when I thought you didn't learn Korean. I was feeling like you make everything about yourself when we're talking. I was mad, but that's not the reason I went with Baron's team. I would never let a spat like that make me turn rogue on a real friend."

I tried not to sappy-smile at *real friend*, and ruminating on the making-everything-about-me part helped there. Maybe I had monopolized a lot of our time together moping about my own problems. Friendships should probably be more give-and-take, and I'd been hardwired to take since birth. "Then why are you on Team Baron?"

She sighed in an exasperated way. "For you, duh!" She sat up. "Obviously Devroe is my friend too, and I didn't want to abandon him. But I know protecting you is still his priority. If he was joining Baron's team, then it was more than likely with the intention of trying to work out some sort of deal from the inside, and for that I thought he might need help."

Did she just say she was going double agent for me?

That was so . . . cool.

I sputtered. "Why didn't you say anything about it? Text me or something?"

"Well, because I was mad at you."

I'd have asked who the hell would hold back information like that just because they were mad, but here I was hiding a whole-ass language, so I couldn't really call her on it.

She spared a glance toward the still-empty hallway before biting her lip and drawing closer to me. "Devroe wants to save you, but he also thinks his mom is going to win this somehow, with or without any of our help. She pretty much bagged this phase for us a couple hours in."

"What do you mean? Whether you want to believe it or not, my team's kind of already racked up the win here."

"Don't be so sure," Kyung-soon said. "Look, Devroe's already gotten Baron to agree to saving your life if we win. I'm trying to get him to give me a wish too, but I'm not betting on that. We're doing the best we can."

"That's not good enough—" I stopped myself, flexing my hands over my lap. Snapping at people never gets you far. "I think you'd be helping me more if you were on my team."

"Maybe. Hate me for it or not, but after meeting Diane, that's not what I believe." She looked away. "She's like a hurricane in a bottle, Ross. You can't stop that once it's let out. I hope you win, but in case you don't . . ." She bit her lip. Enough said.

"I used to think you were the one all about contingency plans . . ." a voice said.

Kyung-soon and I looked up. Devroe stood cautiously at the

entrance of the lounge. He cleared his throat. "Sorry for interrupting."

Devroe and I must have matched gazes for a second too long, because Kyung-soon was the next one to speak. "Now I feel like *I'm* the one interrupting—"

"Wait," I said, reaching for her as she stood. Ditching her because my—uh, Devroe showed up was not good friend behavior.

"It's okay." She reset a slanted barrette and whispered, "By the way, who do you think sent me up there to help you out?"

Then, with a peace sign, she was gone.

I just blinked at Devroe. "You sent her to help me?"

Devroe, brushing some invisible dust off his wrist, meandered my way. "I didn't know who else could. Kiah would have killed you if you lost that bet."

I crossed my arms. "Since when do you know what languages I speak?"

He hovered for a moment before taking Kyung-soon's spot beside me. "You've been practicing for months. I saw you practicing ordering breakfast while we were on that job in the Maldives."

"I never spoke to anyone in Korean while we were in the Maldives."

"No, but you were whispering translations under your breath after you spoke to the waiter in English."

My face flushed. Okay, maybe I had been known to do that when I was studying a new language.

I pulled one of my legs to my chest. God, I loved shorts and pants that gave me the freedom to do that. "So you've been watching me is what you're trying to say, but in a way that doesn't make it sound creepy?"

He rubbed his chin. "How about, I was noticing your beauty from afar?"

"Why don't you go ahead and paste that together with newspaper clippings and mail it to me."

He pouted. "Look what the months of heartache have done to me. I can't even string together a decent flirt."

I couldn't help but laugh a little. "I've been intrigued by your tenacity, nonetheless. If not confused." I pulled my other leg up, hugging both to my chest. "It's not every day or every year that someone, you know, kisses you and then, like, three days later almost kills you but then doesn't and then goes back to flirting with you."

"Really? I never did more than a few weeks at any one school, but I assumed that was more or less how most high-school courting went."

I didn't laugh this time.

He polished his shirt buttons with his thumb. "You know what I've been thinking about a lot over the past few months?"

"Besides all the heists and betrayals and passive-aggressive texts from Count? Because I haven't had much bandwidth for much else."

"If you didn't hate me, and if we didn't have all of the family things to worry about, what it would be like to run away." He said it with a devastatingly devilish grin. "It'd be like the end of one those heist movies. We'd move to Boca, live on a beach, never wear shoes."

"Done the beach thing, not as spectacular when you grow

up next to it. And sorry, even without all the other baggage, Devroe without shoes is not a Devroe I'm as enthralled by."

He pressed a hand to his chest. "Scathing, Ms. Quest. Then we'll have to settle for some lush countryside somewhere, next to a village with the finest tailors, of course. We'll spend our days doing . . . whatever it is people do in quiet villages after the credits roll."

I snorted. "That sounds . . . awful. Who the hell wants to move to a village where no one does anything ever?" My heels clacked together. "Hypothetically, I'd be much happier in a city. A huge one, where there are people everywhere. And lots of tourists to pickpocket on a Sunday stroll. Maybe Brisbane or New York or—"

"London?"

"Sure, London," I said. "I still wouldn't be able to trust you, though."

"You could remind me every day."

"We'd still have to hate each other, though. How would that work?"

He paused. "Just as well as it's working now."

I took a breath. "It wouldn't last. Maybe a year or so until we get dragged back into some other dramatic mission or, god forbid, another Gambit," I said.

"Exactly." He smiled.

"Except it'll probably be more like a week later, knowing you know who."

"I'd just have to use my wish to get us out."

My grin faded. This fantasy was starting to get swallowed up by reality again. I folded my arms. "Why didn't you wish us out of our contract with the organization months ago, then?"

"And give up the only reason I've got to see you every day?"

"So getting to be with me is more important than what I want?"

He didn't answer. We sat quietly, taking in the eerie stillness of Hart's back room. "I don't like what Mum's doing either," he finally said. "I want her to stop just as much as you, if only for her own sake." He fiddled with the cuff of his jacket. "Of course, I don't expect you to believe that, but . . ." He shrugged.

"If things had happened differently before we were born, with my dad. Obviously I used to think about that a lot when I was a kid. Everyone without a dad imagines what it would be like to have one." He swallowed hard, and damn me, I felt his sorrow. It stung my throat too.

He was trying to hold it back, but he couldn't hide his blush. He kept twisting one of the buttons around his cuff. "The last few months, I've been thinking about how else things would be different. If our mums were still friends, I bet we would've grown up together. I probably would have had a crush on you, and if I ever asked you out, Mum would've been over the moon. Maybe there's an alternate reality out there where that Ross and Devroe are living."

I clenched my knees, seeing it myself. My chest hurt. A world where we could've known each other forever. A world where Mom hadn't pushed away all of her friends, Diane included. Where I wouldn't have been alone for so long. It was beautiful. But it was a fantasy.

Because that version of Mom didn't exist. But I wouldn't tell Devroe that.

He sighed, looking infuriatingly handsome as he leaned his head back. "I suppose what I'm trying to say is . . . I wish we lived in a world where I could kiss you and neither one of us would have to feel so treacherous about it."

"Too bad we don't live in that alternate reality, and I'm not allowed to kiss you."

He frowned. "Allowed?"

"*I'm* not allowing myself." I thrummed my fingers against the edge of the sofa. "My mom would never let—"

"Stop it," he said. He rubbed the bridge of his nose, like he couldn't believe what I was saying. "Don't tell me your entire takeaway from the last half a year is that it all happened because you let it happen to you and never trusting anyone ever is . . ." He started laughing.

My jaw dropped, watching him bust a gut. "Screw you." I tried to punch his shoulder, but he dodged. A ridiculous kind of anger was boiling in my chest. "Yeah, maybe that is my takeaway. Sorry if that's what I learned after the attempted family genocide and the fake first romance, because that's what happens when you let yourself be wet-pancake weak and vulnerable, and I lost everything—"

"You got everything you wanted last year."

"Are you drunk?"

He started counting on his fingers. "Independence from your mom. Friends. Dashing first love."

"Almost being murdered along with the rest of my family."

"That didn't actually happen, did it?"

"Well, at least one of the other things you named was a fabrication." I crossed my arms to keep from attacking him.

"Do you think I would've disappointed my mum and backed out of the thing she's been planning for the last twenty years if it was all fake?"

Screw him and his logic.

The couch shifted as he got closer. "You got everything you wanted last year, and you got it because you let yourself be a little vulnerable. Even if you hate me, don't disrespect your other friendships by pretending those don't count."

I suddenly wanted to dissolve into the couch.

"You still lied," I said. One final line of defense.

"Yeah, I did. Sorry, for what it's worth. But I'm a thief, and I was just playing the game." He smiled sadly. "When you tally it all up, I still think you came out on top."

Devroe looked drained, as if explaining to me that being vulnerable got me everything I ever wanted was a hard day's work.

And you know, I was starting to think he was right.

Before I could stop myself, I slipped into his lap. He jumped, sitting up as I fully straddled him. A similar but inverted version of where we'd been at the slot machines.

Just like before, I could feel the heat of his body seeping through our clothes. He was the softest, most comfortable place in the world. His face went even more red. "What are you doing?" he asked. But he didn't ask me to move. Didn't squirm. Didn't do anything.

I rested my hands on his shoulders, matching his gaze. "Being vulnerable, for now." I moved closer until we were only a breath away for the second time that night. "But I haven't decided if I'm doing that long-term yet, so when we leave, this never happened, yeah?"

It took a second, but his hands settled on my hips. I felt him nod.

And he went for it.

His lips crashed into mine, with so much fervor I was glad we were holding on to each other. He devoured me, and I devoured him, drinking up every drop I could get. He tasted like champagne and mint and everything I remembered from our airport kiss all those months ago. I wanted to melt into him, meld us together forever and ever.

Devroe kissed like a man starving. His hands on my hips pulled me even closer, like he was having the same thought as me, a perfect synchronicity. I remembered our last kiss; it'd felt feverish at the time, but compared to this, it had been an innocent thing. Here there was no holding back. No secrets keeping us apart. No lies. I knew what I was getting and he knew what he was getting and we both wanted more.

I don't know how long I was there, in his lap. But at some point, too soon, we were shocked out of it by the yelp of a startled teller.

We broke apart breathlessly, just in time to see him backing away.

"I hate this casino." I buried my face in Devroe's neck for a moment. So I said, but I couldn't help but chuckle.

"You think they'll add this secret to their catalog?" Devroe flexed his fingers over my hips, and I might have died.

"We'll have to steal it back," I said, and went in for another kiss.

TWENTY-NINE

BEING SUMMONED BY Kiah Hart was not my preferred way of ending this forbidden moment with Devroe, but you can't get everything you want. In fact, you usually get very little.

"You should go," Devroe whispered against my neck.

"No hard feelings about me collecting the win?"

"None if you have none."

"Hm." I shimmied off of him, straightened my shorts and my blazer. Still sitting, he drank me in, in an enraptured sort of way that could make any girl swoon. I thought he was going to top off the moment with some sort of joke or flirty compliment, but he stopped himself and opted to rub his neck sheepishly instead.

"Until next time, then, Ross Quest."

I wanted to examine him for a little while. What the hell was up with this sudden nervous act? Was he feeling guilty about kissing me? Honestly, if I'd had more time to think about it, maybe I would have been too.

Questions for later.

One of Kiah's goons was waiting rather impatiently for me in the cashier's lobby. The woman gestured to an open door, which she shut behind me. Kiah leaned against a marble-topped table, which was the only piece of furniture in the room, and took a dab of his vape pen. I pinched my nose.

"Is it bothering you? Do you want me to stop?" Kiah asked, blowing another plume.

A black binder sat in the center of the table. I pulled it toward me. "Don't bother. I won't be browsing long."

I knew what I was looking for.

The pages of the Hart Exclusive catalog binder crinkled like the pages of a photo album as I began to flip through them. Some pages had pictures. Some did not. Every listing included a brief description and price.

Chateau, 250 black chips

Favor from Queen of Luxembourg, 300 black chips

Human Heart, 190 black chips—related:

Discreet Surgical Team, 30 black chips

I couldn't fight the shudder as I came across the first name.

Weston, Jamie. United States. SSN: 421-00-8765.

100 black chips

"Is this an identity for sale or . . . ?"

Or an actual person?

"Buy it and find out," Kiah said, blowing another gag-inducing cloud of vape mist into the air.

I steeled my stomach and moved on. There was a list of things I was supposed to be getting for the organization. Embarrassingly, it took a minute of flipping around aimlessly to notice that the catalog was in alphabetical order. This time I flipped right where I needed to be. Five items were on the slate to buy back. Two of them in the rather packed "secret" category: *Secret: JM #335, 400 black chips*, and *Secret: QG #612, 640 black chips*. I thumbed through almost fifty pages of secrets. None of them had more information. Only a number and a price. I'd have called it bad advertising, but the ambiguity, in a macabre way, piqued my curiosity.

Digging through the pages of secrets, I passed JL only to find it skipped to KA.

What?

I tried for the QG secret. It too was missing.

The other pages I was looking for were a seat on a UK parliament committee that was supposed to be 500 black chips. Gone. SS *Dauntless*, a shipping vessel, contents included, 200 black chips. Gone. Evidence from a Vietnamese criminal court case. Gone.

I slammed the binder closed, glowering at Kiah, who was still vaping with annoying nonchalance.

"Where are they?"

"Excuse me?"

"JM #335. QG #612. The SS *Dauntless*. The parliament committee seat. Evidence from that criminal case in Vietnam. Where are they?" Count had verified that the items were still on the market just an hour before we left for the casino. No way they'd all been bought in the last few hours.

"Oh, *those* . . ." Kiah faked a moment of realization, and I really could've punched him. "Yeah, those items are no longer available for purchase."

"Why the hell not?"

He cut a devious smirk. "Because I gave them back."

I just looked at him. "No."

"How sad for you—you got here just a couple hours too late. But one of your rivals perhaps reached out to me. I was more than happy to give a few items to Mr. Baron in exchange for, well, you don't need to know."

I took a step back, fighting off a minor panic attack. "That's not how this works. You've never negotiated with the organization before." Count had said that was the whole reason we had to do this the illicit way in the first place.

"You mean my great-uncle hasn't," Kiah clarified, rolling his eyes. "Him and his stringent rules. Must stay above the clientele, yadda yadda. I don't think cutting a deal here or there destroys our integrity. And since Uncle Quinton is a bit busy trying to keep his heart beating these days, who exactly is going to stop me?"

Count, all of us, had been playing by the rules set up by the old king. We didn't think about someone else being the one actually in charge. This was what Kyung-soon meant. Even when we won, we lost. We'd lost before we walked in.

I gripped the table for balance. "This whole time . . ."

"Yes, I knew what you were here to do. You and your little friends. By the way, I had your mother escorted out earlier." He chuckled. "Apparently she broke one of my waitresses' hands during the ordeal. No easy feat. I also wasn't expecting the Korean girl to come and help you; I thought she was on the other team. It's still frustrating I couldn't figure out what kind of code you were using, so in fairness, I'll count that as your win. You made it an interesting night if nothing else, Rosalyn Quest."

I wish I could say hearing Kiah address me by my real name inspired some kind of ice-in-veins sensation, but the feeling was more of a throbbing ache than a stab of surprise.

"Why'd you do this dance with me?" I asked. "If you knew what was going on?"

"I wasn't lying when I said I love hunting thieves. Shame on me, I really thought it'd be an easy case, since I *knew* you were pulling something. But it wouldn't have been any fun taking you in without solving the puzzle. You're really good. I still couldn't figure out what you were up to, besides swapping a few forged chips, even though I know that couldn't have been your main tactic."

With a final dab, he tucked the pen away.

Disappointed. That made two of us.

There was nothing else to say. We'd lost. And if Kiah Hart, abiding by his own rules, wasn't threatening my life anymore, then there was no reason to be here. My team needed to figure out what the hell we were doing next.

I pushed the catalog back to the center of the marble table. "Goodbye, Kiah Hart."

"Not making a purchase? There are lots of other curiosities

in here . . ." He thrummed his fingers over the binder's leather cover.

"Another time." Or no time, really.

"Come back soon, please," he said. "I really want another chance to crush you."

THIRTY

THERE ARE LOTS of different types of quiet. Peaceful quiet, like sitting alone on a beach in the middle of the night. Stressed silence, while you're wringing your hands trying to figure out what to say. And then there's defeated silence when there's nothing to say.

We were smothered in that last one. From the edge of this swanky rooftop restaurant, I focused on the bright lights of Hart's building burning through the last of the night. It wasn't quite sunrise, but the sun was starting to appear on the horizon. The party goes on at Hart's, and for Team Kenzie.

The rest of my team wallowed in defeat. Mylo was collapsed on a small wicker bench, his head dangling at a horrible angle off the side. Taiyō stared into the distance, looking as if he was replaying every facet of the night on repeat. Noelia was perched primly on a stool at the abandoned bar, ankles crossed with dead eyes, as if she was a doll someone had turned off. The only person who didn't look completely beat down was Mom, who was applying a top coat to her nails. To anyone else, it might have seemed Mom didn't care, but I knew she was pretending to have herself together.

The brush quivered in her hand. She swore as she dropped it, slapping a speckle of polish on her leg.

I swallowed hard. Oh god, if Mom was tripping up, then we really were screwed, weren't we?

Mylo sat up, sending Count a sheepish glance. He rubbed the back of his neck. "So—"

"Silence!" Count said.

I'd never heard her be so directly abrasive before. We were all falling apart.

Count dropped her tablet on table and flexed her hands at her temples. She looked like she could peel the skin off her own face if that would detach her from reality right now.

"You unobservant, amateur idiots," Count said. "What brilliant work you've done. Now we're all one step closer to the edge of oblivion."

"Yo," Mylo whined. "Okay, I don't think that's fair—"

"Say something else, Mr. Michaelson, and I'll have that trailer park you're from burned down."

Mylo bit his tongue.

"Why don't you cool it?" I hopped down from the ledge I'd been sitting on. "Don't scream at us. We did our best."

"That's the problem, isn't it?"

"It's a lot better than the jack all you contributed."

Count gawked at me. Clearly she still wasn't used to her

toys talking back, but this toy had been wound up enough for one night.

"Are you sure you want to keep speaking to me like that?" she asked darkly. "Keep at it and—"

"And what, Aurélie? You'll kill me and my whole family? Someone's already onto that."

Mom plunked her polish on the table. Or maybe she accidentally dropped it. The way she flinched made me think it was the latter.

I sighed and returned my attention to Count, still fuming, probably even more so realizing that there was absolutely nothing she had to hold over me.

I guess that went both ways.

"Look, we lost," I admitted. "There's no use in whining about it now. Let's move on."

No use in whining about anything that happened. With the heist or the other team. None at all.

"The final phase." Taiyō, the only one of us who was still completely dressed, styled hair, pocket watch, and all, stepped in. "What's it going to be?"

I could always depend on Taiyō to get right to the point.

Count kept eye contact with me, which I returned in total hostility, before turning to Taiyō. "To be delivered shortly." She surveyed the lot of us. Noelia squirmed on her stool. Mylo continued rubbing the crick out of his neck. "This is the last chance. It's one to one now. Whatever it is, I *have* to win." She nodded to me. "We have to win."

At that, Count's shoulders slumped. She picked up her tablet again and retreated toward the access door. I'm sure I was imagining the impossible, but if I'd had to put money on it, I'd have bet she was going to go cry or have an anxiety attack somewhere. Not that it was any of my business.

"She looks the worse for wear," Taiyō noted, watching her go.

"She'll survive."

"Hm." Taiyō pushed up his glasses. "I apologize. My plan . . . didn't work."

"Don't apologize. It was a good plan, we just didn't know all the variables."

"I suppose not." He tilted his head toward the stars for a moment. "Another lesson learned, then. Spend more time investigating the interests of the owners of any major establishment. Make sure you know who's really pulling strings."

I cracked a smile. "At least this'll make a great story for your students."

He fake rolled his eyes.

I spared the sky a glance too, watching a particularly attention-hungry star swell and shrink in the distance.

"I know I said I only owed you if this casino heist worked out, but . . ." I sighed, locking eyes with Taiyō. "As long as I'm still alive at the end of this, I'll hold up my end of the deal. You honestly deserve more than that for the short notice."

Taiyō looked genuinely stunned for a moment, before giving me a fond sort of smile. Weird, I'd never seen that on him before. "Is this one friend taking pity on another?"

"Are you too proud for my pity offer?"

"I'm never too proud to turn down something of overwhelming value. Thank you."

I wrung my hands. "You know, if you ever do get to cash in

on this offer, if you want, I can see if Mom would take my place in our deal." I couldn't help but glance at her, watching the view from the perimeter of the rooftop.

Taiyō looked taken aback. "Why?"

"Well, I mean . . . she's Rhiannon Quest. Bigger name, better plays. She wins."

"But tonight she's sitting in failure like the rest of us."

Okay, fair point.

"Ross, even if your mother somehow managed to swoop in and save the day, I wouldn't want to trade you in for her. That wouldn't be a smart move."

A breeze stung my eyes. Taiyō read the *why?* in my expression.

"I trust you more than her, and that's worth something more."

I bit my lip, preventing it from wobbling. Trust over viciousness. Loyalty over lies. Maybe that route could be just as effective as Mom's.

"Oh!" I scurried past Taiyō to the couch Mylo was sitting on, pushing him aside as I grabbed the purse I'd been carrying all night. Mostly empty now, but there was something left inside.

"Aw, do you need a tissue?" Mylo teased. I shoved him with one hand as I found the box with the other.

"Here." I held the leather box out to Taiyō. Skeptical, he cracked it open.

Taiyo laughed.

"What is it?" Mylo pressed.

Taiyō lifted the black-rimmed glasses out of the box, replacing his current pair with them for a second. They weren't identical to the pair I broke on the train six months ago, but close enough.

"You never did bill me," I said.

"I'll put the prescription lenses on your tab." He blinked half a dozen times before putting his actual glasses back on.

Mylo squirmed. "Argh! I hate not being in on the joke!"

"Thanks for your help, Taiyō," I continued. "But you don't have to stay for the final phase."

"Yes, he does!" Mylo jumped up from his seat, his hair finally looking more tousled than orderly. He ripped off his loose bow tie and pointed at us with it in hand. "He's on the team now. Teams stick together." Mylo gave me a look that said something like *don't ruin this for me.*

"You don't have to stay," I reiterated. Sorry, Mylo. Code of honor first.

"I'd like to stay, if only to see who ends up taking the victory here, though I stand by my thought that neither Count nor Baron deserves it."

Ditto. But like Baron said, it wasn't about deserving it to the organization, but who could get the job done best. But, if I was hypothetically an organization member, was that person even Baron or Count?

A thought, small but powerful, shocked me. "Taiyō, you've got a pretty expansive list of industry contacts by now, don't you?"

"I do. I had quite a bit of time to add to it while I was in the hospital last year. But it's primarily Eastern contacts."

I paced, fiddling with my ponytail. "I bet if we added your list to my family's database and the Boscherts' we'd have a pretty complete-ish contact list for all the major players in the world."

"A great big contact form for criminals. That's cool. Why are we talking about this?" Mylo stretched and cracked his neck.

"Taiyō, I know you just said you're down for the final phase, but could I ask you to do something else instead?"

"Where is this going?"

"Maybe nowhere," I said. "But I'd like to see who everyone would really be behind."

AFTER EXPLAINING EXACTLY what I was thinking to Taiyō and Mylo, and securely emailing Taiyō the Quest contact log, all there was left to do was politely ask Noelia for the Boscherts'. Despite it being a biggish ask, I felt like she was going to say yes. She'd disappeared about half an hour ago, and it took a few minutes before I heard her voice behind the back wall of the bar.

As I approached, I heard an unfamiliar man's voice. On instinct—I swear thieves don't try to be eavesdropping pricks, but when it's in your blood, you really can't help it—I quieted my steps and just barely peeked around. Noelia sat with her back to the wall, posture perfect, holding her phone in front of her. Her face was expressionless as she watched the screen, but the hand that wasn't holding her phone was practically shaking with how tightly it was clenched in her lap.

"I just . . . don't understand," the man went on. And then he sighed in that stupid, condescending way that trash parents, at least in the TV shows I've seen, always do. The way that says more than words ever could how disappointed they are and that it's all your fault.

It really made my stomach churn.

"Perhaps you should have chosen the other team in the first place. I sent you there to work with Diane."

"Yes, Papa," Noelia bravely interjected. "But you're the one who always said how much you respected Rhiannon Quest from your Gambit and that she's super efficient, and so I thought—"

"I know what I said." He sighed again. "I didn't send you to America to enter another Gambit at all. Clearly you and this team can't handle another. Perhaps you should come back before you lose a second. Or were you planning on quitting again?"

Screw this guy.

Noelia blinked one too many times, and I hoped that the prick on the other end couldn't see the faint sparkle of tears in her eyes. "I thought I was doing what you'd want me to last time," she said quietly. Her voice cracked at the end.

"Again with the tears, Noelia?" he sighed.

"I'm not crying. I'm apologizing."

"Apologies don't help anyone, actions do. But you can't give me that, so I really don't have anything else to say to you right now. What am I supposed to do with someone who can't perform, Lia?"

She shrugged, but I imagined that was only because she didn't trust her voice not to quiver.

That's enough of this.

I stormed into the little nook, startling Noelia. She frowned. "What are you—"

I slid to the floor next to her, grabbed Noelia's phone, and angled both of us into the frame. "Hi, Mr. Boschert. What's going on with you today? Besides reaming your daughter, that is?"

Noah Boschert, for the most part, looked exactly how I pictured he would. Annoyingly bright and tidy short-cropped blond hair And what I was beginning to assume was trademark Boschert family blue eyes and fair white skin. I was sure to match Papa Noah Boschert glare for glare.

"You must be Quest's daughter."

"What gave it away?"

He looked over to Noelia. "I don't like being overheard, Lia."

"I didn't know she was there!" Noelia tried to take the phone from me, but I caught her attacking hand and pulled her tight. Noelia's posture slumped, giving up the fight.

"Don't tell me this has become personal, Noelia. Is that why you have been floundering so much lately? You think you've become friends with these people?"

"Not—" Noelia insisted.

I squeezed her tighter, so much so that our faces were practically smushed together.

"*Best* friends, Mr. Boschert. More than that, I think. We're like . . . like sisters. Even if Lia won't admit it." I pinched her cheek tauntingly. She slapped my fingers away, and her face went red, not just from the pinch. She glanced aside.

Papa Boschert paused for a second, and so did I. But she didn't deny it.

I freaking loved Noelia Boschert for that.

"You see," I went on after the brief lull, "we're such best friends, such sisters, that I was thinking if anything ever happened and Lia, I dunno, wasn't appreciated enough in the Boschert family, we'd love to have her as part of the Quest family."

I flashed him a delighted smile. Noelia tensed in my arms, looking from the screen to me and back again.

Papa Boschert went a shade paler, and that was saying something. He opened his mouth, but closed it in favor of a grimace. Again, a beat of silence, while he waited for Noelia to interject.

And again, she didn't. Not for a second, at least.

Then she took a little breath and straightened up. "Noelia Quest isn't as catchy," she said.

"Noelia Boschert-Quest? What do you think, Mr. Boschert?"

"I rather like it," another voice added.

We both turned. Mom was standing on the other side of the bar wall, arms folded, looking down at us. I angled Noelia's phone so Papa Boschert could see as well. Mom gave him a little twinkle wave. Her freshly top-coated nails caught the light as she wiggled them.

"Hi, Noah. Still drowning puppies in your free time?"

"Still cheating your way to victory?"

"I agree with Ross," Mom said, tastefully ignoring his last comment. "I think the Quest family wouldn't mind such a stellar member."

Surely Mom wasn't serious. It was all a bluff. But still, it was nice to know she was willing to go along.

"I see . . ." Papa Boschert said. "Noelia, let's talk later. After someone wins your little game."

After we saw if my family made it out alive or not.

He ended the call. Noelia let out the heaviest breath ever and rubbed her face for a few seconds before taking her phone back.

"Threatening to steal me away if I don't get treated better? Noelia Quest? That's your idea of helping me?" she said.

I squirmed. "Sorry. I should have asked before just butting in, but your dad was being a prick, and I've really had it up to here with—"

She lowered her hands, and her face was slick with tears, but she was smiling through them. "Merci," she whispered. "Thank you."

I could have made a joke, I guess, but instead I just pulled her in for a rib-breaking hug. She giggled and returned it.

"Thank you as well, Ms. Quest," Noelia said to Mom, standing. "But I don't forgive you for what you did to Ross."

"Lucky for me, a Boschert's forgiveness is very low on my wish list."

With that, Noelia dipped away.

I leaned back and eyed Mom. "Look at you, being uncharacteristically generous."

"I'm not a one-note vessel of evil, you know."

"Not convinced."

"Funny."

Mom took a cautious step into my space, and I actually welcomed her. One-note vessel of evil or not, she was being kind tonight. Well, to me at least. It was almost perplexing how she managed to be vicious with one person and Mom of the day with me.

I added a new note about Mom on my If I Live list.

Figure out how Mom manages to be two people at once.

"I'm not actually inviting her to be a Quest, by the way. That, baby girl, was what they call a bluff."

"No duh, Mom."

"Noah will buy it anyway, though."

"How do you know?"

"He's always been afraid to call bluffs. He's a coward underneath all that bravado."

I stretched out my legs. "Why'd you trick me into thinking Noelia hated me when we were kids?" I asked.

Mom shook her head. "I don't really know. Maybe I was scared for you. Friends are dangerous. They can shatter you. I thought it was best if you learned that early on."

Just another reiteration of the famous line: *Don't trust anyone.*

"Noelia wouldn't have," I said. "Never did."

Mom tucked some hair behind her ear. "That's how all the friendships I've had ended."

"Because you were the one who ended them like that."

"Yup," she said. "But who ever said there weren't other people like me out there?"

Ruthlessly efficient. That was how Papa Boschert described Mom. But was there really anyone as excellent at that as Mom?

No, I was sure of one thing. There were no other Rhiannon Quests out there.

"Not everyone, though," I said. "Not everyone in the world is untrustworthy." I weighed my phone in my hands. When I unlocked the screen, my call log, with Kyung-soon's and Devroe's numbers, was still up.

"Sure." Mom flicked her nails. "Maybe . . . you should call your boy."

My head snapped up to Mom. She rolled her eyes. "Don't look at me like that. I just figure getting past your beef with him might make forgiving me that much easier." Mom dropped into a crouch, putting her eye to eye with me. "That's the difference, baby girl—it's only an ulterior motive if they don't admit to you what they're doing. If someone tells you what they're going to do, it's not really backstabbing, is it?"

If the queen of backstabbing said so . . .

Mom suddenly swooped in to kiss to my forehead. I screwed my lips together but didn't try to push her away. When she left me alone, I unblocked Devroe's number and called.

THIRTY-ONE

I KINDA THOUGHT DEVROE was ignoring me. Two times I called and got no answer. It was doing something to my pride to get hit with a voicemail twice.

A text dropped down after the second call cut off early.

Five minutes

I tried to be dramatic and count the stars while waiting, but the sun was burning into the sky by now.

Five minutes passed. Did he want me to call, or did he mean he was going to call—

My phone vibrated for all of two-tenths of a second before I swiped to answer the call.

The other end was quiet for a long moment.

"Hello—"

"Ross—"

Our voices overlapped. Oh right, usually the person who answers a call is the one who talks first.

I pressed a hand into my forehead, hiding my cringe from absolutely no one. Why didn't I know how to act like a normal person?

"I don't know how long I have," Devroe said. I could hear a light wind nipping at the edge of the speaker.

"Where are you?"

"Hiding behind a rooftop access door."

"You're on a roof?"

"Yes, that's usually where rooftop access doors are."

"Me too," I said, ignoring the sass. Getting back to my feet, I turned to face Hart's building, now backlit by the dawn and looking like it had just risen out of the ocean. I was sure that was the rooftop Devroe was on. Why wouldn't his team still be at chilling at Kiah's casino? Was he, maybe, looking this way too?

"It's a gorgeous sunrise," I said.

"I've seen something more stunning."

"Boo. That one was predictable."

"Sorry. Guess I'm rusty."

Being ignored for months would do that to a boy, wouldn't it?

I pressed my toe into the concrete, noting how the morning light seemed to have shifted the shades of everything within a matter of minutes. "Are you going to apologize for beating me?"

"It wouldn't be genuine. Whether you hate me for it or not, it's what's best. What I think is best, at least."

"I don't hate you," I said. The words tumbled out. "I wouldn't have kissed you if I hated you."

"Ah, good to know."

I tried to spot a silhouette on the distant rooftop of the Hart building, but it was like trying to spy a balloon after it had drifted just too far into the clouds. "Everything's so gray," I said. "I don't think I hate anyone. Except for Baron and maybe Count and Noelia's dad on a bad day, but that's not the point." I threaded my fingers through the grate between me and the view to Hart's. "I don't hate you, Devroe Kenzie. I . . . understand all the things going on. Thank you for wanting to save me, but that's not enough. I can't abandon my family."

I heard the faint brush of skin against metal on his end as well. Was there also a safety gate on the top of Hart's? An image of him twining his fingers into the railing on his rooftop popped into my mind. I squeezed the links of the grate. "I talked to Baron privately. He's not going to let me wish for more than one person. I assume just in case Mum found out I was trying to roadblock her plans to end all of the Quests, he doesn't want to risk ticking her off in the last round. I can't save your whole family, Ross, just you."

"Maybe I don't want to be alive if everyone in my family isn't—" I stopped myself, letting the implication sit, dark as it was. "Baron is a snake. Who's to say he won't find a way to backtrack and kill me anyway, especially if he really wants to keep your mom in his debt."

Diane wanted me dead too. We both knew she wasn't just going to stop once I was the only Quest left standing. The beat of silence on Devroe's end told me he had thought the same.

"She's going to win, Ross." Because he thought she would win no matter what. It was more than just being a good son. He had faith in her to pull out a victory and not me. "At least with this arrangement," Devroe said quietly, "I know you'll be okay for now, and it'll buy me more time to keep protecting you. So I'll say it again. I understand if you hate me."

If only it was that easy. But there was something about honesty that made hating him near impossible tonight.

I watched the links of my meteor bracelet twinkle, the shade matching the pastel pink smearing in the sky. Count had been kind enough to have my precious weapon smuggled out of the New Orleans Police's evidence locker, though I suspected it was at Mom's request. "I think I would have hated you, if our moms were still friends. You'd probably be that annoying little boy who was always pestering me with cringey flirting, and I would've thought you were annoying my whole life."

He let out a breath of a laugh. "I think . . . I would have been in love with you for years now."

My breath caught. Would have. Was he saying . . .

Metal creaked behind him. "I have to go."

He ended the call.

THIRTY-TWO

"I **WANT YOU ALL** to know, if we lose this final phase, I'm going to use every remaining scrap of influence in my arsenal to have each of you completely and thoroughly obliterated."

I sighed and took a sip of my water. Ross Quest was already dead, if only in soul, if we lost. Count could get in line.

Taiyō dropped a message into the Wi-Fi group chat. Despite it being 2024, being thirty-two thousand feet in the air still means you have to keep your phone in airplane mode. How the hell is that still a thing?

Taiyō

Overstated threats are often the sign of desperation.

so much energy that could be redirected.

Oh, the messages weren't to the entire chat. Just me.

I typed back.

Are you wondering if Baron would've been reacting better?

Across the slender jet aisle, Taiyō flicked his watch so efficiently I couldn't believe he was done typing until I got the text.

Doesn't matter, we're not on his team.

But that doesn't help Count's case.

He and I locked eyes. Was that a question I saw in his?

"We plan on succeeding, Count," Noelia promised, hands folded in her lap next to me. Her posture was surprisingly less taut than I would have guessed. Since my bluff with her dad, maybe she felt more confident having even a teensy bit of leverage in her family. How nice it was to be able to give that kind of hope to someone else, even if *my* situation was about as hopeless as you could get.

"We'd planned on winning the last phase too," Mylo muttered, shuffling an arc of cards. If only Kyung-soon were here to kick him for me.

But Taiyō, feeling the same, glared harshly enough at Mylo that he messed up his next shuffle. A dozen cards fluttered into his lap. He cleared his throat. "Sorry."

"Don't be." Mom sipped a glass of what was probably ginger

ale, if I knew her. "We all did our best last phase. Of course, it amounted to jack all, but sure, kudos to us for playing it straight and doing our best." She hoisted her glass, cheers-ing an invisible nobody.

"There's no need for the salt, Mom."

She didn't respond, just took another sip. Scratch that—gulp. Mom winced, and I realized that was something a lot stronger than ginger ale. The tremor of the glass in her hand gave away exactly why she needed it.

My heart dropped to my stomach, but I filed the feeling away. I couldn't think about how precarious the situation was and keep a clear mind at the same time.

Maybe *I* needed a drink.

"It's here." Count stopped midpace in the aisle, eyes zigzagging over her tablet. With a swipe of her finger, two screens at the head of the cabin glowed to life.

"Wonderful." Count let out a breath. "Something you should be able to do without being duped by a nineteen-year-old."

"Such faith she has in us," Mylo muttered. I looked close at the screens. On one of them, a picture snapped in the dark. A modern, reflective glass building. I'd have guessed luxurious vacation home, but it was just a touch too large and not quite sleek enough for that. Not to mention an inconvenient location. The angle didn't reveal much, but it looked like I was spying a snapshot on the edge of some sort of elevation. Wires from a distant cable car and the hint of city lights backlit by the horizon.

"This isn't another lab, is it?" Mylo asked.

Count crossed her arms. "It's a visual artists commune. One hosting a very prestigious vintage film collection."

"Quite a swanky retreat," Taiyō noted.

"I'm sure there's some very swanky things stored inside," I said. "Where is this? Given the trees and the cable car, it has to be somewhere warm but with a bit of a mountainous terrain. Big city? Uh . . . South Africa."

Count nodded. "Just outside of Cape Town." Count turned to face us. "There shouldn't be any Kiah Hart–like situations available to manipulate here. The manager of the facility is already a friend of the organization."

Noelia scoffed. "Then why is this necessary at all?"

"He's soon to be a former friend, unbeknownst to him."

"Why's that?" I asked.

"Because I asked him to hand over a certain film reel a few weeks ago. What he handed over was a fake."

So we were stealing an actual old-school film reel, then. How retro.

"What's on the film?"

Count threw us a bone. "Footage relating to an assassination, and a hint that maybe it wasn't perpetrated by the person conventionally thought to have committed it."

Mylo sat up, gripping his armrests. "Whose assassination? JFK? RFK? MLK?"

"Americans really do think the world revolves around them." Noelia cocked her head. "Don't you know any assassinations of world leaders that aren't from the States?"

Mylo scratched his head. "John Lennon?"

Taiyō actually laughed.

"The contents of the film are irrelevant." Count clasped her hands in front of her. "Whoever's the first to acquire it and bring to a yet undisclosed rendezvous location wins this phase. Whoever doesn't win this phase—"

"We know the math," I said.

Do or die. Literally.

"How'd you let a fake get handed over in the first place, Count?" Mom folded her arms. "Sloppy work."

Count turned around slowly. "I've been a little busy in recent weeks."

"Whatever you say, dear." Mom nodded at me. "As for the job, I'll be—"

"Running coms. I know."

Count swiped her tablet up and retreated toward the plane's private cabin. "Brief me in a couple hours."

I barely felt her brush past me.

Mom tilted her head back and closed her eyes. There was a quiver in her eyelids as she closed them. She was certainly more nervous than I was used to seeing her, but not as much as she could have been either.

Noelia received a ding on her smartwatch, which prompted her to rummage in an overhead bin for the tablet Mom had handed off to her days ago. Honestly, I'd forgotten she had it.

Noelia gave a cursory look back toward Count's cabin and its closed door before hooking a finger at me. I followed her toward a set of seats at the other side of the plane, which just so happened to be adjacent to where Mom was sitting.

With the tablet in her lap, Noelia cleared her throat and whispered. "Cousin Freare got back to me about the private chat on the tablet, the one you asked about on the freighter? I owe him quite a pretty penny now, but you can repay me later."

I pursed my lips at her.

"Kidding," she promised. Mom's eye cracked open, and I

had no doubt she was eavesdropping. "He was able to get into the encrypted server they use. I asked him to filter for anything mentioning you or your family especially. He didn't find much in the chat itself, but he was able to isolate what he thinks is Baron's IP address and then dove into that."

"Are we getting to a point here?" I asked. Mom wasn't even feigning lack of attention now.

Noelia huffed. "Correspondence with Diane."

"Is that super unusual? She's been working for him for a while now."

"It originated from Baron," Noelia said slowly. "But it was redirected through your family's black box."

Oh.

Oh.

It was clicking. If Diane thought she was getting messages from my family, I was sure exactly who they were supposedly to be coming from, and what kind of content was in those messages.

"When do they track back to?" I asked.

"Half a year?" Noelia said. "Just after the end of the Gambit."

When Diane would undeniably have been at her lowest. And when it would have made the most sense for Mom to come seeking retaliation after Diane's failed hit on us. Baron had picked the perfect opportunity to stir the pot.

"This . . . this could be good," I whispered. "I mean, it's not good, but if we have proof that Baron was the one who threatened her family, then maybe we can talk Diane out of the last phase." I was on the edge of my seat now, focused on Mom. "You could, like, apologize—"

"No, thank you."

Just like that, Mom laced her fingers and leaned back, going to sleep.

"Mom!" I stage-yelled, glad for the drone of the plane covering my voice.

"Who cares now? She hated me before those messages. Getting on my knees and saying sorry isn't going to save us now. Winning will."

"It's not about saying sorry. God, why can't you ever have any empathy *ever*? Then we wouldn't be in this situation."

"We also wouldn't be in this situation if you'd won the Gambit. But that's where your empathy got us, hm?"

I grabbed her by the arm and pulled her out of her seat. Mom didn't say anything. I ignored whatever Mylo or anyone else was saying behind me as I dragged Mom into the next cabin and clicked the door shut.

Mom rubbed her arm, as if I'd really hurt her. "Such a grip—"

"I don't want to see you anymore."

"You made that clear over the last six months, baby girl."

"Listen to me!" I took a breath. This needed to be said calmly. It wasn't a decision I was making in the heat of the moment. It was logic. It was what was best for me. "Mom, I love you, but I am *never* coming home to you. I . . . I respect you, but I don't want you to rub off on me anymore."

Mom gave up on nursing her fake injury. She examined me as if I were some oddity. Like I didn't make sense. "Just because you think you have friends now—"

"I do have friends. And I'll keep them, because that's where *my* priorities are. Your way works, but being ruthless isn't the only way, and sometimes it's not even the best way, and I don't want to think like that anymore."

Mom's eyes stopped analyzing me. She looked like . . . I broke her.

"You don't mean that." Her voice was heartbreakingly weak.

"I do. I love you . . . but I also kind of resent you. And . . ." I flexed my hands at my sides, fighting the urge to turn away. "If we're about to die, I feel like . . . like my life might have been healthier without you in it." I shook my head, trying to jostle my thoughts into some comprehensible order. "I hate that if I don't have any time left, you took all of my opportunities away from me, and I don't know if I can forgive you for that. If we do get out of this, I can't let that happen again. You need to leave me alone. If you don't, then I'm going to start actively fighting you. You did this to us, and don't try to spin it on me like you did with all that crap last year. We both know it's not the first time you've driven your family to this."

Mom's chin wobbled, staring out into the clouds. "I thought I was going to be alone forever after they cut ties with me. They didn't let Jaya start visiting until she was a teenager. When you were born, I suppose I thought it was like adopting a puppy. They never leave." She turned back to me and smiled sadly. "I can't just let you go. I don't have anything else without my baby girl. You're the only distraction I have from how—" She cut herself off. How what?

How she'd pushed everyone else away? How she deserved it? How lonely she was?

"From?" I pressed.

Mom rolled her lips, giving me a sad smile. "You're the only one I have, Rossie. I refuse to put my emotions on display for anyone, even someone like Diane. I can't trust anyone with that kind of ammunition. Except you . . ." Mom cupped my face. She was . . . crying. Smiling through it, but actually crying. "Who else could I let see me cry and not have to kill them afterward? Who else is going to lift me up when I get caught up thinking about how alone I am? Who else is going to let me babble on a plane about how hard expressing emotions is?" She laughed humorlessly, and used her shoulder to shrug off the tears, turning away for a second. Despite just telling me that I was the one person she could sometimes bear to be vulnerable with, I could tell she was having trouble even now going all in.

Being vulnerable was being human. I wouldn't want to let go of the only person I thought I could be even a little human with either.

"I can't be your everything forever, Mom," I said. "That's not healthy for either of us."

"I didn't say it was."

She knew, but she still couldn't stop herself from trying to tether me to her.

Mom cleared her throat. "How can I let you go when I'm so excellent at momming too?"

I scoffed. "No offense, but you're better at a lot of other things than you are at momming."

"Oh?" She gestured for me to go on.

"Let's see. Grand theft auto, grand larceny, wire fraud."

"Dime-a-dozen skills, baby girl."

"Intimidation, espionage, emotional manipulation, orchestrating kidnappings."

"I guess those are a little more impressive. But what have those gotten me besides a killer reputation? A reputation isn't tangible, it doesn't fill your days. I refuse to be left with absolutely nothing, Ross. I'll die, without someone or something."

Even when I wasn't bolstering her emotionally, being a mom was a perfect distraction—even if being a mom was the opposite of a job she was best suited for.

In a jolt of motion, I peeled Mom's hands off me and stepped back. Mom cocked a brow. "You don't need me. I've found you something better than me. Something that would be so all-encompassing and time-consuming, you'd never have time to think about your pesky little emotions."

Mom chuckled. "Really?"

I nodded. "Promise if I deliver, you'll let me go. Give me the distance I want."

She was skeptical. Hell, I was skeptical. It had only been an idea until now, but it made sense, and I hope she would give me a shot, if nothing else.

Mom crossed her arms. "I'm listening."

THIRTY-THREE

THE LATE-AFTERNOON sunlight glinted off my phone screen, making it almost impossible to read off of. But I had my list almost memorized by now.

> REGRETS AND OTHER STUFF TO FIGURE OUT IF I LIVE:
> *Wth is going on with Devroe and me?*
> *Figure out how I feel about Mom.*
> *Apologize to Kyung-soon.*
> *Get to know Noelia better.*
> *Make up for almost killing Taiyō—*
> *glasses good enough apology?*
> *Figure out how Mom manages to be two people at once.*
> *Who do I want to be?*

Huh. I'd made more progress on this list than I thought.

The wheels of the cable car must have hit a snag. Our carriage jostled. Across from me, Noelia plastered her hand against the window while Mylo laughed in delight. Of course being in a compact car creeping up a mountain wasn't good enough for him. It was the possibility of plummeting into the water below that made it really exhilarating.

"Stop laughing, you maniac," Noelia insisted.

"I've never ridden a cable car before," he defended himself. He had practically pressed his face against the glass windows encircling the car, watching as we ascended higher and higher toward the station at the top of the mountain while the station and city below shrunk beneath us. The water sparkled between the two. "Sick view. We've gotta be halfway up the mountain now. Hey, do you think we'd die if we jumped from this high?"

"Why don't you find out? I'll be sure to let everyone at your funeral know just how eager you were to off yourself," Noelia bit back.

"Can we maybe not joke about funerals right now?" I said quietly.

Noelia and Mylo shut up. They looked worriedly at each other before turning back to me. Noelia put a hand on my knee. "You're not going to die."

"Didn't know you could see the future."

"It's 'cause she only does it on Fridays and Saturdays in front of a crowd." Mylo shrugged. Noelia rolled her eyes, and I gave a sad smile.

This dynamic between friends, it was refreshing. I was going to miss it.

"I wish I had more moments like this before. People moments. I still hate that I didn't get to have this kind of thing before." I swatted a tear away, eyeing my list. "I feel like I just figured out who I am and all the things I want to do. It's not fair that Diane gets to . . . snap it away if she wins."

It wasn't fair what Mom did to her either, but I was thinking about me right now. Me and Mom and all the family I didn't even know that well.

One more thing I'd added to the list:

Get to know the rest of the family.

"Hey." Noelia snapped right in front of my eyes. I startled. "Chin up. I said you're not dying, so you aren't. Personally, I'm offended that you have so little faith in not just your own ability but Mylo's and mine as well. We're taking the win, and there will be no questions asked about that."

Noelia recrossed her legs, a master of the so-sayeth-I form of encouragement. And you know, it actually helped a little.

"Damn straight," Mylo added. He gave me a lopsided grin. "But even if we do die, we're totally robbing the hell out of heaven."

I laughed.

THIRTY-FOUR

ONE OF THESE days, I was going to make it a few months without doing a job that required pretzeling myself into a trunk or cabinet or, in this case, a suitcase.

Noelia's oversized hardback suitcase was more soundproof than I'd expected. I couldn't hear a damn thing beside the wheels whirring over the floor and muffled voices. Contorting my arm, I pressed my com deeper in my ear, tuning in to the conversation outside.

"Ms. Webster," a voice over the com said. I tried not to shift in the suitcase.

"Afternoon," Noelia said, South African accent on point. I imagined her and the person outside shaking hands.

"I'm Dr. Warlen. It's delightful to meet you. Just, wow."

"Hm?" Noelia said.

"Oh, it's just . . . you were the one who turned grayscale color theory on its head. Stupendous, absolutely stupendous."

"Oh my god, thank you," Noelia said smoothly. We'd borrowed some identities from real Noelia and Mylo look-alikes in the photography community, a safer way to guarantee getting access to the facility. Reclusive but renowned vintage photographer Noelia—or Vanessa Webster—and her assistant, Darren, a.k.a. Mylo, had looked quite the part in their artsy black turtlenecks and fraying boho scarves when we left. However, we weren't expecting anyone to be invested in any of the cover stories . . .

"You know, you're a lot younger than I thought." The man laughed, his giggle a touch testy.

This was already going downhill.

Mom's voice cut into the feed. "Make a jab about sexual harassment. If you make it awkward, he'll drop it."

Noelia hmm-ed, and I imagined the pained smile she was putting on. "Are you saying you *like* that?"

There was a breathless pause, and I imagined the dude was *sweating*.

"Oh, no, not at all! That wasn't what I meant, Vanessa. Ms. Webster." Dr. Warlen broke into an uncomfortable laugh. "Um, let me show you around. You and Mr. Thomas, right?"

"How do you do?" I imagined Mylo smiling and shaking his hand in turn.

"That's a rather large overnight bag," Dr. Warlen noted. I swallowed, knowing even though he couldn't see me, he was definitely looking my way.

"He's the best and brightest assistant I could ask for, but a bit of an overpacker. Half of my travel fund goes to checked baggage," Noelia said. Someone slapped the suitcase, and I would've jumped if I'd had the room.

"Do you want someone to take that to the suite for you?" Dr. Warlen asked. "It looks a bit heavy—you probably don't want to haul it around during the tour."

"Oh yeah, *super* heavy," Mylo complained.

Prick.

"They even charged us an overweight luggage fee on the cable car up," he added.

"Apologies." Dr. Warlen let out an exasperated sigh. "The cable cars that run up the mountain and to the station are owned by a third party. They're so finicky, no one would use them if there was another way to get to the retreat. But it's worth the hassle for one of the most stunning views in the country. How inspiring is it to wake up overlooking a cliff and a glistening waterfront? You can get some of the most majestic shots of your career just by rolling out of bed." He snapped. "Oh, speaking of the cable car. The station closes at sunset, so I hope you have everything you need from the city. Also our cell service can be a little iffy up here. Not that we don't *love* the seclusion."

"We read the email," Noelia assured him. "We're just excited for the retreat experience."

"Superb! Then let's get started." Dr. Warlen summoned someone named Leo to take Mylo's suitcase away before beginning the commune tour.

"I've got some special equipment in here," Mylo told Leo. "Be gentle with this."

Leo promised to do just that.

Leo was a liar.

I'd never been prone to motion sickness, nor did I think I could get dizzy when all I could see was black, but the way Leo was jerking and jostling me around was making me question all of my life decisions. The journey couldn't have been more than six or seven minutes, but by the time Leo shoved me to a stop and I heard a door slam, I was dangerously close to Jackson Pollock-ing all over this suitcase. I couldn't get myself out of there fast enough.

The suite was as modern and artsy as you'd expect from a mountaintop communal artist colony. I tumbled out onto a white fur carpet. Holding my stomach, I stood to take in the metallic-accented furniture, paneled wood ceiling, a digital fireplace crackling with multicolor flames. An honestly gorgeous collection of black-and-white portraits covered the walls, but no one in their right mind was looking at those first. Not with the all-glass wall window offering the most spectacular view I might ever see with my own eyes.

I approached the wall, clear enough that I almost thought I could walk through it. The lights of the city below were just starting to glow under the incoming dusk. The water, still and sparkling, reflected the darkening orange and reds in the sky. Suspension lines from the cable car station stretched down toward the city, and one last car was currently making its leisurely way back up toward the retreat. The view was nearly so perfect, it looked like I was suspended in midair, but a sliver of rocky ground below the window assured me that this was just the edge of a precarious cliffside. The sheer drop had to be, what, over a thousand feet?

My phone buzzed. Reluctantly, I took my eyes off the scenery.

Kyung-soon

15 min. Stalling.

I tucked my phone back into a pocket and rubbed my chest. Everything was going to be fine.

The key-card lock on the door chimed. I ducked behind the canopy bed, but quickly stood upon hearing Mylo's groan.

Leaning against the door, he glowered. "I. Hate. Art."

"Don't worry, I'm sure art hates you too."

"Dr. Warlen is taking Noelia to the gray room. Where they keep a bunch of gray candid shots, so they can compare all the different types of gray. Because there are a hundred different types of gray, and that's important." He shook his head in disbelief, patting his pants until he found a folded sheet of paper and a pen. Kneeling at a coffee table between two white fur couches, he opened the paper. Blueprints I'd found were already etched in my mind, but frustratingly the rooms weren't labeled.

Mylo circled one box, the suite we were obviously in now, and drew a line toward another space in the adjacent wing.

"We're in the housing wing right now. According to Dr. Warlen, vintage prints and reels are located here. I didn't get a good look at it. It's off-limits to newbies, but I'm sure a few people were flitting around in there."

"Makes sense." I traced the blueprints, already planning the fastest route through the corridors to get to the room. "Can you cover me while I get there?"

"What do you think I'm here for?" He stood, running a hand over any unruly touches of hair. "You heard from Kyung-soon?"

"She said she's stalling. Let's hope she can do that long enough."

He gave me a goofy smile and poked my shoulder. "Look at you guys, not pretending you're pissed with each other anymore."

"Shut up. Let's go."

Mylo left first. Seeing the hall was empty, he beckoned me out. I let him stay a step ahead of me. At the first hint of a suite door opening, I dipped into the space between two wire sculptures. Mylo was quick to intersect, stealing the woman's attention with a question about looking for a place to meditate. He angled his body in a way that naturally made her turn her back to me, and I carried on down the corridor to another safe spot. He let her go, and we carried on. Rinse and repeat anytime we ran into another artist along the way. In no time at all, we were in the next wing. I held back in an emergency stairwell, com on while Mylo used the key card he most assuredly swiped from Dr. Warlen to enter the vintage films room.

Through the com, I heard the door swing open, and a smattering of pleasant conversation abruptly drew to a halt. "Who the hell are you? This is restricted access only."

"How did you get a key card?"

"Jamie." Mylo introduced himself. "Your names?"

Some hesitation. "Philly. That's Molly."

"Philly and Molly, you're right where Dr. Warlen said you'd be. He asked you to show me around the microfilm room."

"Us? Why us?"

"I dunno, you'd have to ask him. But he's giving my boss a tour now. Do you want me to tell him you said no?"

"No, it's . . . it's fine. We can come back later," Molly, I'm assuming, said.

Peeking out of the emergency stairwell, I watched a lady in an oversized sweater and a guy in overalls escort Mylo back out into the hallway. Overalls was especially careful to pull the door tight behind them. So focused on it in fact that he didn't notice when Mylo silently dropped the key card into the pot of a tree by the door. Once they were out of sight, I retrieved the card and slipped into the restricted room, flicking my com to mute in the meantime, since Mylo and Molly's conversation on deterioration rates of different film types was a bit more distracting than helpful right now.

It was dim in here. About half a dozen individual viewing stations wrapped around three of the walls, with leather chairs and wide screens wired to DVD players, VHS players, and even old-fashioned film projectors. Black curtains divided each space. Shelves here and there displayed stacks of film and discs, along with manuals on film preservation and restoration. The only windows in here were slender and high, just below the ceiling, prohibiting sunlight with black tint.

My gaze settled on a tall black shelf across the room. According to the floor plan . . .

I traced the back of the shelf, feeling carefully. My fingers caught on a dip in the wood. Pulling, the shelf unlatched, and it swung in on itself.

Bingo.

If the first room was dim, then this one was pitch-black. I squinted, trying to get my eyes to adjust. But the second I stepped inside, a puddle of light beamed down on me, drenching me in my own private little circle of luminescence.

In glow-in-the-dark lettering, a sign on the back of the shelf door caught my eye.

WARNING! LIGHT-SENSITIVE FILM STORED HERE.
DO NOT OVEREXPOSE.

Light-sensitive film *and* assassination footage.

I took a baby step forward, and the beam of light followed me, courtesy of a whole layer of motion-sensor lights sitting like bats on the ceiling. Neat, I guess.

About a dozen rows of metal shelves, each around seven feet tall, were spaced unevenly through the room. Approaching one with my beam of light following, I noticed the hand cranks on the side. With ease, I turned one, and the shelf jerked into motion so fast it jumped. An aisle opened between two shelves. A paper note was taped at around eye level.

Sensitive hand cranks. Be careful—

Lot of good a hand-scribbled note did in a near-blacked-out room, but whatever. A glow-in-the-dark plaque on the shelf read A-001 THRU B-056. My target was in the *K*s, so I crept through the dark room accordingly until I was cranking the shelves over to create a new aisle where I needed.

Metal film canisters were arranged in messy stacks from top to bottom, little white tags stickered to the side of each canister labeling them. Thankfully, all the canisters seemed to be in order. I didn't have time to scour through all this film.

At the very end of the aisle, bottom shelf, I picked up film reel K-905. Identical to the rest of the film canisters, but oh, what secrets could be recorded inside. If I'd had time, I might have borrowed one of the projectors in the next room over and found out for myself. Another time, perhaps.

Film in hand, I slipped out of the dark room and started to push the shelf door back in place. I had about twenty minutes until the cable car station shut down for the night. It was just enough time for Mylo to fake a medical emergency and smuggle us down to the city. I was about to com for him to circle back for me, but a crackling sound at the window shut me down. There was a buzzing and a pair of feet pressed against the glass. Someone was breaking in.

THIRTY-FIVE

ON INSTINCT, I dashed back into the dark room, letting the shelf door latch shut after me.

I instantly face-palmed that decision. Why didn't I just leave the damn room entirely? It would've been risky, being seen if someone was outside, but surely that would've been better than boxing myself in. They probably already had the window-pane open by now.

What the hell happened to Kyung-soon's texts? Why didn't she let me know how close they were?

Frustrated, I whipped my phone out, only to see the empty home screen . . . and also the complete lack of signal. Dr. Warlen had said something about the loopy signal, hadn't he?

So, hiding in here it was, then. But for how long? I needed to get back to Mylo so we could get the hell off this mountain. I was not in the mood to play an overnight game of hide-and-seek with Diane.

My fingers curled around the canister. She would realize the target was gone as soon as she got here.

Quickly, I snuck back to the spot where the target had been stashed and grabbed another canister. Thank god I hadn't cut my nails lately. They were just long enough to help me scrape the K-905 sticker off the target and a matching one off K-900. They were wrinkled and a little uneven as I pressed them back on the metal, but hopefully they looked good enough to fool her for a little while.

Featherlight steps crept into the silence. Hide now. There was just one problem.

I looked up, and my heart sunk as I remembered the impossible-to-escape beam of light overhead.

But they were motion lights.

I stepped back into the next open aisle and dropped to a crouch. Someone was feeling around the shelf door, their fingers fumbling on the other side. My beam of light remained. I held my breath.

God, if you ever even liked me a little, do me this one favor now, please.

The door unlatched.

The lights above me switched off. I stayed perfectly still in the dark.

The steps that entered were careful, but assured. In my periphery, I saw the new beam of light spotting a figure as she made her way through the shelves. I couldn't turn for a better angle, though. Even breathing too deeply felt dangerous.

She drew closer, until there was nothing but one movable

shelf between me and her. My mouth went dry as I listened to her pick up the canister. There was a pop as she opened the cylinder.

Take the bait.

After a long minute, she closed the canister and began heading back.

After this, I thought, I was going to start going to church again.

Until I heard one of the hand cranks turning. Of course Diane wanted to close the aisle she'd stolen from. How smart.

And the shelf she just had to pick was the one *I* was between. The shelf adjacent to me, on its hair-trigger crank, started pushing in on the next shelf, ready to pancake me.

With only an inch to spare, I rolled out from the crushing shelves. The motion-sensor lights had me illuminated before I got on my feet.

Looking down the aisle at me, Diane blinked, and then her gaze fell to the canister in my hand.

Well, if you can't hide.

I feinted, heading straight toward her. It drew her in long enough for me to pull back and bolt down the next open aisle instead. She was going to catch up with me; after all, she was closer to the exit. But a few seconds out of her sight was all I needed. I unraveled my bracelet chain. As expected, she threw herself in front of the open aisle, ready to intercept me. I bent and swung my chain around one of her ankles and pulled. She thudded to the floor. I hurdled over her and out the door, pressing it shut behind me. In the viewing room, I scanned the desks at hyper speed before finding a pair of styluses by some tablets, which I dug between the hinges and the doorframe. It shuddered. A binder hit the floor. That wasn't going to hold her for long.

"Whoa." I spun around at the voice to find Kyung-soon by the main entrance, with her phone wired into the locking mechanism of the door. No doubt ensuring the lock wasn't going to work for anyone on the other side while Diane did her thing.

"You're still here! Why?"

"I didn't get your text," I said.

A slam hit the shelf door. Kyung-soon shook her head. "We should go."

"No duh." I ripped her wires out for her and pushed the door open.

Only to come face-to-face with Molly, the guy with the overalls, and Mylo behind them trying to not to make it obvious how he was pressing against the com in his ear.

The com I forgot to unmute when Diane got here.

The five of us were suspended in a moment of disbelief before Diane slammed herself against the secret shelf door again, which prompted Molly to scream, "Call someone, they're breaking in—"

Kyung-soon slammed the door, shutting Mylo and the others out . . . for a bit.

"So, what now?" Kyung-soon asked. Another binder fell off the door. She tensed. "I really don't want to fight Ms. Abara. She's actually really sweet when you're on her good side."

It wasn't like fighting her was going to help us anyway. Getting the hell out of there was the priority, and it was just a matter of time now before people came flooding through the main entrance.

My eyes drifted up to the window Kyung-soon and Diane had come through. I pushed one of the leather chairs underneath it and pushed the pane open. Craning my neck out and up, barely noticeable scuff marks made it obvious they'd rappelled from the roof, sort of like what Noelia and I had done in Antarctica. Judging by the fact that Kyung-soon didn't have the rope they'd used, it was safe to assume Diane had it, so going back up was a no.

I twisted to look below, at the sheer drop and free fall into the water at least a thousand feet down.

And the sliver of rocky ground between the edge of the building and the drop. At least a foot wide. That was enough to walk on. The cable car station was a straight shot across the sliver of ground too. The sun was just starting to tint the sky and the lake a fiery shade of red. We could make it in time.

I turned back to Kyung-soon, holding out my hand.

"I really hate you sometimes," she whimpered, but with no other choice, she took my hand.

THIRTY-SIX

I STUMBLED THE SECOND my feet hit the bumpy ground. Some pebbles tumbled off the cliff's edge.

A wave of dizziness made me sway.

Kyung-soon grabbed my arm, pulling me upright. Even with only one hand on the bricks of the building for support, she was notably sturdy.

"You're good with heights," I said, trying to distract myself.

"No, I've just mastered the art of compartmentalization." Her voice quivered. "You can pay for my therapy."

A breeze hit us, and it felt like a gale-force wind. We both leaned back, taking small but consistent side steps. It wasn't that far to the station, maybe twenty yards max? That was nothing; we just had to keep moving. I kept one hand on the wall behind me and the other bracing the film canister to my chest.

Kyung-soon sucked a sharp breath in.

"What?"

"Oh no, I looked down."

"Why would you do that?"

But because she said it, I did too.

The fall seemed to elongate. My toes were teetering at the edge of solid ground. All it would take was one slip, one unsteady piece of ground. This made the drop from the hotel in Cairo look like a tumble down some stairs. My head shot up, and I pretended I hadn't seen it.

"Why am I friends with you?" I mumbled.

"I was just asking myself the same question."

We kept sliding across the ledge against the wind. Shadows grew as the sky darkened. At some point, Kyung-soon clenched my forearm and didn't let go. If we were going down, I guessed it was together.

On wobbly legs, we somehow managed to make it to the end of the wall. The ground widened a bit leading to a wrought-iron gate that fenced off the cable car station, you know, in case some geniuses decided to do something like scale the rockface.

I gave Kyung-soon a boost over the back gate, then bounded over myself. The platform was empty, except for a station operator, currently balancing on a step stool, examining the wheels and machinery at the front of the car while she spoke into a palm-sized recording device. "Brake check— Bloody hell, where'd y'all come from? The station is closed." She pressed a hand to her chest, then gasped as her gaze landed on our legs. We were completely smeared with dirt from the waist down.

"Oh heavens, did you climb across the rocks—"

"There was a break-in at the retreat!" I blurted out. My words were a desperate rush. "Some woman broke in! And she attacked a bunch of people and"—I threw an arm around Kyung-soon—"she broke my best friend's ribs, and I think she's bleeding internally, and we have to get to a hospital now!"

Kyung-soon gripped her side and howled, crying in full hysteria in under two seconds.

The woman gasped. "Oh, oh my god, get in." I ushered Kyung-soon into the car and shut the door. Through the glass, I watched the operator jump behind the control podium back inside the station. Our car pulled out, clicking into its descent. In a blink, we were gliding over the same ledge we had been trying not to trip over.

Kyung-soon batted some fake tears away. "Fake crying gives me such a headache."

"The thought of losing at the last second gives me a headache." I knelt on the bench, looking out the back end of the car. The film canister was still a comfort held tightly against my heart. I was actually winning this phase.

I stared at the station. No doubt Diane had gotten out of her predicament by now, and if she was able to climb back up and cross the roof instead of taking the dangerous way around, she'd be able to make better time. I was sure she was hijacking a cable car to follow us. But the thing about cable cars is they're slow. And we were ahead of her. No freaking way we were losing with this head start.

I was going to win.

"I just texted Count," Kyung-soon said. "The final rendezvous location is at a pier down there." She handed my phone back to me. When had she taken it?

Kyung-soon put a hand over her eyes and stared at the water. She tapped the glass. "That's it. The place with the loading dock. Count and Baron said the first one to bring the target there wins."

I spared a glance, seeing an isolated dock and an unassuming gray smear of a building connected to it. Looked like it wouldn't be that far of a drive from the cable car drop-off. It should be short enough for us to keep our lead.

I took a shaky breath. *Just don't lose the canister. Stay in the lead—*

A hand squeezed my shoulder, and I startled. Kyung-soon gave me her best calm-down look. "Ross. Relax. We're ahead."

"For now."

"For good!" We both looked back toward the station, just in time to see Diane stumbling onto the platform. There was a two-second argument with the operator before Diane swiped one of those knockout sticks under her nose and she passed out. Diane watched us descending.

"She can't catch up," Kyung-soon assured me.

She entered the next car, but it didn't start moving.

When she came out, she held a seat belt. I watched her loop one of the ends around her right hand, then climb up the car, throw the belt over the freaking cable, and grab the other end.

Oh. My. God.

"Okay, I, uh, wasn't expecting that." Kyung-soon stepped backward. Diane jumped. She was seat-belt zip-lining straight toward us. Double the speed of our cable car.

Even in the darkening evening, the glint of the gun on her hip was undeniable.

"Oh my, uh, what now?" Kyung-soon asked. We still had over half the cable ride left to go—she would have long since caught up with us by the time we hit the bottom.

Unless we started to speed up somehow.

I raced to the front of the car, pressed my face against the window until I could see the wheels connecting us overhead. That was the piece of machinery the operator was examining when she said brake check, right?

A hatch was nestled into the top of the car. I could use the bench to bound up and push it open. "Hold my legs!"

"What?"

As I heaved myself through the open hatch, Kyung-soon thankfully found a grip on my dangling ankles. The wind blew against my face. I checked over my shoulder; Diane was still zipping toward us.

I leaned forward to examine the brake piece, clutching the top of the car as I did. A red latch—bracketed by exclamation points and a REMOVE FOR MAINTENANCE note, followed by a notice that started with something like DO NOT and ended with IN MOTION—seemed like what I was looking for. I strained to reach it, my fingers just a few centimeters out of its grasp.

The sound of Diane's belt screeching over the cable line spurred me on. I strained against Kyung-soon's grip. The tips of my fingers crawled along the machinery toward the hook.

The car jostled.

I grabbed the hook and pulled. A piece clinked away under the wheel. A high-pitched whir cut through the wind. The car accelerated. Fast. Kyung-soon must have tripped, pulling me down with her. As I tumbled back into the car, the high-pitched whirring got louder. Force pushed Kyung-soon and me against the back wall of the car. I could feel my stomach dropping.

Fighting gravity, I twisted to glance at Diane, now yards behind us and getting farther away. I guessed a thousand-kilo cable car had a little more momentum than one lady holding on to a seat belt.

The car jerked. Kyung-soon yelped. The wind passing the open hatch above us sounded like a tornado.

"We're ahead now!" Kyung-soon yelled over the raging wind. "We should slow down."

"They'll stop us at the station!" I said. "There's always an operator at the bottom station there to stop runaway cars!"

Kyung-soon shook her head. "Ross, that station is closed!"

I opened my mouth, but nothing came out.

I flashed back to the operator, reminding us the station below had already shut down for the night. Somehow that had completely slipped my mind.

Oh.

Kyung-soon must have read it on my face, because hers crumpled. "We're gonna die?"

"No!" Fighting the wind force, I pulled myself to my feet. We were now at least fifty yards from Diane, fast approaching the ground station. Where no one would be there to stop us. "The water," I said.

I touched the door to the car, eyeing the rendezvous point below.

"Kyung-soon, we're going to jump."

Kyung-soon was still on the floor and gripping one of the benches. "No, we're not!"

"If we don't jump, we'll die!"

"That's fine."

The floors, the walls, the ceiling started to vibrate. The wheels screeched as we tore across the cable. It was a war with physics just to stay standing and it was only getting worse. Gripping one of the safety handles with one hand, I yanked Kyung-soon up with my other.

She was yelling in Korean while I fought to keep us both upright. "It's too high!" she insisted. "If we hit the water from this high up, it'll be like hitting concrete!"

There was a point there. We were descending, but even if we landed close to the shore, it'd still be a hundred-foot, bone-shattering fall.

Letting her go, I grabbed one of the faux-leather cushions from the benches. A few tugs, maybe fueled by adrenaline, and it peeled up. I tumbled to the other side of the car.

"I really, really hate you right now," Kyung-soon told me.

"That's fine." I kicked the passenger door open. The cushion was just wide and long enough to accommodate us both. All we had to do was land decently, and we'd be okay. Surely.

Kyung-soon reluctantly held on to her side of the cushion, bracing the open door. I did the same. Wind ripped through our hair as we looked down. The encroaching night made gauging the exact distance of the water below impossible, but the light of the rendezvous pier was enough to help us find the shore.

"After we hit the water, swim for the lights at the rendezvous point." Kyung-soon gulped so hard. "You *can* swim, right?" I asked.

"I could five years ago."

"It's like riding a bike."

God, I hoped.

Sparks started to fall from the broken brakes. The water glistened under us. I gave Kyung-soon's hand a squeeze. She squeezed back.

We counted to three and jumped.

THIRTY-SEVEN

I THOUGHT WE WOULD never hit the water, but when we did, I wished we hadn't.

The bench cushion slammed against the water. At least, I thought it was water. The impact felt more akin to hitting solid metal. My chest, my legs, my bones were crushed against the stupid faux leather. The impact knocked my sight into black for a second. My limbs went out of commission.

We did hit the water. We'd landed. Was I broken, though?

Water engulfed me. I felt myself rolling off the bench cushion into the water, and thankfully, that seemed to trigger my arms and legs to reboot. Treading water, I felt inside my jacket. The film canister was still in place, and thankfully sealed tightly.

Above, sparks were flying from where the car was skirting

across the cable. Following behind at a less breakneck speed was Diane. I was sure she wanted to follow us into the water, but she had no cushion to break her fall, and that would certainly not end well for her. It'd barely ended well for us.

Wait, it did, didn't it?

"Kyung-soon!" Slapping the water, I turned around. There was no one else above the surface. Only me and a drifting bench cushion.

I had sucked in a breath to dive under and find her when she broke the surface. Already halfway toward the pier. "Hurry the hell up!" she yelled, then dove back under.

Note to self: Find a way to actually make up for this later.

There wasn't exactly a ladder leading the six or so feet up to the pier, so we swam around to the shore by the outbuilding. We walked soggily toward the darkened door. No one appeared to be waiting outside, but I could swear I made out more than a couple silhouettes lurking in the trees.

"They can't go anywhere without an entourage of bodyguards," Kyung-soon said, wringing water out of her hair. She shivered, and I offered her my jacket, despite it being waterlogged and despite the fact that she had her own equally waterlogged jacket. Kyung-soon stared at the ground. "I didn't think you could win; that's why I didn't back you from the start." She tapped the canister in my hand. "I was wrong. I'm sorry."

Six months ago, I don't think I would've been able to forgive her. But now I just shrugged and smiled. "I believe your intentions were good. And screw what people say, sometimes intention is just as important as impact."

"I feel like I've been thinking that for years . . ." She let out a breath, and we both stopped at a large metal door. The sliver of light slipping out from the bottom made it clear someone was home. Maybe a lot of people. "What are you going to do?" Kyung-soon asked. "You could give Count the win, or . . ."

Or do it my way.

I looked at Kyung-soon, and I think she knew.

She straightened her shoulders. "Well, here we go, then."

THE OUTBUILDING'S HEAVY metal doors groaned as Kyung-soon and I each pushed.

The sound echoed through what was little more than a large concrete-floored open-plan space. Outdoor equipment, kayaks, and paddleboats were stacked against the walls. The place might have been under renovation for something at some point, but into or from what exactly, I couldn't be sure.

Directly ahead, two wooden seating areas almost like pews were situated adjacent to each other. Count and Baron each stood before one, clearly too tense to sit. And lining the room behind them, oh-so many of those armed goons. More than one was holding a tablet, catching the coup de grâce of this final phase from multiple angles.

An audience. Perfect.

"Ms. Shin?" Baron said through gritted teeth.

Kyung-soon tucked some hair behind her ear. "Don't look at me." She made a grasping motion with her hand.

Taking the cue, I handed my phone—I really did have the sturdiest phone case ever—off to Kyung-soon, stepped forward, and held up the film canister.

It looked like a thousand pounds might have been lifted off

Count's slender shoulders. "You pathetic, desperate upstart," she said to Baron, who was absolutely vibrating with fear.

"Tell me, B, would you prefer to spend the next ten or so years of your life in a high-security prison or disappear completely? I'm sure someone in our organization knows someone who needs a crime to be taken off their hands and dumped onto someone else's record. Or maybe we should sell you to Hart's. I wonder how many chips you're worth."

"This is a mistake," Baron sputtered. He stepped backward until his legs hit the pew behind him. His tablet screen was flooding with messages, though they were too distant for me to read. The way Baron paled told me they were not in his favor.

He cleared his throat and tried to recover. "A game is not an accurate way to decide this. This isn't fair—"

"Since when do we care about fair?" Count said, her eyes alight with a manic sort of power that, for all I knew, I could be on the other end of come tomorrow.

Count nodded one of the goons in Baron's direction, but he didn't move.

They were watching me, and the canister in my hand, which I hadn't yet handed off to Count.

Neither Count nor Baron noticed when I found the lighter in my back pocket. They were so hung up in their own moment that no one except the goons seemed to notice as I rubbed the wet wheel dry on my thumb pad, flicked it a few times, then popped open the film canister and lit the reel. It caught fire immediately. A mountain of fire exploded in the film canister, singeing my fingertips. I dropped it, letting the disaster land with a powerful clang on the concrete floor.

Now, that got their attention. Fast.

And it left them both speechless. I walked past Count and Baron and gently took a tablet from one of the wallflower crew. To my surprise, he didn't stop me.

Again, the screen was only a reflection of myself and a chat box hosting over a thousand anonymous viewers and commenters. I gestured toward the burning fire. "I just burned that right in front of Count and Baron, and neither of them even tried to stop me. They didn't even notice."

"I—" Baron started.

"Be quiet," a woman with a side holster said firmly. A faint buzz told me she was just a mouthpiece for whoever was speaking through her ear com.

Baron clenched his jaw, but he sure as hell shut up.

I went on. "I've spent more time than I'd like with Baron and Count over the last few months. Mostly with Count, but just enough with Mr. Baron to decide I personally hate him a little more. You know what I've learned? Yeah, they're both appropriately sinister, calculating, and intimidating enough for the job you want them to fill. But more than that, they're both relentless idiots."

Count's and Baron's death glares were almost strong enough to send me flying, but neither of them said a damn thing.

"I don't know what kind of job application process there is for an organization as . . . unique as yours, but you sincerely need to revamp it. You can do better than someone as petty as Count or as inexperienced as Baron."

The chat was silent. It seemed several people were typing, but no messages were going through. I pinched the tablet to keep the tremor in my hands from showing. This was a big gamble. Being met with silence wasn't on the list of things I was prepared for.

A buzz from the tablet broke the tension. Are you applying?

"No," I said. "You don't want me. As you can see, I have an attitude and am prone to bouts of disobedience. But you're on the right track. Count and Baron don't know a damn thing about ground operations. You need someone who (A) knows how to run a job personally and (B) who still has that calculating ruthlessness you so adore in these two." I gestured half-heartedly to Count and Baron, who were still plotting my murder in their heads if their expressions were any indication.

I cleared my throat, still uninterrupted by any pesky comments in the chat box. Still holding on to their curiosity, at least for the time being.

Baron tried to open his mouth again, but another "Quiet" from one of the goons nipped that right in the bud.

"Ruthless efficiency." The words were simultaneously scathing and flattering. "Someone who never gets tripped up by emotions. Who always gets what she wants." I swallowed. "Someone who'd risk her relationship with her own daughter to make a few million, and the only lesson she'd learn from failing is how not to get caught next time."

"You can't be serious." Count tore toward me, trying to snatch the tablet away, but was promptly caught in a wristlock by the sentinels.

I went on. "Rhiannon Quest is exactly who you're looking for. To be honest, I'm surprised she hasn't joined your gang already." Had there ever been a more fitting shoe?

"You're insane," Baron said. "You can't just replace us with your mummy. No one is going to respect that sort of change.

It makes us look amateurish, we lose credibility—" He was talking more to the organization than me, obviously. But would they bite?

They just needed a little more incentive.

"Ross isn't the only one who supports this," Kyung-soon said. I turned back to her. On the phone, she gave me a nod and a thumbs-up. "Taiyō Itō and I have cross-referenced the Quests', Boscherts', and his personal network of underground contacts over the last twenty-four hours. We did some testing, you could say. We contacted a hefty number of industry heavy hitters and misinformed one-third of them that Count was still in charge of the organization, then told one-third it was going to Baron, and one-third that the position had been given to Rhiannon Quest. Then we asked all of them to complete a job pro bono, out of fealty to the organization, of course. When they thought it was Baron or Count in charge, only fifty percent agreed. But when it was Rhiannon Quest at the helm?

"Seventy-five percent," Kyung-soon filled in. She crept in closer, still holding my phone to her ear. "Taiyō recorded of all the responses. I'm dropping a secure link to a spreadsheet we created with all of this information."

"A fabrication," Count said. Apparently she and Baron were being granted some speaking privileges now. One final desperate gasp for air, I hoped. "A twenty-five percent increase in fealty is—" She broke into a hysterical laugh. "That's just not realistic."

"It's true," I said. "You're not half as intimidating as my mom. No one trusts her, but everyone respects her. On a performance level, I haven't talked to one professional who doesn't want to stay on her good side. She has a reputation for getting stuff done, no matter who she has to mow down. That kind of heartless person you don't want to cross. Now, is that the kind of person you want on your team? Or one of the petty losers who let me embarrass them in front of you because they're too busy bickering with each other?"

A new message vibrated in the chat.

I like these numbers.

Count inhaled sharply.

I know she has her own motives, but I suppose she has a point here.

Do you remember Rhiannon's Gambit? She is absolutely cutthroat.

We love a vicious woman.

A familiar industry face might not be the worst idea??

A poll appeared on the screen.

RHIANNON QUEST? Yes? No?

The numbers added up quickly. I watched unblinkingly, my hands holding on to the tablet for dear life as I watched the yes bar grow and grow and grow. It passed the halfway point and kept going. But once it went past that benchmark, I knew that was enough. As long as this thing was democratic.

"No, no, no!" Count, who'd gotten a tablet from someone, was losing her mind. Baron looked like he wanted to completely evaporate.

The poll ended with a solid 80 or so percent in the yes category. A new message popped into the chat.

It's a yes to Rhiannon Quest . . . for now.

I let out a breath of such relief, I almost laughed. Holy crap, that actually worked.

"How wonderful." One of the goons stepped out of her shadowy post, much to the curiosity of those around her. She slid off her bulky coat, which trimmed about a fourth of her size. Shimmied off her wig and pinched off her boxy glasses. It should have been some kind of metaphor how quickly Mom went from disguised to recognizable. At least I was getting used to it. The goons around her, not so much. One man actually did a double take as Mom walked past him, still a few inches taller than usual in heeled boots.

Mom pressed a kiss to my forehead, which I quickly backed away from, grimacing. "This is the best Mother's Day present ever, you know."

"It's not May."

"Yeah, but you won't be able to top this."

"I didn't do this for you."

She knew that, but accepted happily anyway. So be it. Whatever she was going to do with this newfound power wasn't my concern at the moment. It was more what she wouldn't let happen. The chances of Diane getting her Quest-family-ending favor had now dropped to 0 percent. And if that was the case, then we won. Even if it meant Mom's eye might be on me for the rest of my life now. But I had faith her new gig would also be distracting enough that she wouldn't need me around as much.

Mom pulled her hair out of the ponytail it'd been in under her wig, fluffing it out to great dramatic effect as her attention turned from me to Count and Baron, now completely surrounded by Mom's new army.

"First order of business . . ." Mom dropped her hands on her hips. "About the dissenters. Count, I'd appreciate some guidance on minutiae, so I was thinking of letting you be my assistant. Aren't you honored?"

Count spat the foulest French curses I'd ever heard. "I would never—"

"I was thinking you could be my assistant or you could disappear into option B. I don't think you want to know what option B is."

Count bit her tongue, resigned.

"And me?" Baron managed to keep his head up; I'd give him that.

Mom's back was to me, but her smug smile was audible. "Give me a reason to keep you around."

Baron's brown eyes darted back and forth. "I . . . I can cook."

"No." Marc shook his head from a spot in the shadows behind Baron. "No, he cannot."

The comment box on my tablet was a storm of laughter.

I laid the tablet on the floor and backed away. I let out a breath as I stepped farther and farther from the action.

"Don't pass out." Kyung-soon now lingered near a shelf of dusty towels and floaties. She grabbed my shoulders as if to keep me from teetering. Maybe I was teetering.

"It's fine. You'll catch me, right?"

"If I don't, will your mom have me executed?"

"I honestly have no clue." And I hoped this wasn't a big mistake.

Kyung-soon halfway nodded; then a voice buzzed from my phone in her hand. "Oh, Taiyō's still on."

She pushed the phone into my hand. He seemed to have sensed when it was at my ear. "Congratulations."

"Thanks for the last-minute help."

He tsked. "Don't think of it as a favor. Everything is for a purpose."

I rolled my eyes, though a bud of fondness was behind it. Sure, he was really only helping because (A) the new connections he got helping me out were worth their weight in gold, and (B) kinda, sort of tangentially knowing the new front woman of the organization wasn't such a bad win either. Also, I got the vibe that Mom liked Taiyō, which was saying something.

"Well, I appreciate that your interests have aligned with mine," I said.

"Hm." I imagined him pushing up his glasses. "The facility is being investigated by law enforcement, by the way. I don't believe Noelia and Mylo will have trouble talking their way out of suspicion."

Undercover until the end. Good on them.

"And . . . Devroe?"

Kyung-soon folded her arms. "I texted him the rendezvous point. He's probably on the way." She was wringing out her jacket now.

I huffed a laugh. Wasn't I trying to get Devroe arrested

just a few weeks ago? Oh, how time, a few heists, and some near-death experiences can change things. Across the room, I watched Baron gesturing wildly, trying to demonstrate some kind of value to Mom.

"About Devroe . . ." Kyung-soon said. "I wonder if your mom will still have to—"

My head snapped around as something cut Kyung-soon off. A hand covered her mouth and a snap sounded before a stick was pushed under Kyung-soon's nose. Quicker than I could push the assaulting hand away, Kyung-soon was knocked out cold. On instinct, I dropped to catch her, but an arm snaked around my neck, pulling me in tight.

Yelling, I clawed my nails into the arm. Until the all-too-familiar feeling of a chilly barrel dug into my side.

"Another secret play, then? Quests only know how to win by cheating."

Mom and the rest of the room were facing us now. And Mom's attention only made Diane twist the barrel under my ribs. She started backing up, and with no other option, I backed up with her.

Mom followed. And behind her a dozen goons. "Di, I'mma give you one warning to stop."

Diane didn't stop. I gritted my teeth as we passed through the back doors and onto the dock. Its wooden planks creaked under our shuffling feet. Diane's head pivoted for half a second, and I took in a sharp breath as I felt her finger tightening on the trigger. That stopped any quick thoughts about trying to twist out of her deadly hold before they could blossom.

Mom, with her new militia just one step behind and armed,

had the eyes of a tiger as she kept up with us. Watching me closely, like the predator she was, waiting for the moment to pounce.

"There's nothing but water behind," I said through gritted teeth. "You're backing yourself into a corner."

"You don't know anything about being backed into a corner," Diane said, still pulling me along.

"Don't snap at her, because she's right," Mom said, ears sharp as knives apparently. "You don't have anywhere to go besides the water. Drop the gun and drop her, and we can—"

"What? We can talk?" Diane pulled so hard I almost slipped. I squeaked pathetically. Mom sprinted a good five feet ahead before Diane tightened her arm around my neck and yanked me back, ordering her to halt without saying a single word.

"Talk? I tried to talk to you for weeks after the Gambit! You never wanted to talk about anything then."

"I— You—" Mom fumbled. I knew this was the type of situation she would've avoided before. But, as my constricting throat was reminding me, there wasn't much room for evasion right now.

Diane's steps slowed, as did mine. The sound of water gently lapping against the dock somehow made it over the thrumming of my heartbeat. Only then did I realize how far into the lake we were. We must have hit the end of the dock.

Mom whispered something to her militia, quiet enough that I couldn't hear. She was planning something, and I had a feeling it involved Diane winding up dead.

"Don't do this to yourself," I said, my voice small. "She's going to kill you."

Something shattered. The spotlight at the end of the pier, the one I hadn't realized until now was right behind us, brightened tenfold without the glass lens. Straining to get a look behind me, I caught a glimpse of shattered glass around the floodlight and the sparkling LED bulb inside. Diane had kicked the lens in.

Then she kicked the light so hard, splinters of wood flew up from under it. The light plunked into the water. An electrifying crackle cut through the air. The floodlight, still connected to some underwater power source, lit the water from underneath. The surface might as well have been sparking itself. A fried minnow floated to the surface. Then another, and another.

I winced as Diane pulled us both to the very edge of the pier, and the electrified water.

"Don't shoot!" Mom demanded, calling off whatever attack she'd just tried to put together.

"Mom . . ."

"It's fine." Her face said it was anything but. One rough gust of wind, and Diane and I were both going in.

"Is that really how much you hate me? You gonna kill yourself to get back at me?" Mom asked.

"No . . ." Diane said.

"Then what the hell are we doing here?" Mom snapped back. "Besides making a fool of yourself."

"Tell me why," Diane said. I could feel her shaking her head. Loose strands of her silk-pressed hair nipped my face. "What mattered more than August? Did you ever care about him? Did you ever care about me?"

"Let my daughter go, and maybe I'll talk to you." Mom

pursed her lips. I knew what that meant. After Diane let me go, Mom wasn't saying anything. Even in this situation.

Diane let out a distraught laugh. The incredulous kind. "Even now you think you can just do whatever and get what you want. You always win, and you never look back. Isn't that right?"

Diane spun me. I lost my balance and tripped backward, only to be caught by my shirt collar. I screamed, the toes of my sneakers barely on the dock's edge. My fingers sunk into Diane's arm, and thank god she was planted firm. Frantically, I looked between my grasp on her and the electric water and back again. I swore I could hear the burning LED lights sizzling under the water.

"Don't," Mom said, reaching out but unable to take any steps closer. "Please."

"Please, but no apology?"

"I'm not apologizing to you while you hold my daughter over a death pit."

Diane grimaced and loosened one pinky. I yelped, dropping a couple millimeters before finding my balance. I was heaving in breaths now.

Some poor creature under the surface hit the lights and a crackle pop sizzled under me.

For a second I imagined my skin burning and sizzling on impact. Would I be alive long enough to feel myself being fried?

At least three or four guns clicked. Mom's goons had their weapons up and leveled. "Drop her, and I'll shoot you," Mom said.

"Shoot me, and I'll drop her," Diane countered. I could feel her loosening her ring finger. Her finger continued to loosen, and I shifted my toes frantically, fighting for a better grip on the dock. "You're going to kill me anyway, aren't you? Maybe you should know what it feels like to lose something first, the same way you've been threatening to take my child from me."

"She didn't do that! It was Baron screwing with you!" I insisted. In this situation, it probably sounded like I would make up any bull to help myself.

"Don't put your guns down," Mom said to her goons.

Diane loosened her ring finger completely. I screamed.

A whistle cut through the air, and in a crack of a second, everyone was looking behind Mom. She gestured some of the crew to the side, clearing a line of sight for all of us.

At the other end of the dock, breathing like he'd just been running for miles and miles, was Devroe. Jacket gone, legs smeared with grime. Had he run all the way here?

He skidded to a stop halfway between the edge of the pier and Mom's gang, casting a careful look back at Kyung-soon, who was still unconscious on the floor inside.

Diane sighed. Was she annoyed he'd made his way down here?

"Devroe—" she started.

"Who won?" he asked.

That was the question he was asking right now?

"She always wins," Diane repeated. Like it was a thought constantly drilling into her gray matter.

Devroe's eyes widened as he looked at my mom. He shook off the shock like a pro.

"I want to make my wish."

Mom scoffed. "Not taking requests at the moment."

"They said I could make my wish when the game was over, and I want to make it."

"What is it?" one of the goons behind Mom asked, still with the tablet. I was positive the members were still watching, if only for their own entertainment.

Mom clenched her hands at her sides. I readjusted my grip on Diane's arm, praying my hands weren't getting too sweaty to hold on.

Over my trembling breath, I looked at Devroe. He gave me a sad little smile, and I had the feeling he was about to say something either really sappy or very stupid.

"If anyone harms Ross Quest, or the rest of the Quests, I want you to kill me. That's my wish."

"Devroe!" Diane screamed. I was shocked enough to almost lose my balance. Was he . . . for real?

For me?

"Done," Mom said.

Diane twisted her fist into my shirt and pulled me back onto the dock. I stumbled forward, almost sick with relief. Solid ground, my best friend.

"You win, Rhi," Diane said. She was a tired woman. A tired, tired woman. And I think we might have just drained another decade off her life. "As usual."

Mom shuffled forward, and for a change, I let her put her arms around me. But only for a second. I pushed out of her grasp and reached for Devroe, who'd managed to get past the guards now. He was trying very hard not to make eye contact with his mother.

"Is Kyung-soon okay?" I asked.

"She's just asleep. I gave her my coat," he said quickly.

"You're a chivalrous idiot."

"And you're alive. You're welcome."

There was a thud. Diane had dropped to her knees at the end of the dock. Devroe took a step toward his mom, who was glancing back at the water. She put a hand up, stopping him.

Mom was standing at a distance, arms folded and brow furrowed. She was paying attention, though.

"Mom." I posted myself just a few inches in front of her. No chance of looking away. "You need to tell her. If you ever want to see me again, ever, you need to tell her. You have everything else, at least give her an explanation. What did you wish for?"

"I . . ."

Diane remained silent. Mom pointed back to the outbuilding. "Check on the girl." With that, her new crew obediently shuffled away, and it was just the four of us left on the dock, over a deadly electrified lake.

Mom took a few hesitant paces up to her old friend. "I'm not sorry for what I did. But I wouldn't have done it if it wasn't worth it."

"Nothing was worth more than August."

"No. Nothing I had yet."

I frowned. Until Diane turned and found me. Devroe did too.

Hold up.

"Are you talking about *me*?" I asked.

Mom, the only one who hadn't turned her attention to me, instead looked out over the water with a wistful, sadly nostalgic sort of air and sighed. "Early-onset endometriosis. Practically incurable twenty years ago. It was completely unglamorous. If

I'd said something, you would have figured out what I was doing back then. What I'd wish for."

Diane laughed sadly. "You really aren't sorry, then, are you."

"No, and I never will be. But I do miss him too. And you."

Turning on a dime, Mom straightened her shoulders and headed back down the pier. But when she passed me, she grazed my cheek with her finger. "You look like your daddy," Mom said to Devroe, but kept walking.

THIRTY-EIGHT

"BS." **KYUNG-SOON FLIPPED** over Mylo's latest cards. It was a pair of twos, totally not the eights he'd said they were.

"God damn it." He dragged in a heap of sand along with the pile of cards. I tugged my sunglasses down to get a clearer view of Kyung-soon's chipper smile.

Mylo slapped the sand off his hands. "Stop signaling her."

"I have no idea what you're talking about." Flipping to my back on the beach mat, I closed my eyes, blocking out the drone of laughter and music and beach balls, and just focused on the white noise of the tide, the tickle of the sun on my skin, and the smell of sea salt. I could almost fool myself into thinking I was back home. The illusion didn't last long, though. A few seconds at most. The longer I went without going home, the less I was able to pretend.

Never in my life had I thought I'd ever go twelve months without having set foot on Andros. But here we were. I wondered if they knew it'd been a year to the day since the end of our first Gambit. Was that why they took me to the beach?

Mylo got called on his fake cards two more times, and literally tried to bury his head in the sand. He'd ask Kyung-soon for a rematch later, and to be fair, I'd help him hustle her the next game.

"Devroe's birthday is next week," Kyung-soon said, wiggling her toes in the sand. "I think as a gift we should either help him break into the Vatican archives to steal a book or into a West End tailor to swipe designs for a new custom suit."

"I get the suit sketch thing, not following on the Vatican book," Mylo said.

"It's for his mum," I said. "She started collecting rare books a couple of months ago."

"Ah, so his gift is a gift for his mum?" Mylo asked.

"His gift would be helping him acquire a gift for his mum, and we'd be doing it pro bono," Kyung-soon said.

Rare book collecting wasn't exactly the hobby I thought Diane Abara would pick up when she had to abandon her previous hobby—the quest to murder my whole family. But since that one was off the table now, and with Ms. Abara seeming just a little less enthusiastic about Mom's death knowing what she had wished for, rare book collecting wasn't the worst replacement. Helping him get his hands on something that would make his mum smile was a stellar birthday gift. As for my mom, well, sometimes she called. Sometimes I answered. But she was way more likely to get a response to the job requests she sent to my new black box. Well, the ones sent by her assistant Marc.

“Vatican book it is, then!” Mylo said. “I’ve always wanted to meet the pope.”

“If you get to meet the pope before I do while you’re stealing from his library, then I’ve lost all faith in God,” Noelia’s voice bellowed out of my phone, startling all of us for a moment. She’d been silent for so long, I forgot she was FaceTiming. She did that a lot these days. Call, chat, and then stay on the line while she was doing whatever else on her end and not pop in again until she felt like it.

“Since when do you want to meet the pope?”

“I’m Catholic. Every Catholic wants to meet the pope.” I thought I heard Noelia tapping a pencil. “There’s also a rule in the Boschert family that if anyone ever manages to steal the pope’s rosary, they’ll become the de facto head of the family.”

A smaller voice babbled over the phone. “Nicki says if any of you manage to do that, then you’ll be good enough to join the Boschert family.”

“I think I’d rather die.”

Devroe’s voice slid in behind me. I sat up, and his arm wrapped around my waist, pulling me in between his legs. The sun had been warm, but snug with my back against his chest was so much hotter. “You die, I die, remember. So how about we don’t do that anytime soon?”

Mylo was now arguing with Noelia about whether or not he’d be able to pass off a fake stole and take ownership of the whole Boschert empire, to which Noelia insisted that anything from the pope would be so holy you’d feel the difference, when Mylo went catatonic midsentence, staring in disbelief at his phone.

“What’s wrong?” I asked.

"Oh, he's calling!" Mylo scrambled up and started pacing away.

"Who?" Kyung-soon asked.

"Taiyō! Everybody, shut up." He said that like he wasn't running to take the call yards away from us. I watched him hurdle-jump over a family's blanket before finally landing in a relatively secluded area of the beach.

"I give it three minutes before Taiyō hangs up on him," I said.

"Four," Devroe said.

"Two." From Kyung-soon.

"An hour," Noelia said. I squinted down at the screen, her camera showing her working on a braid at her vanity. It was night on her side of the world, and with the cat's-eye makeup and sliver of a silk evening gown I could see, it was obvious she was headed to something important. "I'm a romantic at heart," she admitted. "Plus, Taiyō was on my team during the Gambit, remember? I got a much better idea of what his real impressions of everyone were. He wouldn't have called if he didn't want to listen for at least an hour." She slid a bobby pin into place behind her ear. "Not that I want that brother kidnapper to be happy—"

"Witch Bitch, will you hurry up?" Nicholi interrupted. "The whole family's almost here. Wait, where's your pointy hat and broomstick?"

I think she threw a mascara tube or something at him.

"Later," she said. "Let me know what I get for winning that bet too." The screen shook as she grabbed her phone and waved goodbye, but before she hung up, she hit the flip screen. "Oh, one last thing."

Below the knee-high hem of her cocktail dress, I could see some of the coolest ankle booties. White leather, with painted ice crystals climbing up from the soles. Bold choice, especially with her entire family meeting for their—how had she put it?—semiannual unofficial ranking dinner?

Let's just hope Papa Boschert remembered that Noelia was perhaps the only person in the family with other career options if she remained underappreciated there.

I pressed the end call button myself, since Noelia seemed to have forgotten, but was surprised to see a string of rubies now attached to my wrist. No, the gems weren't the right shade. They were garnets. I tilted my head up, peering at Devroe.

"Really? I thought we were just here to chill like normal people."

"Couldn't help myself. Besides, Kyung-soon's been swiping sunglasses and phones since we got out of the Uber."

Kyung-soon pursed her lips and nudged her beach bag a little farther away, like that would hide it.

The sunlight sparkled from my bracelet. "They're not even real rubies."

"Give me a break. It's Point Dume, not Venice Beach."

I ran my fingers over the not-so-expensive gems. Pricey or not, I was already treasuring it as much as the dozens of other pieces Devroe had swiped for me in the six months since the Gambit ended. What sort of collection would I have if this went on? In a year, five years, ten years. Twenty.

I shifted around. Devroe's arm stayed snug around me. I drew him in for a soft kiss and slid a pair of Ray-Bans I'd stolen for him over his eyes.

"You're welcome," I said.

Kyung-soon rummaged around in her bag. "Hey, is that from my collection? Not cool, I just found a buyer for those." She strained to snatch them off Devroe's face, but I pulled us both back onto the sand first.

And then we were running, Devroe and I hand in hand across the sand, with Kyung-soon at our heels. Past Mylo, blushing into his phone and not seeming to notice the three of us at all.

ACKNOWLEDGMENTS

Well, well, well, here you are again. You finished the first book and actually came back for more. You, my friend, get all the gold stars.

You know who else deserves a gold star? Chelsea Eberly! You're the glue that keeps my career together. Please don't ever quit agenting, I might literally fall apart.

Stacey Barney, editor supreme, thank you for your patience and for putting up with my rambling anecdotes and tardy emails while I finished Ross and Devroe's story. Thank you mostly for making sense even when I don't make sense. (Did that make sense?)

Thank you also to the entire behind-the-scenes production crew at Penguin. Olivia Russo, Lizzie Goodell, Theresa Evangelista, Suki Boynton, Ana Deboo, Jacqueline Hornberger, Cindy

Howle, Jenny Ly, Sarah Sather, Felicity Vallence, James Akinaka, Shannon Spann, and the probably dozens of others who've worked on this book. You freaking rock.

I'm mailing gold stars across the pond to my overly enthusiastic Simon & Schuster UK team, including but not limited to Lucy Pearse, Dani Wilson, Sarah Macmillan, Emma Finnerty, Olivia Horrox, and Jess Dean. (And you too, Charlotte Bodman and publicist extraordinaire Nina Douglas!) How do you all get more excited about my books every time I see you? Aren't you supposed to keep calm or something?

Thank you a trillion gazillion times to the army of translators and foreign publishers around the world who've brought *Thieves' Gambit* and *Heist Royale* to so many countries. I love love love you all.

Mama and Dada, thank you for never trying to dissuade me from my silly little dream of being an author, even when it took quite a few years to pan out. Keithen and I are who we are because you gave us the room to be ourselves unconditionally and to chase every dream without judgment or doubt. For that, we'll be eternally grateful.

Keithen, speaking of you: thanks for the support through all the highs and lows of the last year, and for listening to me even when I'm being a bit of a prick. But to be fair, you're kind of a prick too, so there you go.

Bianca, I know I can't expect you to go on a deadly, high-risk adventure with me, but I can always count on you to give me an alibi. Thanks for being such a bad influence and an even better friend.

Thank you to my kung fu family at Lee's Kung Fu and Tai

Chi, and to all of you who let me punch you when I was stressed about book things.

Lastly, a gold star for you, reader! Thanks for trusting me with your time and your attention—and for keeping me employed. I hope you come on another adventure with me sometime soon.